IASH Occasional Papers

1. *Europe Redefined.* Richard McAllister. 19
2. *Europe: Ways Forward.* Mark Russell and . ___ _..._._ ...ster. 1992. ISBN 0 9514854 2 3.
3. *Constitutions* and *Indigenous Peoples.* Ninian Stephen and Paul Reeves. 1993. ISBN 0 9514854 3 1.
4. *Indigenous Peoples & Ethnic Minorities.* Peter Jones. 1993. ISBN 0 9514854 4 X.
5. *Educational Values.* Peter Jones. 1994. ISBN 0 9514854 5 8.
6. *Family Values in the Mediterranean.* Peter Jones. 1994. ISBN 0 9514854 6 6.
7. *Post-Communist Transition: Realities and Perspectives.* Ivan Antonovich. 1996. ISBN 0 9514854 7 4.
8. *Value, Values and the British Army.* Patrick Mileham. 1996. ISBN 0 9514854 8 2.
9. *Commonwealth Lectures.* Peter Jones (ed.). 1997. ISBN 0 9514854 9 0.
10. *Darwin's Voyage: Circumnavigation, World History and the Sublime.* Ian Duncan. 2009. ISBN 978 0 9532713 4 4.
11. *Darwin in Scotland.* David Fergusson. 2009. ISBN 978 0 9532713 5 1.
12. *Charles Darwin: Some Scottish Connections.* Walter M. Stephen. 2009. ISBN 978 0 9532713 6 8.
13. *Edinburgh, Enlightenment and Darwin's Expression of the Emotions.* Gregory Radick. 2009. ISBN 978 0 9532713 7 5.
14. *Evolving Creation.* John Polkinghorne. 2009. ISBN 978 0 9532713 8 2.
15. *Conversation: and the Reception of David Hume.* Peter Jones. 2011. ISBN 978 0 9532713 9 9.
16. *Gathering Uncertainties: A Conversation Between Playwright Linda McLean and Susan Manning.* 2011. ISBN 978 0 9568610 0 9.
17. *Hume and Searle: the 'Is/Ought' Gap versus Speech Act Theory.* Daniel Schulthess. 2011. ISBN 978 0 9568610 1 6.
18. *Hume's Intellectual Development: an Overview.* James Harris. 2011. ISBN 978 0 9568610 2 3.
19. *Reason, Induction and Causation in Hume's Philosophy.* Don Garrett and Peter Millican, 2011. ISBN 978 0 9568610 3 0.
20. *The Enlightened Virago: Princess Dashkova through the Eyes of Others* and *Princess Dashkova, the Woman Who Shook the World.* Georgina Barker (ed.). 2019. ISBN 0 9532713 0 6.

To order, please contact:
The Institute for Advanced Studies in the Humanities, The University of Edinburgh,
Hope Park Square, Edinburgh, EH8 9NW, Scotland. Email: iash@ed.ac.uk Web: www.iash.ed.ac.uk

Humanities of the Future

Perspectives from the Past and Present

IASH 50th Anniversary Symposium
Edited by Ben Fletcher-Watson and Jana Phillips

The Institute for Advanced Studies in the Humanities
The University of Edinburgh
2020

Ben Fletcher-Watson and Jana Phillips (eds.)
Humanities of the Future: Perspectives from the Past and Present

This series of occasional papers is published by
The Institute for Advanced Studies in the Humanities
The University of Edinburgh
2 Hope Park Square
Edinburgh EH8 9NW

Published November 2020
Copyright © the authors 2020

All rights reserved. No part of this publication may be reproduced, stored, or transmitted in
any form without the written permission of the author.

ISSN 2041-8817 (Print)
ISSN 2634-7342 (Online)
ISBN 978-0-9532713-1-3
Institute Occasional Papers, 21

The University of Edinburgh is a charitable body, registered in Scotland,
with registration number SC005336.

Printed by Bell & Bain Ltd, Glasgow

Acknowledgements

We would like to thank all those who make our work possible and fruitful, including: the College of Arts, Humanities and Social Sciences, and its twelve Schools, which provide funds, professional services, governance and strategic direction for the Institute; various trusts and supporters, who fund Fellowships and support community activities for the Fellows; and our partners and stakeholders outside the University. In particular, we would like to recognise the contributions made by our authors, who have worked to very tight deadlines during the pandemic to produce these fascinating papers. Our staff, notably Pauline Clark, Donald Ferguson and Isabelle Gius, have all helped to make this publication a reality. The book has also benefitted hugely from Bill Walsh's design skills.

Contents

PETER MATHIESON

Foreword

It gives me great pleasure to introduce this essay collection which marks the 50th anniversary of the Institute for Advanced Studies in the Humanities (IASH). Whilst the University's own history is around ten times as long, fifty years is an appreciable time for a research institute to be operating in the current academic environment. Given this volume's focus on 'humanities of the future' it is interesting to observe how IASH's own future has been shaped by its past.

In what, even by today's standards, looks like an innovatively cross-disciplinary move, IASH was first proposed in 1968 by an extraordinary natural scientist and by a leading humanities scholar: Professor Conrad Hal Waddington (Professor of Animal Genetics) and Professor John MacQueen (Professor of Scottish Literature and Oral Tradition). The following year IASH was founded within the then Faculty of Arts at the University of Edinburgh and in 1970, IASH hosted its first fellows and supported its first conference: *Scotland and the Enlightenment*. The novelty of this proposal is indicated by the fact that IASH is still Scotland's only Institute for Advanced Study (IAS) and one of the oldest IASs in the world.

As its ethos, IASH drew inspiration from other Institutes for Advanced Studies in the USA and Ireland as a place of inclusivity, independent from the university structure, where academics could come together and conduct research free from the responsibilities of teaching. Unlike its two predecessors (in Princeton, New Jersey and Dublin, Ireland), IASH was anchored within a university. As the overall emphasis on research productivity in UK universities intensified in the 1980s and 1990s, all

i

faculty were encouraged to be engaged in 'advanced studies' and IASH could no longer present this as its distinctive raison d'être. In this context IASH highlighted once again its focus on interdisciplinarity, a legacy which remains today.

IASH also developed a thematic specialisation. It was not intended to 'be concerned exclusively with Scottish projects' (in Professor MacQueen's words), but rather a centre that would benefit other universities and intellectual communities, both in Scotland and beyond. However, IASH's first conference (*Scotland and the Enlightenment*), its highly successful and wide-reaching Institute Project on the Scottish Enlightenment (1986), later projects and events, and the general interests of its directors and fellows, have all made IASH an important site in the recovery and revival of academic interest in Scottish culture, literature, history, arts and philosophy from the 1970s onward.

In response to these developments, the 1980s witnessed a growing community of fellows supported by IASH. Mrs Sophia M.W. Gifford made two generous donations (of £250,000 each) on behalf of her late husband, T.J. Carlyle Gifford, which still form the foundation of the Institute's external income and which underwrote the relative independence of the Institute. IASH also moved to its present-day location in Hope Park Square, giving it a distinct location and fostering the idea that IASH is a place that brings scholars into a community which encourages them to share ideas, make connections, and support each other's work. Then-Director Professor Peter Jones introduced several new initiatives to forge and intensify connections with international scholars and institutions, raising the international profile of IASH.

In the 2000s, based on feedback from current and former fellows, IASH began to shift its focus from older, established academics to supporting early or mid-career researchers. The changing research culture and rapid growth in humanities PhDs meant that there was a demand for new forms of postdoctoral opportunity and also that there were more women in the postdoctoral cohort. In 2005, Professor Susan Manning was the first woman to be appointed Director of the Institute. During her time as Director, the percentage of female fellows at IASH grew to nearly 50%; currently female academics are in the clear majority. With this new model IASH was able to increase its annual intake of fellows and in 2015 IASH welcomed its 1000th fellow, celebrating with an open day and reunion.

In recent years IASH has become the host for genderED, a project led by Professor Fiona Mackay which aims to connect work in gender and sexuality studies across different schools and make it accessible to students, researchers, and the wider community.

Now, at its 50th anniversary, IASH continues to focus on inclusivity, including race equality, and interdisciplinarity – offering diverse fellowships across the arts, humanities, and social sciences, sponsoring interdisciplinary events, planning new projects, and encouraging its research Fellows to fully participate in the collaborative atmosphere that IASH fosters. The last three years have seen renewed efforts to recruit fellows from all around the world, and IASH continues to be an important supporter of early-career researchers and academia in Scotland.

I do hope that you will discover something new and thought-provoking, and above all enjoy reading this collection of essays.

Professor Peter Mathieson
Principal and Vice-Chancellor of the University of Edinburgh

STEVEN YEARLEY

Shifting Perspectives and the Humanities of the Future

It's a slightly uneasy pleasure to write this introduction to this symposium volume since, though there's a great deal to celebrate in IASH having reached its 50ᵗʰ anniversary, it also calls to mind our frustration in finding that we had timed our anniversary celebrations to coincide exactly with the 2020 peak of COVID-19 infections in the UK. That timing meant that the live symposium and festivities had to be cancelled. But many scholars from the IASH community had prepared papers for the anniversary symposium, and so we offered people the chance to have them published in this special edited collection. This volume is therefore a celebration and commemoration of that anniversary, but it also serves as an opportunity to speak to an even wider audience or readership than could have participated in the planned symposium. This selection of papers gives a flavour of the wide range of scholarship undertaken at IASH and, at the same time, illustrates and allows us to reflect a little on possible futures for the humanities (and related fields) and on the contribution of institutes of advanced study.

IASH is now officially 50 years old. This clearly places it among the oldest IASs in the world. As the Vice-Chancellor's Foreword points out, the role of an institute of advanced studies in the humanities has changed a great deal over IASH's first half century. One big trend over the last 50 years is that, early on, IASs were a way of creating space for concerted research activity in the humanities. But as university departments themselves all sought to become centres of excellence in research (as well as teaching) there arose a question about the distinctive role for IASs: if everyone aspires to carry out advanced research, IASs look less distinctive. Clearly IASH

1

(and IASs generally) had to offer something with or for the humanities that was unlikely to be done in a department of literature or philosophy or history. Interdisciplinary endeavour became IASH's answer to this question. From about its second decade, IASH aimed to respond to the realisation that humanities research was changing: becoming more interdisciplinary, more likely to require external funding, and likely to depend on broad international scholarly networks.

Naturally, the situation of the Institute has continued to develop over the last 20 years or so, in part because of new possibilities and themes. At the time of writing, IASH is strongly encouraging work in the digital humanities, calling on emerging methods to carry out and extend customary forms of humanities research and exploring endeavours which are more or less unthinkable without digital connectivity and forms of digital analysis. Many Fellows are also working in the area of environmental humanities, re-examining the links between cultural practices and ecological change. Moreover, systematic attention to the environment is part of the widening-out and recognition of diverse perspectives which has been such a key feature of change within the academy in recent years. The humanities are also continuing their interactions in the area of medical and health humanities, and they are involved in new conversations with informatics and the natural sciences about the nature and specificity of the human condition, as well as the ethical and legal innovations that may be required to handle humans' interventions into human nature. These themes are strongly represented in the papers in this volume, and they are already incorporated in the focus points which we highlight on our IASH website; we also have specific fellowship schemes in most of these areas. Two further powerfully cross-cutting topics are also explored in several of the chapters in this volume: gender and sexualities studies, on the one hand, and race and decoloniality, on the other.

We would like to thank all our contributors, and especially Rosi Braidotti, who would have been the keynote speaker at the anniversary symposium. She has happily agreed to share her reflections in this collection. Professor Braidotti has served on IASH's Advisory Board for many years and is a stalwart friend of the Institute. Her superb scholarship plants a suitably bold and interdisciplinary flag at the heart of the humanities, and many of the themes she explores are developed further by her fellow authors.

Colin Johnson puts the art into artificial intelligence with his chapter, **New Aesthetics in Artificial Intelligence Art**. He probes into the linkages between aesthetics, algorithms and AI, positing some possible new directions for computer-made artworks. For Dr Johnson, 'machinehood' can fruitfully be compared with the autobiographical and viscerally personal art of recent years, perhaps in time situating the computer as equivalent to the human creative professional. His rich case-studies demonstrate the fertility of this ever-changing field and highlight the speed of change in the digital humanities.

In her chapter **Autism, Neurodiversity, and the Humanities**, Catherine Crompton outlines the history of our (popular and scientific) understanding of autism, the foundations of the present-day neurodiversity movement, the study of autism within various humanities disciplines, and how the humanities can integrate the message of the neurodiversity movement within future studies of autism. The paper focuses on the move to include autistic people within autism research ('nothing about us without us'), and it identifies the need to investigate intersectionality for autistic people and to diversify autism studies in relation to gender, race, and sexuality.

Kathryn Simpson's contribution (**The Digital Archive as Space and Place in the Constitution, Production and Circulation of Knowledge**) examines the digital archive and how it 'curates knowledge', looking especially at how archives are defined and compiled, as well as the way power imbalances and gender and ethnic bias operate within this process. In relation to the project she is currently working on, she specifically focuses on 'digitised archives of women's writing in the long nineteenth century'. She identifies some issues with digital archives that are shared by other researchers too – these include: unequal representation; the subjectivities involved in curating a collection; and the issue of how to maintain or preserve digital information, as projects are abandoned, certain digital formats fall out of use, and archives run out of digital storage space. Digital archives will become an ever-greater part of scholarly collections, and this chapter anticipates key methodological and practical challenges to which this will give rise.

Noémie Fargier's paper **Global Sound Archive** examines sound maps and their potential use for research in the humanities in the future. She looks at the world-wide, place-based sound project Aporee as the model many collaborative global sound maps follow, noting the limitations in this model in terms of search filters and capabilities. She highlights the question of who is making the recordings and the process of curation, the dual representation of space by organising an auditory medium in a physical way (recordings located on a map), and the question of how to continue to digitally store recordings as collections grow. The paper emphasises the potential value of sound maps for preserving the past and 'lost sounds', and – by linking digital and environmental humanities – makes a case for re-examining wild soundscapes as part of what we consider as environmental protection.

The history of concert life in Edinburgh is explored in Elizabeth Ford's chapter **Steil's Tavern and the Musick Club**. This covers the Edinburgh Musical Society as it evolved from Musick Club (which is said to have met at the Cross Keys Tavern in Edinburgh early in the eighteenth century). She also discusses the project she worked on (part of the AHRC-funded 'Space, Place, Sound, and Memory: Immersive Experiences of the Past' project), which used digital techniques to recreate a scene from the Cross Keys as an immersive VR experience. She describes some of this project's difficulties due to the lack of historical documentation about the Musick Club. Dr Ford's project melds historical research with technology in order to better understand a site-specific history that is difficult to construct based purely on archives.

In his chapter **The Future of History and its Recent Past**, Sam Cohn aligns his personal experience and reflections on history-writing with historical trends over the past 50 years. His analysis, which includes a reflection on changes in history scholarship at IASH, leads him to two predictions for the future of research: that historians will continue to cross 'the humanities/science divide' and that, due to the coronavirus pandemic, there will be an increased interest in previous plagues (e.g. the Great Influenza). The paper's identification of a continued intersection between historical studies/historiography and the sciences and technology links directly to Soraya de Chadarevian's discussion of the use of DNA in historical research and to Elizabeth Ford's engagement with digital reconstruction of a vanished historical location.

Natalie Goodison and Deborah Mackay write as a discipline-spanning team – a medievalist and epigeneticist – reviewing their joint work identifying an anomalous birth that takes centre-stage in a medieval romance (the 14th century tale, *The King of Tars*) as a molar pregnancy. They identify the steps which led to their partnership – as their title **An Unlikely Research Partnership between a Medievalist and a Geneticist** indicates – and what they have found to be the benefits of their working together. For Professor Mackay, their work has enabled her to able to better convey the concepts of epigenetics and reproduction to a broader audience, to make new diagnoses and identify genetic diseases, and to realise that there needs to be a greater focus on fertility in medical care and research. For Dr Goodison, the partnership has changed her perception of romance, making her 'analyse the extent to which romance may reflect prevalent theories of conception' and 'reconsider the *longue durée* of congenital abnormalities birthed by women'.

In her chapter on **DNA and History,** Soraya de Chadarevian discusses the use of ancient DNA (aDNA) and genetic studies to assist in researching historic populations. She frames her paper specifically in relation to a project she undertook with another historian about a decade ago, which looked at the Longobard migration in sixth-century Europe. Her emphasis on using scientific data (genetic research) only in conjunction with other disciplines and forms of evidence is a key point from this chapter, highlighting the critical role of insights from the humanities in cross-disciplinary research.

For his chapter, **Holocaust Studies in the Era of Climate Change**, Tomasz Łysak looks at the previously suggested connection between climate change and Holocaust studies, and he takes this discussion further by looking at Holocaust memoirs and fiction, both literary and in film, to identify links in vocabulary and experience between the Holocaust and climate change. He focuses primarily on the literary works of Primo Levi and the films *Der Rat der Götter* (*The Council of the Gods*) and *Snowpiercer*, identifying common themes in those disparate works. His chapter ends with a look at the way studies of the past can directly inform our understanding of the future and speaks directly to conceptions of the role of the environmental humanities.

In her chapter, **Setting Rumi: Casting the Intangible,** Margaret McAllister discusses her process of composing a piece of music, specifically a piece for cello and voice (commissioned by cellist Rafael Popper-Keizer), setting four poems by Jalāl ad-Dīn Muhammad Rūmī to music. She aims to set out a lucid account of her process of composing and touches on the different elements that must be considered when writing music, including the collaborative aspect of creating music. Throughout her explanation, she makes a point of demonstrating the way in which music – and its constituent parts, such as rhythm – links to lives and cultures. In this way, this chapter is a natural complement to Elizabeth Ford's chapter, as both authors situate music in historical terms.

From this very wide-ranging set of chapters we can see that this IASH symposium has inspired novel conversations about the trajectory of the humanities and has encouraged ideas and directions for the next 50 years to prepare IASH and the scholarly community for key trends in humanities futures.

ROSI BRAIDOTTI

The Transversal
(Post)Humanities
in the 21st Century

For Susan Manning

Introduction

Writing about the humanities in the midst of the COVID-19 pandemic means addressing an embattled field in a grieving world. There is no easy way to keep a balanced approach, given the alternation of exhilaration and suffering that marks our times. I have described this internally contradictory state as the posthuman convergence, that is to say the intersection of an intense sense of emergency with one of hope and resilience. We are swinging between the excitement at the advanced technologies that drive the Fourth Industrial Revolution (Schwab, 2015) and the anxiety about the damages inflicted by the Sixth Great Extinction (Kolbert, 2014). The effect of this convergence – technological development on the one hand, environmental degradation, climate change and new epidemics on the other – is felt on both the human and non-human inhabitants of this planet.

The COVID-19 emergency exemplifies the conflicting aspects of the posthuman condition (Braidotti, 2013). The planetary contagion, itself the result of environmental degradation and abuse of animal and other species by global capital, paradoxically resulted in increasing our collective reliance on the very technological apparatus that drives advanced capitalism. This is expressed in the collective hope – and scientific competition – for vaccines and other bio-medical solutions. But it also informs our global dependence on internet-backed communication and exchange of basic services and provisions, not least in education. All the contemporary humanities are digital humanities and, sadly enough, the ecological roots of this coronavirus are obscured in the mist of the public health emergency. All the contemporary humanities should also be environmental humanities, but regretfully they are not. And the death-toll is rising, across all species. At the time of writing, the coronavirus casualty list has reached the 1.5 million mark, while an estimated 1-3 billion animals died in the 2019 Australian bushfires alone. The world is in mourning.

How does one even begin to speak of the future of our field, amidst such intense grief? There is so much that we need to both embrace and heal, acknowledge and resist: the collective and personal loss of lives, the evidence of harsh socio-economic inequalities, the uncertainties about the future. Finding an appropriate language – both critical and humble – for such an endeavour entails taking in and on the pain of this damaged planet, without giving in to the pretentions of knowing better.

A deep sense of fatigue, at times even of hopelessness, is the prevalent mood; faced with such a sense of exhaustion, words in many ways fail us. The strength of those who think and research in the humanities is that we are experts at using ordinary language to achieve extraordinary levels of accuracy, precision and accountability. To express the extraordinary in ordinary language requires knowledge, inspiration and stamina. In such effort, at times our language practice slips into over-precise technical language, which the critics brutally dismiss as jargon. But mostly, we all remain accessible and strive to be comprehensible, while making ordinary language work overtime. Over the last decades, a consensus was reached within the humanities community that it is inappropriate to speak of a 'crisis' of our field. But nobody is denying that we do spend a disproportionate amount of time actually justifying or defending our existence, methods and terminology to the public.

To situate the humanities in the contemporary world requires therefore multiple balancing acts, respect for complexity, and an extra effort to develop cross-species solidarity. This is a time for collective mourning of our dead, both humans and non-humans; a time for solace and regeneration.

The traditional humanities mission of pastoral care needs to be extended transversally to encompass the planet as a whole, with its multiple non-human dwellers. The affective and social climate we are in calls for a collaborative ethics of inter-dependence and cross-species egalitarianism. 'We' are truly in this together, but 'we' are not one and the same. In what follows, I will single out some fragments of a meditation upon our grieving present, and end up striking an affirmative note.

After Humanism
The coronavirus emergency shows the impossibility of delinking both human welfare and our scientific thinking from their ecological roots. We are all part of an environmental ecosystem that we have disrupted at our own risk and peril. This is not an essentialist statement, because not only does it not entail the superiority of nature over culture, but it questions this entire divide as obsolete. An anthropogenic virus like COVID-19 is best understood within a nature-culture continuum. It emerges from environmental sources, but moves as a social actor and an indicator of structural social and economic inequalities. Public health has always been an intensely political issue, and the 'capitalocene' – that is to say, the greed of consumers' society – is primarily responsible for the abuses that triggered the epidemics. To address these intertwined issues, the humanities need to develop a new relationship to the so-called 'natural' sciences and vice-versa. A culture of mutual respect is urgently needed.

Post/decolonial and Indigenous philosophies working within different parameters have a great deal to teach us as well. While they stress that for most people on earth, the nature-culture distinction does not hold (Descola, 2009; 2013), they also show that the experience of death and extinction is an integral part of colonised cultures. For many Indigenous people on earth, epidemics, dispossession and environmental devastations were the mark of the colonial conquests and of the Europeans' appropriation and destruction of First Nations cultures (De Castro, 2015). Catastrophes on this scale are for many people on earth an everyday reality: not only do Europeans have a lot to answer for, but also a great deal to learn from the South on how to endure and prosper.

Consequently, the humanities at this point in time cannot smugly cling to an implied notion of a universal 'human' as an allegedly neutral category. The human is rather a normative category that indexes access to rights, privileges and entitlements. Appeals to the 'human' are always discriminatory: they create categorical distinctions among different categories of sub/in/infra-humans. Humanity is a quality that is distributed according to a hierarchical scale centred on a humanistic idea of Man as the measure of all things. This dominant idea of Man is based on a simple assumption of superiority by a subject that is masculine, white, Eurocentric, practising compulsory heterosexuality and reproduction, able-bodied, urbanised, speaking a standard language (Deleuze and Guattari, 1987; Irigaray, 1994; Braidotti, 1994; Wynter, 2015).

But humanism cuts both ways and you can be critical of western humanism in the name of humanism (Said, 2004); be an anti-humanist and remain perfectly anthropocentric (Foucault, 1977); you can also critique anthropocentrism but re-instate humanistic values (Singer, 1975; Nussbaum, 2006). I propose instead a critical posthumanist stance that takes the criticism all the way, across both categories. The convergence of posthumanism and post-anthropocentrism is never a harmonious synthesis; it rather entails negotiations and a chain of theoretical, social and political effects. My argument is that this process amounts to a qualitative leap in new conceptual directions: the transversal humanities, also known as the critical posthumanities. This is the most effective and ethical response to the contemporary conjuncture (Braidotti, 2019).

The convergence-factor needs to be stressed in order to avoid the risk of separation in contemporary knowledge production. For instance, scholarship – on AI; on the Anthropocene; on the new political economy of post-work; on climate change and extinction, etc. – is producing its respective takes on the human/non-human, independently of one another. Not only are there few crossovers between these domains, but they also tend to remain isolated from the critical work of speaking truth to power. These new separations do not help to construct the kind of transdisciplinary taskforce we would need to address the complexity of issues confronting us in the posthuman predicament.

Exposing the power-ridden assumptions of the dominant category of the human also results in relocating the subjects who have come to represent the dialectical opposite of this normative vision of 'Man'. These are the less-than-human others, dehumanised or excluded from full humanity – these qualitatively minoritarian subjects actually very often are quantitatively the majority. Historically, they have been the sexualised others (women, LGBTQ+); the racialised others (non-Europeans, Indigenous); and the naturalised others (animals, plants, the Earth). The others of the dominant subject – the Man of reason (Lloyd, 1984) – are the feminists, queer, anti-racists, Black (Hill Collins, 1991), Indigenous (Rose, 2004), postcolonial (Mies and Shiva, 1993) and ecological activists (Plumwood, 2002) and thinkers who have been criticising that regime for decades.

They have introduced theoretical innovation in the humanities through interdisciplinary practices that called themselves 'studies'. Women's, gay and lesbian, gender, feminist and queer studies; race, postcolonial and subaltern studies, alongside cultural studies; film, television and media studies; science and technology studies; these are the prototypes of the radical epistemologies. These 'studies' voice the situated knowledges (Haraway, 1988) of the dialectical and structural 'others' of the humanistic 'Man'. They have criticised the undifferentiated, universalist idea of the human upheld by the academic humanities on two grounds: structural anthropocentrism on the one hand, and inbuilt Eurocentrism or 'methodological nationalism' (Beck, 2007) on the other.

Methodological nationalism is inbuilt into the European humanities' self-representation as bastions of national languages, cultures and identities across the multi-lingual landscape of Europe and the world. As a method, it hinders the humanities' ability to cope with the distinctive features of our times: cultural diversity, notably between different geo-political areas but also within each one of them: global mobility, migration and the legacy of colonialism. Edward Said reminded us that humanism must shed its smug Euro-centrism and become an adventure in difference, exile and democratic criticism. This shift of perspectives requires consciousness-raising on the part of humanities scholars, a becoming-nomadic of sedentary mental habits (Braidotti, 1994). It is important to replace discriminatory unitary categories, based on Eurocentric, masculinist, anthropocentric and heteronormative assumptions, with robust alternatives, counter-knowledges, methods and affirmative values.

The critical 'studies' focus on the limitations of Eurocentric humanism and expose the compatibility of rationality and violence, of scientific progress on the one hand and practices of structural exclusion on the other. No privilege of extra-territoriality is granted to scientific reason and practice (Braidotti, 2011a; 2011b). Academic disciplines are held accountable not only to the disciplinary past, but also to the dynamic and transdisciplinary conditions of the present. Critical – in speaking truth to the power of dominant visions of subjects and knowledge – and creative at once, feminist and race theories propose alternatives forged by the experience, the unrealised insights and multiple competences of marginalised subjects (Braidotti, 2002; 2006). Their point of reference is thinking of, in, for and with the lived experience of others, in a becoming-world of knowledge production practices. The critical studies voice robust criticism, offering qualitative shifts of perspectives; as such they constitute an asset and a laboratory in the quest for a new role for the humanities in the 21st century.

Clearly, not all these 'studies' simply oppose humanism to embrace the posthuman: they also offer alternative visions of the humanist self, knowledge and society. Notions such as a female/feminist humanity (Irigaray, 1993), queer in-humanism (Halberstam and Livingstone, 1995), and Black humanity (Fanon, 1967; Wynter, 2005) are part of this tradition of more inclusive humanism (Braidotti and Gilroy, 2016). And just as obviously, not all these studies were inspired by the philosophical, linguistic, cultural and textual innovations introduced by the French post-structuralist generation since the 1970s. The sources of the critical humanities are multiple and they depend on the different locations of the knowing subjects. This methodology is not relativistic, but rather immanent and materialist. I have also defined it as a form of critical perspectivism – the politics of locations (Rich, 1994). The key idea is that disciplinary purity must give way to trans-disciplinary connections.

In a concomitance of events that marks the extraordinary period we are living through, the voices, experiences and perspectives of multiple de-humanised and excluded others are being expressed all around us. The power of viral formations has become manifest in the pandemic, stressing the agency of non-human forces and the overall importance of Gaia as a living, symbiotic planet (Margulis and Sagan, 1995). But at the same time a global revolt against endemic – and indeed viral – racism has also exploded in the fateful year 2020, crystallised around the Black Lives Matter movement. As these multiple crises unfold, the politics of the sexualised, racialised, naturalised others are moving centre stage, pushing the old Eurocentric *Anthropos* off-centre. It's time to move on.

After anthropocentrism
The humanities are also structurally anthropocentric, and this translates into sustained negotiations and discussions with the culture, methods and institutional practice of science and technology. The unique or exceptional nature of 'Man' – *Anthropos* – and his culture of humanism is challenged today not only because of his discriminatory practices – as argued by gender, race and postcolonial studies – but also in relation to contemporary science and technology. What is the place of the humanities as a scientific enterprise in this globalised, networked, technologically-mediated culture that no longer upholds the humanist unity of space and time as its governing principle?

Decentring anthropocentric patterns of thought, however, is particularly difficult for the humanities, in that it positions terrestrial, planetary, cosmic concerns, as well as the conventional naturalised others, animals, plants and the technological apparatus, as serious agents and co-constructors of collective thinking and knowing. Humanities scholars were not accustomed to asking such questions – 'what do you mean by human?' or, 'are we human enough?' or, 'what is human about the academic humanities?' Tradition and the force of habit encourage us to delegate to anthropologists and biologists all scientific discussions about *Anthropos*, while we in the humanities focus on Mankind, as culture, polity or civilisation.

The proliferation of critical 'studies' morphed with the posthuman convergence, when 'Man' came under further criticism as *Anthropos*, that is to say as a supremacist species that monopolised the right to access the bodies of all living entities. What has emerged in the last 15 years is a second generation of 'studies' areas, genealogically indebted to the first generation in terms of critical aims and political affects and commitment to social justice, while addressing more directly the issue of anthropocentrism. They range from animal studies to eco-criticism, green studies and critical plants studies. The anthropocentric core of the humanities was also challenged by the ubiquity of technological mediation and the capitalisation of Life through data mining (Asberg and Braidotti, 2018).

Media studies is almost emblematic of the post-anthropocentric shift, as it evolved from standard media, film and television studies into a galaxy of its own, encompassing game studies, internet studies, software studies, critical code studies, algorithmic studies, etc. A related and equally prolific field of posthuman research concerns the inhuman(e) aspects of our historical condition: conflict and peace research studies; post-Soviet/communist studies; human rights studies; humanitarian management; migration and mobility studies; trauma, memory and reconciliation studies; security, death and suicide studies; extinction studies; and the list is still growing.

Today, environmental, evolutionary, cognitive, biogenetic and digital critical studies are emerging around the edges of the classical humanities and across the disciplines. They rest on post-anthropocentric premises and technologically mediated approaches, which are very promising for new research in the field. They spell the end of the idea of a denaturalised social order disconnected from its environmental and organic foundations and call for more complex schemes of understanding the multi-layered form of interdependence we all live in (Tsing et al., 2017). Secondly, they stress the specific contribution of the humanities to the public debate on climate change, through the analysis of the social and cultural factors, the power mechanisms, the ethical values and aspirations that underscore the representation of these issues. Humanities and more specifically cultural research are best suited to provide a rigorous analysis of the social imaginary and help us think the unthinkable, both in the negative and the affirmative sense. The successive generations of 'studies' areas therefore are both institutionally and theoretically a motor of critique and creativity that can prove inspirational for the transversal humanities.

In a further development, several interdisciplinary areas of study in the humanities today no longer start from the centrality and the exceptionalism of the human; rather, they problematise it. These new fields call themselves: ecological, sustainable, Anthropocene or environmental humanities, sub-divided into blue (water) and green (earth) humanities; digital, computational, algorithmic or interactive humanities; medical, neural or bio-genetic humanities; public, civic, community or translational humanities, and the list is open and growing.

Their emergence was sudden, but did not go unnoticed. Meta-discursive analyses have been articulated in terms of: the posthumanities (Wolfe, 2010); the inhuman humanities (Grosz, 2011); the digital humanities (Hayles, 1999); the transformative humanities (Epstein, 2012); the critical posthumanities (Braidotti, 2013) and the nomadic humanities (Stimpson, 2016). Innovative and threatening in equal measure, the phenomenon of what I call the critical posthumanities represents both an alternative to the neo-liberal governance of academic knowledge, dominated by quantitative data and control, and a re-negotiation of its terms.

What are we to make of them?

My first comment is that, far from being the symptom of crisis and fragmentation, these new discourses are a sign of great vitality and innovation in the field. There is no crisis of the humanities in terms of content and research energy, though the field suffers from a negative public image and lack of government support.

Secondly, the transversal (post)humanities open up new eco-sophical, posthumanist and post-anthropocentric dimensions for research in the humanities. And these developments are empirically verifiable; they are already here. They are not the result of mere influx of capital. The transversal and critical humanities today are rather the result of the hard work of communities of thinkers, scholars and activists that reconstitute not only the missing links in academic knowledge practices but also a missing people.

The critical posthumanities assume that the knower – the knowing subject – is neither *homo universalis* nor *Anthropos* alone, but a collective assemblage, collaboratively linked to human and non-human agents as a complex zoe/geo/techno-mediated ensemble. The subject of knowledge

15

is no longer only Man/*Anthropos*, but rather a complex zoe/geo/techno-mediated ensemble. What this means is that the objects of study in the humanities today, in addition to human diversity, also extend to animals, eco- and geo-elements, forests, fungi, bacteria, dust and bio-hydro-solar-techno powers. We have meta-objects and the hyper-sea, while 'human/imal' and algorithmic studies ignite the imagination of our graduate students.

However, what is significant is not just the new objects of enquiry they introduce, but rather the qualitative shifts at the conceptual and methodological levels. These discourses take on the vital materialism, the life-making capacities of organic entities, but also of inorganic devices. They teach us how to think the vitalist immanence of non-anthropomorphic life-systems, 'smart' things and 'live' connections. Posthuman scholarship celebrates the diversity of zoe/geo/techno-mediated, that is to say, non-human lives, in a non-hierarchical matter; it recognises the respective degrees of intelligence, ability and creativity of all organisms not as a 'flat ontology', but as a materially embedded, differential system within a common matter.

This implies that thinking and knowing are *not* the prerogative of humans alone, but take place in the world, which is the terrestrial, grounded location for multiple thinking species and computational networks – we are all eco-sophically connected. Of course there is a qualitative difference between accepting the structural interdependence among species and actually treating non-humans as knowledge collaborators. My point is however, that, in the age of computational networks and synthetic biology on the one hand and climate change and erosion of liberties on the other, this is precisely what we need to learn to do, in addition to all that we know already. We need to de-familiarise our mental habits.

The creative proliferation of critical 'studies' as an institutional phenomenon was met with mixed reactions and even open hostility during the 1990s 'theory wars' in the USA (Redfield, 2016). This coincided not only with the emergence of the new political Right, the consequences of which we are all experiencing today, but also with the rise of digital culture, and support for bio-genetic and cognitive capitalism (Moulier-Boutang, 2012). This also resulted in a profound transformation of the university structure through the adaptation to neoliberal governance and emphasis on the monetarisation of knowledge. The result was the creation of classes of both academic stars, contiguous with the circuit of the media (Shumway, 1997), and the academic 'precariat'. This neologism merges precarious with proletariat, to designate the bottom social classes in advanced capitalism. This includes adjunct lecturers and other temporary, under-paid and over-worked non-staff members of the contemporary academy (Gill, 2010; Warner, 2015). What the position of these underpaid – and mostly younger – academics will be in the contemporary university is a matter of great concern.

The missing peoples' humanities

A pandemic on the scale of COVID-19 brings home to the western world an ancient truth: that 'we' are all in this planetary condition together, whether we are humans or others. But it is also high time for this heterogeneous and collective 'we' to move beyond the Euro-centric humanist and anthropocentric representational habits that have formatted it. Nowadays we can no longer start uncritically from the centrality of the human – as Man and as *Anthropos* – to uphold the old dualities. This acknowledgment, however, does not necessarily throw us into the chaos of non-differentiation, nor does it awaken the spectre of extinction. It rather points in a different direction, towards some other middle-ground, which expresses the awareness that 'we' – all living entities – share the same planetary home.

Yes, we are connected, that is to say ecologically interlinked through the multiple interconnections we share within the nature-culture continuum of our terrestrial milieu. But we differ tremendously in terms of our respective locations and access to social and legal entitlements, technologies, safety, prosperity and good health services. The posthuman subjects of today's world may be internally fractured, but they are also technologically mediated and globally interlinked. It is important to stress the materially embedded differences in location that separate us, but also stress the shared intimacy with the world that creates a sense of belonging together, within webs of ever-shifting relations.

A diversity of perspectives is crucial and today the critical posthumanities are in motion towards more inclusive horizons, led by multiple 'missing people'. Historically, all sorts of communities were already empirically missing. Whether we look at women and LBGTQ+, Indigenous knowledge systems, queers, otherwise enabled, trailer-parks, non-humans or technologically mediated existences, these are real-life subjects whose knowledge never made it into any of the official cartographies. Their struggle for visibility and emergence also affects the knowledge they are capable of generating. But the other missing people are the virtual ones, those that can emerge only as the result of a neo-materialist praxis of affirmation, aimed at constructing the plane of composition for such an assembly. By this, I mean a people in the process of becoming *not-One*: 'we-are-in-*this*-together-but-we-are-not-one-and-the-same' kind of posthuman subjects.

The emerging 'missing people' are the commons to come. They point to new clusters of research and knowledge production organised around a heterogeneous assemblage of devalorised human and non-human others, for instance: non-nationally indexed humanities; feminist/queer humanities; Black humanities; migrant/diasporic humanities; poor/trailer park humanities; decolonial humanities; a child's humanities; otherwise-abled/disabled humanities.

Since Rob Nixon's seminal work on slow violence (2011), the missing links between postcolonial theories, the environmental humanities and Indigenous epistemologies have been exposed and analysed, resulting in growing convergence between them. At the level of the political economy of the posthumanities, this results in the production of new areas of studies that crossover the convergence that constitutes the post-human turn.

This produces planetary differential posthumanities, such as: Indigenous environmental and digital humanities; postcolonial green; decolonial futures of digital media; transnational environmental literary studies; queer neo- and in-humanisms; Indigenous knowledges and cosmologies. Similar developments are on the way to fill in missing links in the digital humanities. For instance, relying on the work of pioneers like Lisa Nakamura (2002), Ponzanesi and Leurs (2014) claim that postcolonial digital humanities is now a fully constituted field, digital media providing the most comprehensive platform to re-think transnational spaces and contexts.

Mignolo's (2011) decolonial movement has struck new alliances between environmentalists and legal specialists, Indigenous and non-western epistemologies, First Nations peoples, new media activists, IT engineers and anti-globalisation forces. They have produced the decolonial digital humanities. Different assemblages are being formed, along the convergence of posthumanism & post-anthropocentrism, but adding in the social, ethical and political dimensions. They follow an encounter between feminist, LGBTQ+ and gender studies; postcolonial, de-colonial and Indigenous studies; critical legal studies; media activists; hackers and makers; First National land rights activists.

These encounters are transforming both the environmental and digital posthumanities. The assemblages they compose are as multiple as their lived experience, producing new areas of transversal research.

A posthuman university?

All these developments indicate the good state of health of posthuman knowledge in the humanities, but what do they mean for the contemporary university?

I remember long conversations with the late and much missed Susan Manning about the intellectual and civic missions of the university today, about the forgotten status of non-profit organisation, or charity, that is so much part of our history. I shared with Susan the idea that social relevance is an inbuilt attribute of academic excellence in higher education, and not an optional extra. I still believe that we, researchers in this field, need to work harder to restore an aura of cultural authority to scholarship in the humanities and to highlight the impact of university research upon citizens in extra-academic environments and in society as a whole.

Historically, relations between the universities as the location of academic research and their social, cultural and political contexts have been a matter of perennial concern. Every university has its own situated history of 'town and gown' relationships: always close, often troubled, the academic and the civic have always been mutually complicit. Their interaction reveals a society's self-representation, values, anxieties and their joint aspiration to train literate and discerning citizens. No amount of commitment to economic globalisation should alter this ideal. The fast rate of technological mediation, especially in these times of pandemic isolation, revive the humanities' mission to provide guidance, solace and care. This is a fundamental form of intergenerational solidarity that has no price, and which cannot be reduced to vocational training and support for a business economy. These values shape the very idea of what counts as fundamental 'research' and its value to society.

The contemporary humanities are at the core of these crucial concerns and are perfectly suited to provide insightful and workable solutions to the dilemmas of the posthuman convergence. In fact, they are already doing so through the surprising and inspirational transversal developments I have outlined here. The posthuman predicament does not mean that 'human' should become an obsolete category – rather, what we need is to update our understanding of what counts as 'human' and what new forms humanities research is able to acquire.

The humanities are negotiating their present predicament and contradictions by finding the self-confidence and the willingness to review some of their traditional assumptions and premises on behalf of scholarly excellence and commitment to society at large. Whether one believes in the intrinsic rationality of the humanities and their dialogical method as perfectly suited to the challenges of social accountability, or in the extrinsic need to elaborate an accountable epistemology for the humanities, extra work is needed. This entails a serious discussion of what, of the humanist past, can and should be salvaged. Of course the past and its canonical texts should be respected, but they should not be frozen into sacred nationalistic icons. The past of humanism is too rich and important to be monumentalised: it should be brought to bear upon the present, transversally and in a broad, planetary perspective. This supposes delinking the classical canon from ethnocentric, patriarchal and exceptionalist premises to be re-framed in a different social imaginary.

We need an active effort to sustain the academic field of the humanities in a new global context and to develop an ethical framework worthy of our times. Affirmation, not nostalgia, is the road to pursue. The humanities need to embrace the multiple opportunities offered by the posthuman condition and set new objects of enquiry, free from the traditional or institutional assignment to humanistic reflexes. We know by now that the field is richly endowed with an archive of multiple possibilities which equip it with the methodological and theoretical resources to set up original and necessary debates with the sciences and technologies and other grand challenges of today.

The question is what the humanities can become, in the global civic arena in a posthuman era. It seems urgent to organise academic communities that reflect and enhance an ethically empowering vision of the emergent posthuman subjects of knowledge, especially the 'missing peoples'. Transversal interconnections across the disciplines and society – shareable workbenches – are the way to implement an affirmative ethical praxis that aims to cultivate and compose a new collective subject. This subject is an assemblage – 'we' – that is a mix of humans and non-humans, zoe/geo/techno-bound, computational networks and earthlings, linked in a vital interconnection that is smart and self-organising, but not chaotic. Let us call it, for lack of a better word, 'life'.

Death is an essential part of it. So many lives today are the object of biopower's thanato-politics, or new ways of dying: think of the refugees dying on the edges of Fortress Europe. We are all vulnerable to viruses and other illnesses, to the effects of climate change and other devastations – and many of the exposed lives are not human. Fortunately, humans are not the centre of creation. This is the insight of affirmative thought as a secular, materialist eco-philosophy of becoming. Life is a generative force beneath, below, and beyond what we humans have made of it. It is an inexhaustible generative force that potentially can transmute lives into sites of resistance – all lives, including the non-human.

An adequate response to a crisis on the scale of COVID-19 calls for community-based experiments to see how and how fast we can transform the way we live and die. That means facing up to the negative conditions, the social and environmental inequalities and the collective responsibility towards exposed or vulnerable populations. It is a praxis that promotes action and critical self-knowledge, by working through negativity and pain. This proactive activism manifests living beings' shared ability to actualise and potentiate different possibilities and generate multiple and

21

yet unexplored interconnections. This is the immanence of life as jointly articulated in a common world. Not some transcendental and abstract notion of Life with capital letters, but rather the more patient task of co-constructing one's life, alongside so many others: just a life.

This praxis of forging communal solutions through the confrontation of uncomfortable truths is central to the ethics of affirmation. Accepting our shared exposure to ways of living and dying together, amidst environmental and public health human-led disasters, is also the starting point for a process of assessing what binds us together as an academic community. This is a task for the transversal humanities. This approach expresses a sort of epistemological humility that reiterates the never-ending nature of the processes of becoming-humans, even and especially in posthuman times.

BIBLIOGRAPHY

Asberg, C. and Braidotti, R., eds., 2018. *A Feminist Companion to the Posthumanities*. Cham: Springer International Publishing.

Beck, U., 2007. The cosmopolitan condition: why methodological nationalism fails. *Theory, Culture & Society*, 24(7/8), pp.286–90.

Braidotti, R., 1994. *Nomadic Subjects: Embodiment and Sexual Difference in Contemporary Feminist Theory*. New York, NY: Columbia University Press.

Braidotti, R., 2002. *Metamorphoses: Towards a Materialist Theory of Becoming*. Cambridge: Polity.

Braidotti, R., 2006. *Transpositions: On Nomadic Ethics*. Cambridge: Polity.

Braidotti, R., 2011a. *Nomadic Subjects: Embodiment and Sexual Difference in Contemporary Feminist Theory*. New York, NY: Columbia University Press.

Braidotti, R., 2011b. *Nomadic Theory: The Portable Rosi Braidotti*. New York, NY: Columbia University Press.

Braidotti, R., 2013. *The Posthuman*. Cambridge: Polity.

Braidotti, R., 2019. *Posthuman Knowledge*. Cambridge: Polity.

Braidotti, R. and Gilroy, P., 2016. *Conflicting Humanities*. London: Bloomsbury.

Descola, P., 2009. Human natures. *Social Anthropology*, 17(2), pp.145–57.

Descola, P., 2013. *Beyond Nature and Culture*. Chicago, IL: University of Chicago Press.

Epstein, M., 2012. *The Transformative Humanities: A Manifesto*. New York, NY: Bloomsbury Academic.

Foucault, M., 1977. *Discipline and Punish*. New York, NY: Pantheon Books.

Gill, R., 2010. Breaking the silence: the hidden injuries of the neoliberal universities. In: R. Gill and R. Ryan Flood, eds. *Secrecy and Silence in the Research Process*. New York, NY: Routledge, pp.228–44.

Grosz, E., 2011. *Becoming Undone*. Durham, NC: Duke University Press

Halberstam, J. and Livingston, I., eds., 1995. *Posthuman Bodies*. Bloomington, IN: Indiana University Press.

Haraway, D., 1988. Situated knowledges: the science question in feminism as a site of discourse on the privilege of partial perspective. *Feminist Studies*, 14(3), pp.575-99.

Hayles, K., 1999. *How We Became Posthuman*. Chicago, IL: University of Chicago Press

Hill Collins, P., 1991. *Black Feminist Thought: Knowledge, Consciousness, and the Politics of Empowerment*. London/New York: Routledge.

Irigaray, L., 1993. *An Ethics of Sexual Difference*. Ithaca, NY: Cornell University Press.

Irigaray, L., 1994. Equal to Whom? In: N. Schor and E. Weed, eds. *The Essential Difference.* Bloomington, IN: Indiana University Press.

Kolbert, E., 2014. *The Sixth Extinction.* New York, NY: Henry Holt Company.

Lloyd, G., 1984. *The Man of Reason: Male and Female in Western Philosophy.* London: Methuen.

Margulis, L. and Sagan, D., 1995. *What Is Life?* Berkeley, CA: University of California Press.

Mies, M. and Shiva, V., 1993. *Ecofeminism.* London: Zed Books.

Mignolo, W., 2011. *The Darker Side of Western Modernity: Global Futures, Decolonial Options.* Durham, NC: Duke University Press.

Moulier-Boutang, Y., 2012. *Cognitive Capitalism.* Cambridge: Polity.

Nakamura, L., 2002. *Cybertypes: Race, Ethnicity and Identity on the Internet.* New York, NY: Routledge.

Nixon, R., 2011. *Slow Violence and the Environmentalism of the Poor.* Cambridge, MA: Harvard University Press.

Nussbaum, M., 2006. *Frontiers of Justice: Disability, Nationality, Species Membership.* Cambridge, MA: Harvard University Press.

Plumwood, V., 2002. *Environmental Culture.* London: Routledge.

Ponzanesi, S. and Leurs, K., 2014. Introduction: on digital crossings in Europe. *Crossings, Journal of Migration and Culture,* 4(1), pp.3–22.

Redfield, M., 2016. *Theory at Yale: The Strange Case of Deconstruction in America.* New York, NY: Fordham University Press.

Rich, A., 1994. *Blood, Bread and Poetry: Selected Prose 1979-1985.* New York, NY: Norton.

Rose, D.B., 2004. *Reports from a Wild Country.* Sydney: University of New South Wales Press.

Said, E., 2004. *Humanism and Democratic Criticism.* New York, NY: Columbia University Press.

Schwab, K., 2015. The fourth industrial revolution. *Foreign Affairs,* 12 December.

Shumway, D.R., 1997. The star system in literary studies. *PMLA,* 112(1), pp.85–100.

Singer, P., 1975. *Animal Liberationism.* New York, NY: Avon Books.

Stimpson, C.R., 2016. The nomadic humanities. *Los Angeles Review of Books,* 12 July.

Tsing, A.L., Swanson, H.A., Gan, E. and Bubandt, N., eds., 2017. *Arts of Living on a Damaged Planet: Ghosts and Monsters of the Anthropocene.* Minneapolis, MN: University of Minnesota Press.

Viveiros de Castro, E., 2015. *The Relative Native: Essays on Indigenous Conceptual Worlds.* Chicago, IL: HAU Press.

Warner, M., 2015. Learning my lesson. *London Review of Books,* 37(6), pp.8–14.

Wynter, S., 2015. *On Being Human as Praxis.* Durham NC: Duke University Press.

Wolfe, C., 2010. *What is Posthumanism?* Minneapolis, MN: University of Minnesota Press.

COLIN JOHNSON

New Aesthetics in
Artificial Intelligence Art

Abstract

In recent years artists have engaged with artificial intelligence (AI) as a subject of their art, both by building AI-based machines that make art and by using AI as a medium in which to make art. This paper explores this through the lens of aesthetic theories that explain the impact of such AI art on the audience. Four ideas are explored in detail: the revisiting of representational aesthetics through AI simulation and the rescaling of natural phenomena; works that explore the inner workings of AI algorithms; guided self-expression facilitated by AI as a medium in interactive, relational artworks; and, the aesthetics of mass and repetition seen through AI processes of search and classification.

Introduction

In the last few years, a number of visual and conceptual artists have begun to interact with the materials and methods of artificial intelligence (AI): treating AI as a medium with which to make art, building machines to make art, or focusing on AI as a subject for art. Behind these recent developments by artists are decades of research in computational creativity (Colton, López de Mántaras and Stock, 2009; Veale and Cardoso, 2019), Internet art (Greene, 2004), technologically-grounded art, data art (Harrison, Waters and Jones, 2005), etc.

Such works have included the use of AI as an artistic medium, for example in the neural network works of Mario Klingemann and the Obvious collective, who exercise artistic skill through their choice of training examples for an AI system and the choice of parameters for that system. Other AI artist practitioners see themselves as meta-makers, people who make machines or software that in turn make the art. This is exemplified by the *Painting Fool* system by Simon Colton and colleagues (Colton, Valstar, and Pantic, 2008; Krzeczkowska et al., 2010; Colton, 2012) and by Harold Cohen's *AARON* system, developed over several decades (McCorduck, 1991; Cohen, 1995). It is often the case in such examples that the artists throw away some of their control – whilst they have programmed the system themselves, deliberate randomness or the complexity of the code as it executes can produce results unpredictable to the creator. For artists such as Sougwen Chung, Rob Saunders and Leonel Moura, who work with physical robots, the roughness of the physical world and the difficulty of accurately controlling machines (particularly wheeled mobile robots) adds to the unpredictability.

In the background of this artistic work is a body of research into computational creativity (Colton, López de Mántaras, and Stock, 2009) – the attempt to build and understand AI systems that can demonstrate creative intelligence and work in creative domains such as the arts. This has not only produced a slew of work aimed at building creative machines, but also the very existence of such machines, and the development of techniques required to build them, has provoked new theories about creativity and a more detailed understanding of its nature.

Much of the writing on this topic has focused on the technical means of producing the artworks. In this paper, the focus instead is on aesthetic concerns. In particular, four aesthetic theories are presented that represent recastings of traditional aesthetic ideas. Representational theories of art are given new life by considering AI and artificial life artworks that simulate natural phenomena at a new, immediately perceivable scale and by representing the inner workings of algorithms. Expression-based aesthetic theories are revisited in the context of works that use AI to guide the audience in finding new ways to express themselves. Finally, modernist aesthetics of mass and repetition are examined in the context of computer systems that can create masses of material based on meaning and connotation rather than on visual similarity.

The Purpose of Aesthetic Enquiry

Why do cultures around the world have a distinctive category of objects that are *artworks*, objects created specifically for attention and contemplation in their own right? What is it that distinguishes such artworks from mundane objects? What is the process of 'making special' by which people exhibit certain behaviours towards artworks (Dissanayake, 1995; 2013)?

A number of philosophical and psychological theories have been devised over the years to explore aesthetic experience (Carroll, 1999; Dutton, 2009; Gaut and Lopes, 2013) – dating back to Plato (n.d.), who first raised the idea that there might exist a wider theory of aesthetics beyond pointing out the aesthetic properties of individual objects, each regarded as having an aesthetic value *sui generis*.

One set of theories focuses on imitation – objects that have aesthetic value because they accurately reproduce, and bring to our attention, aesthetically engaging imagery and focus our attention on a particular aspect of it. A related set of aesthetic theories concentrates on the skill of the artist in conveying the image with accuracy and conviction. Both of these have faded somewhat in recent times as photographic means of capturing the visual likeness of an object have rendered the value of reproduction by hand less significant (Benjamin, 1969; Carroll, 1999). Nonetheless, artistic skill is still valued – indeed, whilst mechanical means of reproduction might be available, the effective operation of them remains a skill, and the choice of what to photograph under what conditions remains a complex aesthetic decision. Moreover, the decision to draw attention to specific aspects of a visual scene is still a powerful part of artworks, and there is a rise (post-photography) in artistic movements that are grounded in ideas of reproduction – but, now, non-literal reproduction designed to shine a new light on some aspect of a visual scene that is not immediately available through a naïve reproduction.

Another set of theories focuses on formal aspects of an artwork. In these, the subject of the work is more-or-less irrelevant. Instead, it is how the formal properties of space – colour, shape, angle, alignment distribution – are used that is important, whether applied to a figurative depiction or in a more abstracted way. This set of theories is particularly focused on explaining why, given two objects with superficial similarity – say, two photographs depicting the same objects – one might be regarded as an artwork capable of provoking aesthetic behaviour, whilst the other is a workaday depiction.

The final main class of theories are concerned with expression, most importantly emotional expression. These theories revolve around the idea that art is a distinctive way in which the artist can express their emotional state (or, memories or imagination of such a state) to another person.

In a recent paper (Johnson, in press), I have outlined ways in which these aesthetic ideas can be applied to artworks involving AI and the challenges involved in doing so. In this paper, I focus instead on the way in which AI art pushes these aesthetic ideas, creates new aesthetic concepts and revisits existing aesthetic concepts in new ways.

New Aesthetics for a New Medium

How might aesthetic theories change in light of AI art and computational creativity? The remainder of this paper explores four new aesthetic ideas that are particularly relevant to the way in which AI art has an aesthetically engaging effect. These ideas are: the use of simulations of life and intelligence to re-represent natural phenomena on a scale that is appreciable to the immediate senses; the exploration of the inner workings of AI systems; the use of AI as a technology to work with an audience to amplify, distort and provoke their own creativity; and the ability of search engines to generate masses of material.

Representational Aesthetics and Aesthetic Rescaling
Some of the earliest aesthetic theories were concerned with *representation*. Accurate representation of a visual field was seen as a reason for aesthetic appreciation, whether through appreciation of the artist's skill or by the brute fact of being able to bring a representation of an aesthetically valued object into the viewer's purview. With the rise of mechanical means of generating representations, such as photography, such theories have faded in importance. That is not to say that such representations are uncomplicatedly objective – but, with the rise of them, aesthetic theories

based solely on the value of reproduction and imitation began to fade.

However, recent advances in computer art might cause us to revisit representational theories. That is, works that use computer/ AI technologies to rescale phenomena that would otherwise be unappreciable by the immediate senses. Consider a work such as *Eden* by Jon McCormack (2001). This is an installation piece which projects onto a number of panels and includes a soundtrack. Both the visual images and the soundtrack are generated in real-time by a simulation algorithm that replicates (in a very abstracted form) the ecological interactions between a population of creatures and plants: plants grow, creatures move, creatures eat plants, predator creatures eat prey creatures and new creatures are born. A representation of this activity is projected onto the screens, and the soundscape is generated by sounds associated with the various actions.

One aspect that makes this aesthetically engaging is the *scaling* (in both time and space) of an aesthetically-appreciable phenomenon from something that happens over weeks, months or years, over many square miles, to something that can be appreciated on a scale appreciable to the immediate senses. A viewer of the work in a gallery can spend a few minutes looking at the work and can gain an appreciation of these phenomena on an aesthetic level.

It is common for scientists to describe the phenomena that they study as having an aesthetic value. Theories and observations are described using aesthetic terms such as 'beauty' and 'awe-inspiring'. Yet, this aesthetic appreciation is gained only by detailed study of the subject and by building a rich mental model of the scientific phenomenon of interest. By building these representations that reduce the phenomenon to a scale in time and space where it can be appreciated by the senses, these works give a glimpse into this aesthetic world without the need to build these internal mental models.

Works such as *Eden* are sometimes described as *artificial life* (alife) artworks (Penny, 2010; McCormack, 2012). Artificial life is an approach to the biological and ecological sciences that tries to understand the natural world by building simulations of phenomena on the computer (Levy, 1993). However an important part of alife research is trying to understand a broader set of principles underlying the biological sciences; one difficulty with understanding general principles of biology is that there is only one example of the origin of life, and so it is hard to create a comparative biology where different forms of life could exist. By building computer simulations that allow us to rerun the origin and development of life over and over again, perhaps with variations in conditions (e.g. climate), a broader understanding of biology can be developed, based not just on life as it is on Earth, but on 'life-as-it-could-be' (Langton, 1989, p.2). This provides another potential direction that has been rather under-explored in alife art so far. Rather than aesthetic scaling of existing natural phenomena, there is the potential for such 'simulations' of ideas yet to be found in nature to represent more abstract ideas from theoretical biology.

Another direction to pursue in understanding these works is through the well-developed theories of *environmental aesthetics*, which attempt to explain why people find natural scenes aesthetically engaging. These theories fall into two broad categories. The first are those that argue that our aesthetic appreciation of the natural environment is grounded in and enhanced by our understanding of natural history and environmental science (Carlson, 1979; Saito, 1998). In the second category, Noël Carroll (1993) instead argues that aesthetic appreciation of nature is more visceral and that it is a different kind of aesthetic appreciation to that of artworks, because people cannot readily separate themselves from the environment (Berleant, 1988), and therefore they cannot take the disinterested stance that is often seen as a prequisite for aesthetic judgement (Kant, 1790). Works such as *Eden* place complex ecological phenomena into the gallery and provide a mid-ground between these two theories of environmental aesthetics, allowing rich scientific theories to be appreciated, but from a visceral/perceptual stance rather than an intellectual appreciative one.

Exploring the Inner Workings of Algorithms
Another way in which AI art has revisited the aesthetic of reproduction and imitation is in those works that explore the inner workings of AI algorithms. For example, Penousal Machado, João Correia and Juan Romero (2012) present an algorithm that explores a space of visual representations: the

algorithm contains a collection of formulæ that describe which pixels in an image should be which colour, and these formulæ change over time by a process of mutation and exchange of components inspired by biological evolution. The driver for these changes is similarity of the images to a collection of images of human faces. The end results of such a process are rather prosaic; the algorithm learns, within the constraints of what its space of formulae can express, how to represent the typical features of a person's face. The interesting examples, though, are those that are generated by stopping the process before it has reached its final level of expertise; the resulting images are distorted abstractions of the concept of a face.

The well-known deep dreaming images are generated by a similar process (Simonyan, Vedaldi and Zisserman, 2014; Spratt, 2017). In these, an AI algorithm known as a deep neural network is used. These networks are used for many tasks in AI, with the canonical one being the problem of labelling photographic images with words describing what can be seen within the visual field. In the deep dreaming images, this process is cut off early, whilst the network is still trying, only partially successfully, to fit its previous store of images to the current image. These partial successes expose the inner workings of the algorithm in an interesting, and often uncanny, way.

These examples offer one interesting general approach to creating AI art from algorithms, which is to take a system that is trained to imitate or understand the world and then sample from the middle of that process of imitation, giving a somewhat abstracted representation that nonetheless is grounded in the objects being imitated. This approach has echoes of the automatism of the surrealist movement, such as the automatic drawings of André Masson and others (Montagu, 2002). These artists attempt to expose aspects of hidden processes, in this case the processes in the pre-conscious areas of the mind, through the exercise of mental discipline aimed at removing the conscious control of the artist's movements. Similarly, these AI works attempt to expose aspects of the inner workings of algorithms.

Aesthetic Self-contagion

A number of AI artworks are based around an idea of interaction with an audience. In these, the work is active – what is displayed to the audience depends on the actions of the audience member, most commonly through the modality of movement or voice. Such interactive works date back to the early days of technological art – one of the earliest works of robotic art was Edward Ihnatowicz's *Senster* (1970), a giraffe-like robotic creature equipped with a control circuit inspired by the response of animals to the environment (Kac, 1997; Zivanovic, 2005). Despite the simplicity of the behavioural model (essentially, the creature demonstrated 'curiosity' towards quiet sound and movement and 'fear' by moving quickly away from loud sounds and sudden movement), it gave an impression of life-like behaviour and, in turn, inspired curiosity from the audience about how it behaved.

More recently, such interactions have been through the computer screen. This idea was initially introduced by Richard Dawkins (1990) (the *Biomorphs* system) as a way of helping people to understand how biological evolution works. *Biomorphs* consisted of a system that displayed a number of graphical images of creatures on the computer screen. The users of the system then chose some of the images to act as 'parents' of the next generation; these 'parents' were paired at random and 'genes' – sequences of numbers specifying different elements of the creature's graphics – were exchanged and mutated, producing a new screen of virtual creatures. Similar ideas were explored around the same time in a collaborative project between programmer Stephen Todd and artist William Latham (Todd and Latham, 1991; 1992), in which this interaction-evolution cycle was used to allow the artist to explore the space of possibilities in a complex computer graphic system.

More recent works, such as NEvAr (Machado and Cardoso, 2002) and the ant paintings by Sébastien Aupetit et al. (2003) involve the audience in evolving the appearance of the work. In such systems, audience members choose (e.g. by clicking on examples) which of a number of images they want to see used as the basis for creating the next generation of images. Thus, the image displayed is evolved in a collaboration between the audience and the system (and the constraints and possibilities placed into the system by its creator). Typically, such systems will present the current images on screen and the audience members will click on them; however, some works have embedded this interaction into a different kind of environment. For example, Duncan Rowland and Frank Biocca's (2002) *Genetic Sculpture Park* embeds a number of virtual sculptures in a virtual reality environment, where audience members can explore, remove disliked sculptures from the plinth, and then generate a new set of sculptures from the ones remaining. More recently, eye-tracking systems have been used to drive the selection (Holmes, 2010; Makin et al., 2016) – the audience member is presented with a visual environment, and the parts of that environment that they attend to most strongly are used as the basis for the next generation of examples.

What aesthetic idea is underpinning these works? A new aesthetic is emerging here which is related to expression-based theories of aesthetics. Expression theories of art focus on the idea that art is a distinctive and effective way for the artist to express their feelings to their audience – more so than communicating those feelings descriptively in words. There are many variants of such theories; in particular, there is a significant debate about whether such expression requires the artist or audience member to actually *feel* the emotions being expressed, or whether artwork primarily acts as a trigger for a memory of those emotions. Regardless of the details of the expression theory under consideration, such theories come to a juddering halt when attempting to analyse computer-based art – computers simply do not have any emotional qualia to express, and so expression theories cannot explain the aesthetic effect of computer-based art.

There are workarounds to regain some kind of expression theory for AI art. Perhaps the computer is being used as an expressive medium by the artist. Perhaps it is sufficient for the computer to be able to simulate aspects of emotional expression, without actually being capable of feeling those emotional qualia. These interactive works, though, open up a new kind of aesthetic, where the expression is coming from the audience member but being reflected, restricted, amplified and distorted through the interactive computational process. An audience member might not have the artistic skills to directly express a certain emotional state through art. Nonetheless, by using such interactive systems, they can recognise when an approximation to what they want to express is being displayed, and by a repeated process of audience member choice alternating with the AI artist generating new examples based on those choices, a human-machine collaboration gradually helps the audience member to make an act of artistic expression. Indeed, the audience member may not have started out with any particular emotional state that they wanted to express, but instead they gradually worked towards that expression through this cycle.

Artistic expression has been described as a process by which 'the artist infects others' with their feelings (Tolstoy, 1904, p. 39). Noël Carroll (2014, p. 164) has noted the link between these ideas and the concept of *emotional contagion* in psychology (Hatfield, Cacioppo and Rapson, 1994). In these interactive artworks there is a kind of emotional *self-contagion*. The audience member will be able, through the sequence interactions, to create things that they wouldn't have been able to create by themselves – the artwork is partially acting as a spur to the audience member's creativity (albeit a kind of ostensive creativity, where they are being creative by selection rather than by directly doing). Yet, this creativity is not unconstrained – the creator of the work has put certain ways of mark making and certain visual styles into the system.

Such systems can be seen as a very direct example of the *relational art* described by Nicolas Bourriaud (1998). In such works, the artist acts not as the direct creator of the work but, rather, as the 'catalyst' for interactions that would not happen otherwise. The term has typically been applied to artworks based around human relations, e.g. where participants come together and, by the layout and structure of the event or by participants following a set of rules, interact in a way that they would not in day-to-day life. In these systems, the audience member is still interacting through such a catalyst system, but they are interacting with the consequences of their previous decisions.

Mass Aesthetics

A commonly explored aesthetic in twentieth-century art has been one of *mass*. Minimalist artists such as Sol LeWitt, Carl Andre and Michael Landy have explored the differential aesthetic impact between a single object and many copies of the same object, perhaps displayed in a formal structure. Some of this is an aesthetic of form – for example, a mundane object such as the brick being 'made special' by its use in a tessellation (Dissanayake, 1995; 2013). Sometimes, it is the impact of the analogy with processes of mass production or large-scale commerce that forms the aesthetic nub of the work, as in Landy's *Market* and *Appropriation 1* or Ai Weiwei's *Sunflower Seeds*.

These are very concrete, physical examples of mass aesthetics. Other artists have collected information about their lives in a persistent way. For example, works such as Ellie Harrison's *Tea Blog*, where she records her thoughts every time she has a cup of tea, or *Eat 22*, a record of everything she ate over the course of the year (Harrison, Waters and Jones, 2005; Harrison and Jones, 2009), gather the mass together not by visual similarity but by the category to which those objects belong.

The development of AI art and the development of large-scale connections between data allows for works that expand this mass aesthetic. Most of the examples presented so far in this section could be characterised as examples of *syntactic* mass – it is the direct, surface characteristics of an object that are replicated at scale to achieve the aesthetic effects that emerge when many identical or similar things are placed in the same visual field.

However, there are other kinds of mass that AI and large-scale computer networks allow us to exploit. The Ellie Harrison pieces discussed previously could be characterised as having a mass aesthetic, but one based on *semantic mass* – that is, the collection of objects by meaning or category rather than by visual similarity.

One way in which technology has transformed the creation of masses of semantically linked objects is through web search engines such as Google and Bing, which provide a ready route for the creation of semantic mass. Web search has been used as part of the creative process in a number of recent artworks (Johnson, 2013). For example, the image search function in Google allows for the ready creation of grids (formal arrangements) of images associated with a particular word. Such pieces could be presented as visual artworks in their own right.

This raises interesting issues about authorship and creativity. The collection of items with some hidden (or not-so-hidden) theme is a well-known way for humans to make art. For example, Hong Hao's *Long March in Panjiayuan* series consists of photographs of large collections of tourist tchotchkes on the theme of Mao Tse-Tung. This has impact because of the visual coherence of the material used – e.g. the colour palette – as well as the kitsch value of the objects themselves.

When it comes to semantic mass that is computer-created, issues of the locus of creativity come to mind. A literature on computational creativity – the ability of computers to act in a way that would be regarded as creative if carried out by humans – has developed over the last couple of decades (Wiggins, 2006; Ritchie, 2007; Colton, López de Mántaras and Stock, 2009). Interestingly, the vast majority of the work on computational creativity has focused on old media forms of creativity, with little exploration of computational creativity in new media or technological artforms (Johnson, 2013).

One explanation for this might be that it is difficult to pin down the origins of creativity in a richer, interactive, networked computational process (Johnson, 2012). Consider my own piece *Blank*, which consists of nine panels of giclée prints from the top Google Image Search results for the word 'blank'. Panel seven contains a powerful image; in the middle of a grid of neutral, emotionally unsalient images is an image of several bullets, presumably arising from the association of the word *blank* with blank cartridges. If this has been created by human agency, we might well have noted the violent effect of placing this image – relevant yet a salient contrast – in the middle of this set of otherwise rather bland images. Should the computer be credited with this artistic act? One argument against that is that it is a human that decided that the images were worth displaying and that until a computer can make these evaluative value judgements we should not regard it as being truly creative (Charnley, Pease and Colton, 2012).

Perhaps the richest answer is that we are faced here with a truly joint creation, and that audiences need to adjust to an artform in which the boundaries between creator and medium are increasingly blurred. We are not used to paint or clay pushing back into the creative process to anything like the same extent as the networked computer environment asserts itself in this context.

Syntactic mass often reflects on the idea of mass production. By contrast, semantic mass can reflect on the more recent notion of mass customisation. For example, Aaron Koblin's piece *The Sheep Market* consists of 10,000 drawings of sheep (Koblin, 2006; Doan, Ramakrishnan and Halevy, 2011). Each of these drawings were created by workers using the Amazon *Mechanical Turk* system, which matches up workers with requests for work. Each of the drawings were created by a different worker, who was paid $0.02 for their drawing.

A specific kind of semantic/connotational mass is where the connotation is a person's name. In particular, several works have explored the idea of how internet search and social networking allows the discovery of many people with the same name. One example is Jennifer Mills' piece *What's in a Name?*, where the artist has taken a collection of image search results for her own name and then painted pictures based on those images. This 'transcoding' into a different medium adds depth to this work (Manovich, 2002).

A final form of mass is one based on the coincidence of how a collection comes together in time or space, rather than by some link between the appearance of the objects in the collection or an underlying connotation or meaning. Call this *propinquitic* mass.

Anywhere where people come together – physically or virtually – has the ability to create such a mass. The collection of conversations in a café is an example. However, it is difficult to collect and re-present such material to create an artwork, and it is also intrusive to privacy. However, online sources make this both technically more feasible and reduces privacy issues, as users voluntarily contribute information that is intended to be viewed publicly in some form.

One place where such a propinquitic collection can be found is in the live feed of Google searches displayed in the foyer of Google. This displays a random selection of terms that have been recently typed into the Google search engine (presumably slightly censored for taste and decency).

There is some artistic merit in displaying propinquitic information in such a direct way. Viewers can be provoked by unexpected items or combinations within the search stream and, by contrast, be surprised at how common certain topics are. There is scope for viewers to take a more readerly approach to the construction of meaning from the stream and find connections between items in the stream. By contrast, more distilled ways of presenting such material, such as summaries of hot topics, seem less artistically interesting, as too much work has been done for the viewer.

Photography in Abundance by Erik Kessels demonstrates how a physical work, facilitated by technology, can draw upon this idea of propinquitic mass. The piece consists of a printout of every photo uploaded to the photo-sharing website Flickr on one (arbitrary) day: enough to fill a couple of rooms with piles of photographs.

This work can be looked at in a number of ways. Visitors to the work are encouraged to enter the room and look at individual photos, encouraging 'ah-ha' moments. Other views of the work treat the collection as a mass. The transcoding of the work from virtual into physical makes concrete the sheer amount of material that is being shared using these services, working against the difficulty that people have with comprehending large numbers. Nelson Goodman (1976) has noted that, whilst the thing that is most like a painting is another painting, we don't see this – instead, we say that a painting is representative of a castle or a dog or whatever its subject is. Interestingly, in this example, the sheer quantity of photos reimagines this. Instead of the photos being seen as individual representations of subjects, they are once again just photos.

Future Directions
What are some future directions for AI art and its aesthetics? One direction is the creation of works that engage with the growing political and ethical analysis of AI algorithms. Such works have been few in number to date, but are beginning to emerge, as highlighted in a recent article by Daphne Milner (2019). She highlights two works in particular: *ImageNet Roulette* by Kate Crawford and Trevor Paglen, which highlights offensive and stereotypical labels generated by a popular AI image labelling system; and *Not The Only One* by Stephanie Dinkins, an AI chatbot that is trained with

the oral history of her family, engaging with issues of race and AI.

One interesting aspect of such AI works that engage with and critique AI is that they draw attention to the presence of AI as a medium. Art that draws on the personhood, autobiography and identity of the artist has been a common part of art of the twentieth and twenty-first centuries, but AI art has rarely drawn attention to the 'machinehood' of its creation.

One reason for this may be that, as present, AI art is often evaluated and critiqued through a computational creativity lens (Colton, López de Mántaras and Stock, 2009). That is, the point of the evaluation is to analyse which dimensions of creative intelligence are being exhibited by the machine that created the work. Under such a lens, it is hard to value works that engage in a deliberate way with technology. Human creativity is often held up as being the prototypical example of creativity (for example, Colton, López de Mántaras and Stock (2009, p. 11), define computationally creative systems as 'software that exhibits behavior that would be deemed creative in humans'). As such, results that could just as well have been created by a human are valorised, while results that expose the software's computer-ness fail to convince. There is something of the legacy of the Turing test here (Moor, 2003), where (in the most common interpretation used today) the ability to pass as indistinguishable from a human in conversation is seen as a landmark test of intelligent behaviour.

As a result, we are stuck in a situation where work that reflects on technology is seen as having a 'technical fetish or fascination' (McCormack, 2005, p. 434), being valued because a computer can do it at all, rather than because of the actual value of the art produced. Perhaps AI art needs to go through a cycle – initially, the argument that computer-generated art is valuable needs to be made by comparison with, and passing off as, human generated art; but as AI-made art becomes more acceptable, the need to prove its value by comparison with human art might become less urgent, freeing up the medium to engage with its origins in a more direct way.

One area where such a transformation might exhibit itself is in the realm of AI as a generator of conceptual art. It is notable that AI art has made almost no attempt to engage with this kind of art making before. Given the richness with which the AI field has explored the idea of knowledge representation (Brachman and Levesque, 2004), there would seem to be much scope for extracting interesting pieces of knowledge to use as the basis for conceptual art works.

Conclusions

This paper has examined some recent examples of AI art in the light of aesthetic theories. In particular, four examples have been given of where AI art provokes the adaptation of aesthetic theories: artificial life artworks that bring complex scientific observations to a scale where they are appreciable by the immediate senses; artworks based on exposing the inner workings of algorithms; artworks that use AI as a catalyst to enhance the audience's creativity; and, artworks that draw on AI search and classification algorithms to create new kinds of mass aesthetics. Finally, we have presented some underexplored directions for AI art: making AI art that critiques and analyses the political and ethical aspects of AI, and AI as a medium for and creator of conceptual art.

BIBLIOGRAPHY

Aupetit, S., Bordeau, V., Monmarche, N., Slimane, N. and Venturini, G., 2003. Interactive evolution of ant paintings. In: *The 2003 Congress on Evolutionary Computation, 2003. CEC '03.* Canberra, Australia, 8-12 December 2003. s.l.: IEEE.

Benjamin, W., 1969. The Work of Art in the Age of Mechanical Reproduction. In: H. Arendt, ed. 1969. *Illuminations.* Translated by Harry Zohn. New York, NY: Schocken Books. pp.214-218.

Berleant, A., 1988. Environment as an aesthetic paradigm. *Dialectics and Humanism,* 15, pp.95-106.

Bourriaud, N., 1998. *Relational Aesthetics.* Dijon: Les Presses Du Réel.

Brachman, R.J. and Levesque, H.J., 2004. *Knowledge Representation and Reasoning.* San Francisco, CA: Morgan Kaufmann.

Carlson, A., 1979. Appreciation and the natural environment. *Journal of Aesthetics and Art Criticism,* 37, pp. 267-276.

Carroll, N., 1993. On being moved by nature: between religion and natural history. In: S. Kemal and I. Gaskell, eds. 1993. *Landscape, Natural Beauty and the Arts.* Cambridge: Cambridge University Press. pp. 244-266.

Carroll, N., 1999. *Philosophy of Art: A Contemporary Introduction.* London: Routledge.

Carroll, N., 2014. The arts, emotion, and evolution. In: G. Currie, M. Kieran, A. Meskin and J. Robson, eds. 2014. *Aesthetics and the Sciences of Mind.* Oxford: Oxford University Press. pp.159-180.

Charnley, J, Pease, A. and Colton, S., 2012. On the notion of framing in computational creativity. In: M.L. Maher, K. Hammond, A. Pease, R. Pérez y Pérez, D. Ventura and G. Wiggins, *Third International Conference on Computational Creativity.* Dublin, Ireland, 30 May - 1 June 2012. s.l.: computationalcreativity.net.

Cohen, H., 1995. The further exploits of AARON, painter. *Stanford Humanities Review,* 4(2), pp.141-158.

Colton, S., 2012. The painting fool: stories from building an automated painter. In: J. McCormack and M. d'Inverno, eds. 2012. *Computers and Creativity.* Heidelberg: Springer. pp.3-38.

Colton, S, López de Mántaras, R. and Stock, O., 2009. Computational creativity: coming of age. *AI Magazine,* 30(3), pp.11-14.

Colton, S., Valstar, M.F. and Pantic, M., 2008. Emotionally aware automated portrait painting. In: S. Tsekeridou, A.D. Cheok, K. Giannakis and J. Karigiannis, *DIMEA '08: Third International Conference on Digital Interactive Media in Entertainment and Arts.* Athens, Greece, September 2008. New York, NY: Association for Computing Machinery.

Dawkins, R., 1986 *The Blind Watchmaker.* Harlow: Longman Scientific & Technical.

Dissanayake, E., 1995, *Homo Aestheticus: Where Art Comes from and Why.* Seattle, WA: University of Washington Press.

Dissanayake, E., 2013. Genesis and development of 'making special': is the concept relevant. to aesthetic philosophy? *Rivista Di Estetica*, 54, pp.83-98.

Doan, A., Ramakrishnan, R. and Halevy, A.Y., 2011. Crowdsourcing systems on the world-wide web. *Communications of the ACM*, 54(4), pp.86-96.

Dutton, D., 2009. *The Art Instinct: Beauty, Pleasure, and Human Evolution*. Oxford: Oxford University Press.

Gaut, B. and Lopes, D.M. eds., 2013. *The Routledge Companion to Aesthetics*. 3rd ed. London: Routledge.

Goodman, N., 1976. *Languages of Art: An Approach to a Theory of Symbols*. 2nd ed. Indianapolis, IN: Hackett Publishing.

Greene, R., 2004. *Internet Art*. London: Thames and Hudson.

Harrison, E. and Jones, H., 2009. *Confessions of a Recovering Data Collector*. Plymouth: Plymouth College of Art.

Harrison, E., Waters, J. and Jones, H. eds., 2005. *Day-to-Day Data: An Exhibition of Artists who Collect, List, Database and Absurdly Analyse the Data of Everyday Life*. Nottingham: Angel Row Gallery.

Hatfield, E., Cacioppo, J.T., and Rapson, R.L., 1994. *Emotional Contagion*. Cambridge: Cambridge University Press.

Holmes, T., 2010. *Interactive Evolutionary Computation Driven by Gaze: A New Paradigm for Experimental Aesthetics and Beyond*. PhD. Royal Holloway, University of London.

Johnson, C., 2012. The creative computer as romantic hero? Computational creativity systems and creative personæ. In: M.L. Maher, K. J. Hammond, A. Pease, R. Pérez y Pérez, D. Ventura and G.A. Wiggins, *Third International Conference on Computational Creativity 2012*. Dublin, Ireland, 30 May - 1 June 2012. s.l.: computationalcreativity.net.

Johnson, C.G., 2013. Artistic and musical applications of internet search technologies: prospects and a case study. *Digital Creativity*, 24(4), pp.342-66.

Johnson, C.G., (in press). Aesthetics, artificial intelligence, and search-based art. In: J. Romero, P. Machado and G. Greenfield, eds. (in press). *Handbook of Artificial Intelligence and the Arts*. Heidelberg: Springer.

Kac, E., 1997. Foundation and development of robotic art. *Art Journal*, 56(3), pp.60-67.

Kant, I., 1790. *Critique of Judgement*. Edited by Nicholas Walker, 2007. Translated by James Creed Meredith, 1952. Oxford: Oxford University Press.

Koblin, A., 2006. The Sheep Market. [online] Available at: <http://www.thesheepmarket.com> [Accessed August 2020].

Krzeczkowska, A., El-Hage, J., Colton, S. and Clark, S., 2010. Automated collage generation - with intent. In: D. Ventura, A. Pease, R. Pérez y Pérez, G. Ritchie and T. Veale, *First International Conference on Computational Creativity 2010*. Lisbon, Portugal, 7-9 January 2010. s.l.: computationalcreativity.net.

Langton, C.G., 1989. Artificial Life. In: C.G. Langton, ed. 1989. *Artificial Life*. Boston, MA:

Addison-Wesley.

Levy, S., 1993. *Artificial Life*. Harmondsworth: Penguin.

Machado, P. and Cardoso, A., 2002. All the truth about NEvAr. *Applied Intelligence*, 16(2), pp.101-118.

Machado, P., Correia, J., and Romero, J., 2012. Expression-based evolution of faces. In: P. Machado, J. Romero and A. Carballal, *Evolutionary and Biologically Inspired Music, Sound, Art and Design, First International Conference, EvoMUSART 2012*. Málaga, Spain, 11-13 April 2012, Berlin/Heidelberg: Springer.

Makin, A.D.J., Bertamini, M., Jones, A., Holmes, T. and Zanker, J.M., 2016. A gaze-driven evolutionary algorithm to study aesthetic evaluation of visual symmetry. *i-Perception*, [e-journal] 7(2). https://doi.org/10.1177/2041669516637432.

Manovich, L., 2002. *The Language of New Media*. Cambridge, MA: MIT Press.

McCorduck, P., 1991. *Aaron's Code: Meta-art, Artificial Intelligence, and the Work of Harold Cohen*. San Francisco, CA: W.H. Freeman & Co.

McCormack, J., 2001. Eden: an evolutionary sonic ecosystem. In: J. Kelemen and P. Sosík, *Advances in Artificial Life, 6th European Conference, European Conference on Artificial Life 2001*. Prague, Czech Republic, 10-14 September 2001. Heidelberg: Springer.

McCormack, J., 2005. Open problems in evolutionary music and art. In: F. Rothlauf, J. Branke, S. Cagnoni, D.W. Corne, R. Drechsler, Y. Jin, P. Machado, E. Marchiori, J. Romero, G.D. Smith and G. Squillero, *Applications of Evolutionary Computing, Workshops 2005: EvoBIO, EvoCOMNET, EvoHOT, EvoIASP, EvoMUSART, and EvoSTOC*. Lausanne, Switzerland, 30 March - 1 April 2005. Berlin/Heidelberg: Springer.

McCormack, J., 2012. Creative ecosystems. In: J. McCormack and M. d'Inverno, eds. 2012. *Computers and Creativity*. Heidelberg: Springer. pp.39-60.

Milner, D., 2019. How art holds AI to account. *It's Nice That*, [online] Available at: <https://www.itsnicethat.com/features/how-art-holds-artificial-intelligence-to-account-digital-art-041219> [Accessed 17th August 2020].

Montagu, J., 2002. *The Surrealists: Revolutionaries in Art and Writing 1919-35*. London: Tate Publishing.

Moor, J.H., ed., 2003. *The Turing Test: The Elusive Standard of Artificial Intelligence*. Heidelberg: Springer.

Penny, S., 2010. Twenty years of artificial life art. *Digital Creativity*, 21(3), pp.197-204.

Plato, n.d.. *Cratylus. Parmenides. Greater Hippias. Lesser Hippias*. Translated by H. N. Fowler, 1926. Cambridge, MA: Harvard University Press.

Ritchie, G., 2007. Some empirical criteria for attributing creativity to a computer program. *Minds and Machines*, 17(1), pp.67-99.

Rowland, D. and F. Biocca, 2002. Cooperative design methodology: the genetic sculpture park. *Leonardo*, 35(2), pp.193-96.

Saito, Y., 1998. Appreciating nature on its own terms. *Environmental Ethics,* 20(2), pp.135-49.

Simonyan, K., Vedaldi, A., and Zisserman, A., 2014. Deep inside convolutional networks: visualising image classification models and saliency maps. In: *Workshop Proceedings, International Conference on Learning Representations (ICLR) 2014.* Banff, Canada, 14-16 April 2014. s.l.: s.n.

Spratt, E.L., 2017. Dream formulations and deep neural networks: humanistic themes in the iconology of the machine-learned image. *Kunsttexte.de,* 4.

Todd, S. and Latham, W., 1991. Mutator, a subjective human interface for evolution of computer sculptures. IBM United Kingdom Scientific Centre Report 248.

Todd, S. and Latham, W., 1992. *Evolutionary Art and Computers.* London: Academic Press.

Tolstoy, L., 1904. *What Is Art?.* Translated by Aylmer Maude, 1904. New York, NY: Funk and Wagnalls.

Veale, T. and Cardoso, A., eds. 2019. *Computational Creativity: The Philosophy and Engineering of Autonomously Creative Systems.* Heidelberg: Springer.

Wiggins, G.A., 2006. Searching for computational creativity. *New Generation Computing,* 24(3), pp.209-22.

Zivanovic, A., 2005. SAM, the Senster and the Bandit: early cybernetic sculptures by Edward Ihnatowicz. In: *AISB'05: Social Intelligence and Interaction in Animals, Robots and Agents: Proceedings of the Symposium on Robotics, Mechatronics and Animatronics in the Creative and Entertainment Industries and Arts.* Hertfordshire, England, April 2005. s.l.: AISB Press. Available at: <https://aisb.org.uk/wp-content/uploads/2019/12/4_CreatRob_Final.pdf> [Accessed 18th August 2020].

CATHERINE CROMPTON

Autism, Neurodiversity, and the Humanities

Over the past 50 years, our understanding of autism has undergone a dramatic metamorphosis. We have seen a significant progression in autism research and a seismic paradigm shift in our understanding of autism. However, to understand how to move forwards, we must examine and appreciate the progress that has already been made, while recognising there is still a long way to go.

This progress is a culmination of research in many fields, with the humanities making some of the most significant contributions to our modern understanding of autism. The work of autistic writers and self-advocates has also had a critical impact on moving forward the discourse around autism, including introducing the concept of neurodiversity.[1]

To continue this progress, researchers can embrace the concept of neurodiversity and embody the principle of 'nothing about us without us' through participatory and inclusive research practice. The humanities are fertile ground for neurodiversity research and are uniquely placed to deepen and broaden our understanding of the range of neurodivergent experience.

Our evolving understanding of autism

Origins

'Autism', from the Greek '*autos*', meaning 'self', was first used to describe

---

1 The neurodiversity umbrella incorporates a range of neurodivergences including autism, ADHD, dyslexia, and dyspraxia. This chapter will focus on autism, situating it within the wider context of neurodivergence.

social withdrawal in adults with schizophrenia (Bleuler, 1908). In 1943, the landmark paper 'Autistic Disturbances of Affective Contact' was written by psychiatrist Leo Kanner, describing a young child who was 'happiest when he was alone', 'oblivious to everything around him', who enjoyed spinning toys, and was distressed by disruptions in routine (p.242). Kanner later recognised these patterns in a small group of his patients, and thus autism was first recognised as a clinical condition. In parallel to this, Hans Asperger had identified a group of Austrian children with a similar, shared set of features (Asperger, 1944). Both Asperger and Kanner noted differences in the social behaviours of the children, alongside focused special interests – a lack of eye contact, a preference for routine and structure – and that these features persisted into adulthood.

Aetiology

In the absence of any biomedical explanation, Kanner believed that autism was caused by 'refrigerator mothers' and a 'genuine lack of maternal warmth' (1949, p.422). This remained unchallenged for many years. It was believed that the autistic child's behaviour was caused by withdrawing from their environment and seeking comfort in solitude (Kanner, 1949). This theory was embraced by the medical establishment in the 1950s, with numerous publications describing the effects of a lack of parental affection and the impact of life experiences on autistic development (Bettelheim, 1959). This concept was disproved in the 1960s and 70s, as a growing body of evidence indicated the biological underpinnings of autism and its relationship with brain development.

In 1977, the first study of autism in twins established that autism is partially genetic in nature. Folstein and Rutter (1977) found that when one twin is autistic, the other twin is significantly more likely to also be autistic if they are identical twins rather than non-identical twins. Subsequent studies have consistently replicated this finding, showing a significant genetic influence (Bailey et al., 1995; Le Couteur et al., 1996). However, the genetic influence on autism is not related to a single gene and is instead likely to be related to many genes of small effect size (Bailey et al., 1995). The majority of medical research since this seminal 1977 paper has focused on identifying the complex polygenic underpinning on autism and understanding the biological differences of autism as a lifelong neurodevelopmental condition (Pellicano, Dinsmore and Charman, 2013).

Diagnostic criteria

Changes in diagnostic criteria have reflected our evolving understanding of autism. Initially described as a psychiatric disorder of 'childhood schizophrenia' (American Psychiatric Association, 1968), autism was characterised by a detachment from reality. As our understanding of the biological and neurodevelopmental basis of autism became established, diagnostic manuals were updated. Autism was established as a separate diagnosis in 1980, distinct from schizophrenia, and described as a 'pervasive developmental disorder' by the American Psychiatric Association (1980). The diagnosis was then defined by a lack of interest in others, communication impairments, and unusual responses to the environment – all emerging before the age of two-and-a-half.

As understanding of the heterogeneity of autism grew, the notion of autism as a 'spectrum' became reflected in the diagnostic criteria. In 1994, autism was separated into five conditions, each with distinct features (American Psychiatric Association, 1994). This included those with no intellectual or clinically significant language delay, which was defined as 'Asperger's Disorder'. Further updates to the diagnostic criteria conceptualised autism as a continuous spectrum, with the latest iteration identifying only one condition of 'Autism Spectrum Disorder' and eliminating the previous separate conditions (American Psychiatric Association, 2013).

This new framing recognises that there are core autistic similarities, while also understanding that these may present as a range of traits. It inherently addresses that, as well as differences between autistic people, there are likely to be differences *within* an individual autistic person, depending on, for example, the environment they are in.

Centring the autistic experience through autistic narratives

For a long time, autism was described by clinicians, researchers, or parents of children with autism (Rose, 2008; Hacking, 2009). Over the past 30 years, many first-hand accounts and autistic narratives have been published which have enabled a much deeper understanding of autism. Seminal texts by Temple Grandin, Donna Williams, Tito Rajarshi Mukhopadhyay, and Daniel Tammet have provided rich descriptions of the experience of being autistic. These texts, in particular the early books by Grandin and Williams, were revolutionary in describing first-hand experiences and autistic peoples' own stories (Rose, 2008; Hacking, 2009). In a foreword to Grandin's *Thinking in Pictures*, neurologist Oliver Sacks described Grandin's writing as: 'Unprecedented because there had never before been an "inside narrative" of autism; unthinkable because it had been medical dogma for forty years or more than there was no "inside" or inner life, in the autistic' (Sacks, 2006, p.11).

Around the time that Grandin and Williams' work was published, Jim Sinclair, an autistic advocate and academic, emerged as an early leader of the autistic community. Sinclair co-created Autism Network International, an advocacy organisation run by and for autistic people in 1992. In 1993, Sinclair gave a speech to the International Conference on Autism in Toronto entitled 'Don't Mourn for Us', which has since been considered neurodiversity's first manifesto (Pripas-Kapit, 2020).

> Autism isn't something a person has, or a "shell" that a person is trapped inside. There's no normal child hidden behind the autism. Autism is a way of being. It is pervasive; it colors every experience, every sensation, perception, thought, emotion, and encounter, every aspect of existence. It is not possible to separate the autism from the person–and if it were possible, the person you'd have left would not be the same person you started with.

> (Sinclair, 1993, cited in Sinclair, 2012, p.1)

In recent years, advances in technology and the internet have meant that a hugely diverse range of autistic voices and perspectives are now easily accessible. This has particularly enabled autistic people who do not use spoken language to tell their own stories.

The Neurodiversity Movement

Many autistic people are at the forefront of the 'neurodiversity' movement. Neurodiversity is the phenomenon of neurological diversity, a naturally occurring feature of the human race. Just as diversity in ethnicity and gender are part of humanity, so too is diversity in our neurology, including brain structures, connections, and functions. Neurodiversity incorporates a range of differences in how our brains function and how this translates into behaviour, and it regards all of these differences as normal variation within the human population (Fenton and Krahn, 2007; Kapp et al., 2013).

Neurodiversity also gives rise to defined categories in brain differences, which result in diagnostic labels like autism and ADHD. Neurodiversity includes everyone: 'neurodivergent' people (those whose neurocognitive functioning differs from the norm in some way, such as autistic people, people with ADHD, and people with dyslexia) and 'neurotypical' people (the majority neurotype, describing people whose neurocognitive function falls within a 'socially acceptable range') (Kapp, 2020). Neurotypical people differ from each other at an individual level, as do autistic people or people of any other neurotype.

The neurodiversity movement advocates for a range of goals, including greater acceptance of neurodivergent (including autistic) behaviours and the ability for neurodivergent people to embrace their natural behaviours and not have to conform to neurotypical social norms. It also advocates for research and services that focus on improving the quality of life and upholding the rights of neurodivergent people (Jaarsma and Welin, 2012; Kapp, 2020). Key to this is the principle of 'nothing about us without us', involving neurodivergent people at all levels of decision-making to lead to meaningful change.

The definition of autism in 2020

To receive a diagnosis of 'Autism Spectrum Disorder', a person must be assessed by a medical professional as having persistent difficulties with social communication and social interaction, restricted and repetitive behaviours, and activities and interests that have been present since early childhood and 'limit and impair everyday functioning' (American Psychiatric Association, 2013, p.26). As the diagnostic criteria for autism have evolved and become more inclusive, autism has moved from being seen as a rare condition of childhood to being understood as something that affects between 1-4% of the population across the lifespan, in myriad different ways (Yeargin-Allsopp et al., 2003; Russell et al., 2014). It is unlikely that this will be the last change in the autism diagnostic criteria. Changes to date have been progressive and welcome; however, there is still more to know and understand.

While the medical terminology is 'Autism Spectrum Disorder', the language around autism is constantly evolving. The autism community, including autistic people, their families, friends, and those who support them, often have differing views about how to describe autism (Kenny et al., 2016). A lack of consensus on this may reflect the heterogeneity of autism and the widely varying support needs of people on the spectrum. The idea of autism as a disorder is rejected by many, who instead view it as a difference.

While medical autism research has moved forward our understanding of the biological mechanisms of autism, much of our understanding of the autistic experience has come from the work of autistic writers and self-advocates. Alongside this, much of the distance between Kanner and Asperger's understanding of autism and how autism is now conceptualised has been gained through research in the humanities and social sciences.

Autism and the humanities: the past fifty years

By focusing on trying to understand what life is like for autistic people and the challenges they face, the humanities and social sciences have significantly changed our definition and perception of autism over the last 50 years – arguably more so than medical research. Indeed, Pellicano, Dinsmore and Charman (2014) found that many of the top research priorities for autistic people and their families were questions that could be best addressed by the humanities, despite the fact that the majority of research funding is allocated to biomedical research (Pellicano, Dinsmore and Charman, 2013).

Following is a short overview of some of the key research in the humanities and social sciences that has shaped our knowledge and understanding of autism. This is not an exhaustive or comprehensive overview, more an introduction to some of the key research in each field.

Psychology

Psychology is the study of the mind and how its development, functions, and interactions with the environment underlie human behaviour. Naturally, a significant amount of progress in our understanding of autism has come from psychological research. Early psychological work on autism focused on case studies and small group research, with the first robust and large-scale study in 1979. Wing and Gould's (1979) theory of a 'triad of impairments' was based on a screened sample of over 900 children and clustered autistic features into three categories of 'deficit': social interaction, communication, and imagination. This 'triad of impairments' fundamentally shaped modern understanding of autism and was (and still is) the basis for the diagnostic criteria.

Subsequently, psychologists searched for a single unifying theory of autism, and though several have been proposed (e.g. Baron-Cohen, 2002; Frith, 2003; Markram and Markram, 2010), a cohesive and inclusive framework has not been established. In 1996 Wing published *The Autistic Spectrum*, which described the heterogeneity of autism and the high degree of variability between autistic people. This conceptualisation of autism as a spectrum reflected that there may be vast dissimilarities between autistic people who are still connected by a common similarity. This ground-breaking development had a seismic impact on how autism is diagnosed by clinicians and understood by the general public.

Until recently, psychology largely focused on the social and cognitive aspects of autism, comparing autistic and other groups based on standardised and experimental measures. For example, many psychological studies have compared how autistic and non-autistic people perform on 'theory of mind' tasks, which test the ability to understand and predict other people's behaviour (Baron-Cohen, Leslie and Frith, 1985; Frith and Happé, 1994). This kind of research has tended to focus on tasks which may be harder for autistic people (Morrison et al., 2019). While this can be useful in progressing understanding of autism and helping design supports for autistic people, it can lead to overly simplified views of autism and misconceptions: for example, that autistic people lack empathy (Aaltola, 2014; Fletcher-Watson and Bird, 2020). In recent years, qualitative studies have been more common, which have deepened our understanding of autistic people's experiences of the world (Sedgewick, Hill and Pellicano, 2019; Crompton et al., 2020).

Linguistics

Linguistics is the study of language and its structure, along with the social, cultural, and political factors that influence how we use language. Research into autistic differences in language development and use has been integral in understanding autism. This has included research exploring concepts such as pronoun reversal (using 'you' when 'I' was intended and vice versa), echolalia (repeating a word or phrase) and production-comprehension lag (speakers producing more or less sophisticated speech than they can comprehend) (Gernsbacher, Morson and Grace, 2015). This has contributed to the development of speech and language therapies for autistic people, as well as improving understanding of autistic people who communicate differently, for example those who do not use spoken language.

Linguistics research has also explored autistic social interaction in depth and the relationship between language skills and social communication (Hale and Tager-Flusberg, 2005). Recently, linguists have examined areas such as the effect of bilingualism on autistic language acquisition and use (Drysdale, van der Meer and Kagohara, 2015). These areas of research have direct real-world applications for individuals, families, and communities.

Sociology

Sociology is the study of society, social relationships, interaction, and culture, including social policy and welfare. Sociologists have made significant contributions to our understanding of autism, particularly through studies of social movements and autism advocacy groups (Silverman, 2008). This has included studying and documenting the evolution of the social model of disability, which re-frames disability as being caused by the way society is organised instead of by a person's impairment.

> In the broadest sense, the social model of disability is about nothing more complicated than a clear focus on the economic, environmental and cultural barriers encountered by people who are viewed by others as having some form of impairment – whether physical, sensory or intellectual. The barriers disabled people encounter include inaccessible education systems, working environments, inadequate disability benefits, discriminatory health and social support services, inaccessible transport, houses and public buildings and amenities, and the devaluing of disabled people through negative images in the media – films, television and newspapers.

> (Oliver, 2004, p.18)

More recently, sociologists have examined the specific barriers experienced by autistic people and the experience of being oppressed by societal views of normality. Some propose that the primary difficulties for autistic people are in understanding a confusing social world (Aylott, 2003). Others have highlighted the double standard of labelling autistic difficulties understanding non-autistic communication as 'impaired' while not framing non-autistic difficulties understanding autistic communication in the same way (Milton, 2012). Sociology is uniquely positioned to use epistemological and phenomenological frameworks to provide insight into the autistic experience (Leveto, 2018), including exploring the relations between autism and identity (Davidson and Henderson, 2010).

Literary and cultural studies

Research into how autistic people are characterised in literature and popular culture has helped us understand the positive and negative impacts of representation for autistic people. The representation of autistic characters (or characters with autistic traits) can contribute to increased autism awareness and understanding in the general population, though it can also be stereotypical and one-dimensional (Nordahl-Hansen, Øien and Fletcher-Watson, 2018). Children's books, popular novels, mainstream television shows, and popular movies often portray autistic characters as geniuses or heroes (Belcher and Maich, 2014), and show autistic characters as having savant-like skills (Nordahl-Hansen, Øien and Fletcher-Watson, 2018). However, the estimated prevalence of savantism in autistic people is very low, at between 10% and 30% (Rimland, 1978; Howlin et al., 2009).

By failing to accurately represent a broader spectrum of the autistic experience, misconceptions about autism become prevalent in the general population. Media can be a powerful tool for increasing understanding of autism, but it is important that the stories that are portrayed reflect a range of different realities.

Neurodiversity and the humanities

The neurodiversity movement advocates for acceptance of difference in how brains function. Research questions in the humanities are often defined by characterising a specific group (e.g. autistic adults) or comparing and contrasting two groups (e.g. autistic teens and non-autistic teens). Combining these approaches is possible, and in doing so, the humanities can play a key role in furthering our understanding of neurodiversity. Potential fertile areas for neurodiversity research across the humanities include:

• moving away from a deficit-based model of comparing neurodivergent and neurotypical groups
• examining disabling aspects of the environment and how they can be minimised for neurodivergent people
• enhancing understanding of the neurodivergent experience
• aligning research agendas with the priorities of neurodivergent communities.

One way to engage with the principles of neurodiversity and 'nothing about us without us' is to utilise participatory methods and inclusive research practice across all research endeavours relating to neurodiversity.

Participatory and inclusive research practice

Participatory research happens *with* members of a relevant population, rather than simply *to* them or *for* them (Israel et al., 2005). For example, in autism research, this is characterised by the meaningful inclusion and involvement of autistic people in the research in an empowered way. Participatory research is not a research methodology in and of itself, but rather is a framework of defining characteristics that can be incorporated into a range of different methodologies. On a practical level this might involve an autistic project consultant providing oversight and expert advice on the research, collaborating with an autistic researcher, or a researcher joining an autistic community group to work on a specific project.[2]

Participatory research must include representatives with first-hand lived experience of the relevant neurodivergence. For example, in autism research, this involves the inclusion of autistic people, rather than, for example, the non-autistic parents of an autistic child or professionals who work with autistic children. This is not to say that these groups do not have relevant and important expertise, skill and insight, but for work to be truly participatory, the opinions and experiences of those with first-hand experience must be centred.

Researchers must ensure that they are attentive and accommodating to the access and communication supports that may be required by community members involved in research.[3] As the aim of participatory research is to engage and involve those who have been voiceless and powerless in research, it is of practical, ethical, and moral importance to ensure the opportunity to engage in participatory research is available to all, regardless of access or support needs.

Directly involving neurodivergent people using participatory research paradigms can have positive practical impact. Including community

2   Though researchers themselves may be neurodivergent, it is still important to utilise participatory methods in order to present researchers with perspectives different to their own.

3   See Chown et al., 2017, Fletcher-Watson et al., 2019 and Milton et al., 2019 for more comprehensive guidance, including redressing the power dynamic between researchers and community members.

members can ensure that research is asking useful, feasible, and acceptable questions, and it can help humanities researchers learn *how* to ask these questions, particularly to people who may have differences in communicative style or method. In humanities studies requiring data collected via human participation, for example in psychology or linguistics, autistic involvement in recruitment, development of test materials, and interpretation of data can minimise common research risks, such as failing to recruit, participant dropout, and misinterpretation of findings. Using participatory methods can also ensure that research has practical relevance for neurodivergent people, their lives and communities, and is sensitive and respectful to their needs. It can also enhance the translational impact of research outputs.

Neurodivergence is defined by the fact that people who are neurodivergent process and respond to information differently than neurotypical people and experience the world in a fundamentally different way (den Houting, 2019). Without directly incorporating their views in research, it is not possible to increase our understanding of neurodevelopmental diversity (Robertson, 2009). Additionally, participatory research done well increases the skill, understanding, and empathy of the researcher, provides an enriching and empowering experience for the community members, improves the quality of research, its impact and reach, improves engagement between academic and non-academic communities, and builds trust with marginalised communities.

Participatory research in the humanities

The humanities provide a multitude of frameworks to enable rich explorations of the human experience of neurodivergence. Participatory methods can be embedded into many of these frameworks. While participatory research may find more obvious applications in some humanities fields, for example psychology or linguistics, some creative thought can result in its meaningful and beneficial application in other fields.

For research that involves studying sources such as text, art, or transcripts, it may seem that it is not necessary or beneficial to include autistic insight into the project as the research does not involve collecting human data. However, including a participatory element in this type of research could be beneficial.

For example, to a humanities scholar examining the representation of autism in twentieth-century British literature, it may not seem pertinent to include a participatory element. The researcher would likely be looking for representations in the literature that align closely with clinical diagnostic criteria. However, involving autistic people in this process could improve the researcher's understanding of how these clinical criteria translate into real-world behaviours, interactions, and experiences. This would result in a more nuanced understanding and interpretation of the literature. Including a participatory element enriches the research, builds researcher skills, builds engagement with the community, and enhances the impact of the work.

Neurodiversity and the humanities of the future

The humanities are concerned with studying aspects of society and culture, and how the human experience is processed and documented. Humans use many media to understand the world and record experiences, including philosophy, art, literature, music, drama, and language. The myriad of research methodologies and academic frameworks from across the humanities can enhance our understanding of neurodivergence as well as our ability to document the experience of being neurodivergent. The contribution of the humanities over the coming years can be to further conceptualise how we think about neurodiversity: enshrining its values within society and exploring and documenting the lived experience of neurodivergence, including disabling aspects of society. As outlined above, participatory and inclusive research practices can improve the quality and significance of these endeavours.

To date, most autism research has focused on North American and European populations (Norbury and Sparks, 2013), while autistic people from minority backgrounds are under-represented in research (West et al., 2016). Due to a long history of autism being understood as a predominantly male disorder, most research has also included a majority of male participants (Shefcyk, 2015). These biases mean that many autistic people's experiences have not been represented by work that has been done to date. The humanities of the future should actively seek to address these imbalances and engage with under-represented and unrepresented groups.

The humanities can also provide insight into how aspects of society, culture, diversity and identity intersect and impact neurodivergent people. For example, autistic people are more likely to identify as being non-heterosexual, non-binary, or trans (Cooper, Smith and Russell, 2018; George and Stokes, 2018), to live with mental health conditions, physical disabilities, or learning disabilities (Hirvikoski et al., 2018; Kinnear et al., 2019), or to be in a relationship with a neurodivergent person (Nordsletten et al., 2016). In addition, little is known about the influence of cultural and religious values and expectations on the identification and support of neurodivergent people. Taking an intersectional approach to research will further enhance our understanding of neurodivergence in multiple dimensions, reflecting the richness and complexity of the neurodivergent experience. These areas are fertile ground for new research in the humanities and social sciences.

Conclusions

While our understanding of autism has progressed substantially over the past 50 years, it is clear that there is still much work to be done. We are now at the point where many significant topics for future research have been identified; however the quality and impact of this research will rely on researchers in all fields understanding the value of participatory methods. Future research should involve autistic people and people with other neurodivergences at all stages of the research process to make sure it has relevance and meaning for neurodivergent people.

The humanities aim to study, understand, and document the human experience, and this should include the full breadth of neurodiversity. The humanities of the future could, and indeed should, enrich our knowledge and understanding of what it means to be neurodivergent and can achieve this by working in an intersectional and participatory way.

*, 6(6),

, U., 1985. Does the autistic child have a "theory of
*, 21(1), pp.37-46.

2014. Autism spectrum disorders in popular media: storied reflections of
views. *Brock Education: A Journal of Educational Research and Practice*, 23(2), pp.97-

Feral children and autistic children. *American Journal of Sociology*, 64(5),

The prognosis of dementia praecox. In: J. Cutting and M. Shepherd, eds. 1987. *The
*. Cambridge: Cambridge University Press. pp.25-26.

, J., Beardon, L., Downing, J., Hughes, L., Leatherland, J., Fox, K., Hickman,
MacGregor, D., 2017. Improving research about us, with us: a draft framework for

, L.G. and Russell, A.J., 2018. Gender identity in autism: sex differences in
affiliation with gender groups. *Journal of Autism and Developmental Disorders*, 48(12),

, Hallett, S., Ropar, D., Flynn, E. and Fletcher-Watson, S., 2020. 'I never realised

59

everybody felt as happy as I do when I am around autistic people': a thematic analysis of autistic adults' relationships with autistic and neurotypical friends and family. *Autism*, [e-journal]. http://dx.doi.org/10.1177/1362361320908976.

Davidson, J. and Henderson, V.L., 2010. 'Coming out' on the spectrum: autism, identity and disclosure. *Social & Cultural Geography*, 11(2), pp.155-170.

den Houting, J., 2019. Neurodiversity: an insider's perspective. *Autism*, 23(2). pp.271-273.

Drysdale, H., van der Meer, L. and Kagohara, D., 2015. Children with autism spectrum disorder from bilingual families: a systematic review. *Review Journal of Autism and Developmental Disorders*, 2(1), pp.26-38.

Fenton, A. and Krahn, T., 2007. Autism, neurodiversity, and equality beyond the "Normal". *Journal of Ethics in Mental Health*, 2(2).

Fletcher-Watson, S. and Bird, G., 2020. Autism and empathy: what are the real links?. *Autism*, [e-journal] 24(1), pp.3-6. http://dx.doi.org/10.1177/1362361319883506.

Fletcher-Watson, S., Adams, J., Brook, K., Charman, T., Crane, L., Cusack, J., Leekam, S., Milton, D., Parr, J.R. and Pellicano, E., 2019. Making the future together: shaping autism research through meaningful participation, *Autism*, 23(4), pp.943-953.

Folstein, S. and Rutter, M., 1977. Infantile autism: a genetic study of 21 twin pairs. *Journal of Child Psychology and Psychiatry*, 18(4), pp.297-321.

Frith, U., 2003. *Autism: Explaining the Enigma*. 2nd ed. Oxford: Blackwell Publishing.

Frith, U. and Happé, F., 1995. Autism: beyond "theory of mind". In: J. Mehler and S. Frank, eds. 1995. *Cognition on Cognition*. Cambridge, MA: MIT Press. pp.13-30.

George, R. and Stokes, M.A., 2018. Sexual orientation in autism spectrum disorder. *Autism Research*, 11(1), pp.133-141.

Gernsbacher, M.A., Morson, E.M. and Grace, E.J., 2015. Language development in autism. In: G. Hickok and S.L. Small, eds. 2015. *Neurobiology of Language*. San Diego, CA: Elsevier. pp.879-886.

Grandin, T. and Scariano, M., 1986. *Emergence: Labeled Autistic*. Novato, California: Arena Press.

Hacking, I., 2009. Autistic autobiography. *Philosophical Transactions of the Royal Society B: Biological Sciences*, 364(1522), pp.1467-1473.

Hale, C.M. and Tager-Flusberg, H., 2005. Social communication in children with autism: the relationship between theory of mind and discourse development. *Autism*, 9(2), pp.157-178.

Hirvikoski, T., Mittendorfer-Rutz, E., Boman, M., Larsson, H., Lichtenstein, P. and Bölte, S., 2016. Premature mortality in autism spectrum disorder. *British Journal of Psychiatry*, 208(3), pp.232-238.

Howlin, P., Goode, S., Hutton, J. and Rutter, M., 2009. Savant skills in autism: psychometric approaches and parental reports. *Philosophical Transactions of the Royal Society B: Biological Sciences*, 364(1522), pp.1359-1367.

Israel, B.A., Parker, E.A., Rowe, Z., Salvatore, A., Minkler, M., López, J., Butz, A., Mosley, A., Coates,

L., Lambert, G. and Potito, P.A., 2005. Community-based participatory research: lessons learned from the Centers for Children's Environmental Health and Disease Prevention Research. *Environmental Health Perspectives*, 113(10), pp.1463-1471.

Jaarsma, P. and Welin, S., 2012. Autism as a natural human variation: reflections on the claims of the neurodiversity movement. *Health Care Analysis*, 20(1), pp.20-30.

Kanner, L., 1949. Problems of nosology and psychodynamics of early infantile autism. *American Journal of Orthopsychiatry*, 19(3), pp.416-426.

Kanner, L., 1943. Autistic disturbances of affective contact. Reprint 2012. *Nervous Child: Journal of Psychopathology, Psychotherapy, Mental Hygiene, and Guidance of the Child*, 2(3), pp.217-250.

Kapp, S.K., 2020. *Autistic community and the neurodiversity movement: Stories from the Frontline.* Singapore: Springer Nature.

Kapp, S.K., Gillespie-Lynch, K., Sherman, L.E. and Hutman, T., 2013. Deficit, difference, or both? Autism and neurodiversity. *Developmental Psychology*, 49(1), pp.59-71.

Kenny, L., Hattersley, C., Molins, B., Buckley, C., Povey, C. and Pellicano, E., 2016. Which terms should be used to describe autism? Perspectives from the UK autism community. *Autism*, 20(4), pp.442-462.

Kinnear, D., Rydzewska, E., Dunn, K., Hughes-Mccormack, L., Melville, C., Henderson, A. and Cooper, S.A., 2019. Relative influence of intellectual disabilities and autism on mental and general health in Scotland: a cross-sectional study of a whole country of 5.3 million children and adults. *BMJ Open*, [e-journal] 9(8). http://dx.doi.org/10.1136/bmjopen-2019-029040.

Le Couteur, A., Bailey, A., Goode, S., Pickles, A., Gottesman, I., Robertson, S. and Rutter, M., 1996. A broader phenotype of autism: the clinical spectrum in twins. *Journal of Child Psychology and Psychiatry*, 37(7), pp.785-801.

Leveto, J.A., 2018. Toward a sociology of autism and neurodiversity. *Sociology Compass*, [e-journal] 12(12), 10.1111/soc4.12636.

Markram, K. and Markram, H., 2010. The intense world theory – a unifying theory of the neurobiology of autism. *Frontiers in Human Neuroscience*, [e-journal] 4(224). http://dx.doi.org/10.3389/fnhum.2010.00224.

Milton, D.E., 2012. On the ontological status of autism: the 'double empathy problem'. *Disability & Society*, 27(6), pp.883-887.

Milton, D.E.M., Ridout, S., Kourti, M., Loomes, G. and Martin, N., 2019. A critical reflection on the development of the Participatory Autism Research Collective (PARC). *Tizard Learning Disability Review*, 24(2), pp.82-89.

Morrison, K.E., Pinkham, A.E., Kelsven, S., Ludwig, K., Penn, D.L. and Sasson, N.J., 2019. Psychometric evaluation of social cognitive measures for adults with autism. *Autism Research*, 12(5), pp.766-778.

Norbury, C.F. and Sparks, A., 2013. Difference or disorder? Cultural issues in understanding neurodevelopmental disorders. *Developmental Psychology*, 49(1), pp.45-58.

Nordahl-Hansen, A., Øien, R.A. and Fletcher-Watson, S., 2018. Pros and cons of character portrayals of autism on TV and film. *Journal of Autism and Developmental Disorders*, 48(2), pp.635-636.

Nordsletten, A.E., Larsson, H., Crowley, J.J., Almqvist, C., Lichtenstein, P. and Mataix-Cols, D., 2016. Patterns of nonrandom mating within and across 11 major psychiatric disorders. *JAMA Psychiatry*, 73(4), pp.354-361.

Oliver, M., 2004. The social model in action: if I had a hammer. In: C. Barnes and G. Mercer, eds. 2004. *Implementing the Social Model of Disability: Theory and Research*. Leeds: The Disability Press. pp.18-31.

Pellicano, E., Dinsmore, A. and Charman, T., 2013. *A Future Made Together: Shaping Autism Research in the UK*. London: Institute of Education.

Pellicano, E., Dinsmore, A. and Charman, T., 2014. What should autism research focus upon? Community views and priorities from the United Kingdom. *Autism*, 18(7), pp.756-770.

Pripas-Kapit, S., 2020. Historicizing Jim Sinclair's "Don't Mourn for Us": a cultural and intellectual history of neurodiversity's first manifesto. In: S.K. Kapp, ed. 2020. *Autistic Community and the Neurodiversity Movement*. Singapore: Palgrave Macmillan. pp.23-39.

Rimland, B., 1978. Savant capabilities of autistic children and their cognitive implications. In G. Serban, ed. 1978. *Cognitive Defects in the Development of Mental Illness*. New York, NY: Brunner/Mazel. pp.43-65.

Robertson, S.M., 2009. Neurodiversity, quality of life, and autistic adults: shifting research and professional focuses onto real-life challenges. *Disability Studies Quarterly*, [e-journal] 30(1). http://dx.doi.org/10.18061/dsq.v30i1.1069.

Rose, I., 2008. Autistic autobiography or autistic life narrative?. *Journal of Literary & Cultural Disability Studies*, 2(1), pp.44-54.

Russell, G., Rodgers, L.R., Ukoumunne, O.C. and Ford, T., 2014. Prevalence of parent-reported ASD and ADHD in the UK: findings from the Millennium Cohort Study. *Journal of Autism and Developmental Disorders*, 44(1), pp.31-40.

Sacks, O., 2006. Foreword. In: T. Grandin, 2006. *Thinking in Pictures*. London: Vintage, pp.xiii.

Sedgewick, F., Hill, V. and Pellicano, E., 2019. 'It's different for girls': gender differences in the friendships and conflict of autistic and neurotypical adolescents. *Autism*, 23(5), pp.1119-1132.

Shefcyk, A., 2015. Count us in: addressing gender disparities in autism research. *Autism*, 19(2), pp.131-132.

Silverman, C., 2008. Fieldwork on another planet: Social science perspectives on the autism spectrum. *BioSocieties*, 3(3), pp.325-341.

Sinclair, J., 2012. Don't mourn for us. *Autonomy, the Critical Journal of Interdisciplinary Autism Studies*, [online] Available at: < http://larry-arnold.net/Autonomy/index.php/autonomy/article/view/AR1> [accessed 20 May 2020].

West, E.A., Travers, J.C., Kemper, T.D., Liberty, L.M., Cote, D.L., McCollow, M.M. and Stansberry Brusnahan, L.L., 2016. Racial and ethnic diversity of participants in research supporting evidence-based practices for learners with autism spectrum disorder. *Journal of Special*

Education, 50(3), pp.151-163.

Wing, L., 1996. *The Autism Spectrum*. London: Constable.

Wing, L. and Gould, J., 1979. Severe impairments of social interaction and associated abnormalities in children: epidemiology and classification. *Journal of Autism and Developmental Disorders*, 9(1), pp.11-29.

Yeargin-Allsopp, M., Rice, C., Karapurkar, T., Doernberg, N., Boyle, C. and Murphy, C., 2003. Prevalence of autism in a US metropolitan area. *Journal of the American Medical Association*, 289(1), pp.49-55.

KATHRYN SIMPSON

The Digital Archive as Space and Place in the Constitution, Production and Circulation of Knowledge

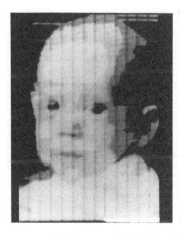

The first digital image was a scan of a photograph of Walden Kirsch by Russell A. Kirsch[1]

63 years ago, Russell A. Kirsch, one of the designers and users of America's first programmable computer (SEAC), used a drum scanner to digitise a photograph of his young son. This grainy image was made with 176 by 176 square pixels. What Kirsch created became the standard for the next half century. Kirsch's ground-breaking work has led to a revolution in how we engage with content: we live in the age of the digital archive.

1   Licensed under Public Domain via Commons - "National Institute of Standards and Technology Digital Collections, Gaithersburg, MD 20899."

This digitisation has led to 'images being connected, mobile and instantly reproducible', a deluge of images of texts, manuscripts and objects that are consistently available on the web to be used, re-used and adapted (Martínez Luna, 2019, p.43). The digital archival space has become a vast repository into which more is being put every day. Such a wealth of information should be providing new knowledge structures and frameworks, its very indiscriminateness bringing in the narratives of those who are marginalised or not recognised by the dominant knowledge structures. However, we have to ask what it is that is being created and re-created: are we unknowingly re-creating the dominant ideology structures of physical libraries and archives?

Over 40 years after creating the first digital image, Kirsch realised that, 'What I did was not the best thing that could have been done because someone had a better idea a thousand years before' (2011). Over 1,500 years prior, in antiquity, people had been using tesserae to create mosaics, that is, pixels in different shapes to suit the image being created. Yet, in the subsequent half decade of digitisation no-one thought to change Kirsch's square pixels, until Kirsch himself, in 2010, created variable shaped pixels, built on six by six pixel arrays. This new pixel array Kirsch suggested ultimately used fewer pixels and improved accuracy. However, no-one had thought to challenge the status quo of how the digital image was created previously, '[b]ecause people have always believed that if you used more little square pixels you'd get better accuracy' (Kirsch, 2011). As with the digital image, we have to ask: has doing more of the same thing regarding the generation of digital content opened up the possibilities of knowledge creation, or is there just *more* content?

The digital archive has become intrinsic to contemporary academic research, whether that be accessing digital surrogates of primary source material or finding articles online, and, as such, it has a weighted responsibility in the constitution, production and circulation of knowledge. In this paper I will look at how the digital archive curates knowledge. I will use data from an ongoing survey of digitised content created by women in the long nineteenth century to talk around issues of access and sustainability. I will particularly focus upon how these digital archives enable text and object to be 'read' in new ways, to behave in ways un-proscribed and malleable, and to reveal their intangible human emotional archaeology. I will examine how the digital archive works through or around issues of agency, permission and power; who is surveilling and supporting these digital archives; and how good or successful archives are defined. I will explore the very real issues surrounding whether we are creating problems for future critical research as digital archives continue to be created in the knowledge that there are few long-term or sustainable pedagogical and fiscal practices currently in place to support the continued maintenance and growth of such archives. Finally, I will suggest ways in which the digital archive can move forward and develop. In many ways, the researcher is still beholden to the digital archive coming out of the physical archive's materiality, its authority, and its suggestion of completeness of content – a digital overlay on the physical archive, the archive as a singular thing, un-human, passive and yet expert in its curation.

The Role of the Digital Archive in the Constitution of Knowledge

The digital archive has come to be understood as something which is curated, with not everything in it deriving from the same physical location or its material being chosen for its interpretive value; edited, with the primary material manipulated in some way, for example transcribed or cut from surrounding context; and, front-facing and interactive, for example the possibility of happening upon a book or object which may be physically next to the item the user is looking at is reduced and the user often must search for a specific thing (Price, 2009; McGann, 2014; Nail, 2019). The digital archive has become intrinsic to the creation, curation and analysis of text and object, but like its physical forebear the digital archive is not a complete record. The digital archive is a place of power imbalances; it often represents and is centred around the overt and exceptional subject, and that subject is often male, white and western. An inherent flaw of this paper and the case study it comes from is that it focusses on English language textual archives and that in doing so it perpetuates 'an absence of the standpoints of marginalised people' (Baijnath, 2019, p.33). As a mono-lingual, white, female scholar I acknowledge that, in arguing against the systematic power imbalances within archives, I too am writing from a position of power and privilege and that I and other scholars in my position must utilise our opportunity to develop more comprehensive and systematic approaches to inclusive and multi-lingual digital archives.

This paper has come out of an ongoing collaborative macro-historical survey, in which we explore digitised archives of women's writing in the long nineteenth century.[2] The primary aim has been to 'search' for these archives, to understand how they represent their content and to understand how accessible that content is. Expressly, the survey has not been systematic but opportunistic and based upon the basic search function of multiple search engines, including Google, Duck Duck Go, Bing, Dogpile and so on. Our work is predicated on four zero-sum hypotheses which state that, given the drive to negate the gendered bias in archives, digital archives of women's writing would be free at the point of use, easily found, accessible, and that there would be no discrete differences in the form and function of women's writing archives as with comparable digital archives of men's writing. The historical timeframe chosen for the search was selected with the intention of providing the greatest scope for responses, predicated on the rise of recorded women writers in Anglophone countries in the long nineteenth century, commensurate with their increased active role in public society. In the survey we are anxious to understand how easy it is to access new histories, new data and new narratives that can then be used to re-engage with historical narratives.

The first and most striking outcome is that even the use of the term 'archive' is problematic – little of what can be accessed could be considered an archive: 'Increasingly the boundaries between what has been known as 'archive' and everyday practices of creative media management with internet technologies have become blurred' (Ibrus and Ojamaa, 2020, p.51). As such, 'archive' becomes a malleable term, and the survey looks instead to access or identify the location of records of English language women's writing in the long nineteenth century. Kate Theimer notes that,

2   'Illuminating the Archive: women, convention and presumption' is a joint project between Heather F. Ball (St John's University), Lois M. Burke (Edinburgh Napier University) and Kathryn Simpson (University of Glasgow).

in actuality, the digital archive as a term can be used to describe four discrete functions: 'for collections of born-digital *records*, for websites that provide access to collections of digitised materials, for websites featuring different types of digitised information around one topic, and for web-based participatory collections' (2015, p.158). This can be seen to be one of the dynamic aspects of collating and curating women's histories, that by existing in multiple organisational forms on the web, the records become discontinuous with the past methods of archival hierarchies and power (Bishop et al., 2003). Traditional power dynamics in archival theory and practice can be authoritarian and bureaucratic. The digital archive and its variants can enable people to take greater control over their own histories.

As cultural theories of the archive have repeatedly noted, the function of archives exceeds the mere storage and preservation of data, as the epistemological decisions made in the compilation of an archive fundamentally define what is archivable, what is knowable, and hence what is deemed disposable and forgotten.

(Agostinho et al., 2019, p.424)

The web provides a digital space to challenge traditional regimes of knowledge, power and control.

Finding the woman writer in history can be problematic as she might not have written much, she might have stopped writing when she became a wife or mother, or maybe her work would be subsumed into the work of a male partner – for example, the Scottish novelist Willa Muir, *née* Anderson (1890-1970). There are Muir papers held in the archive at the University of Edinburgh Library. Muir is a prime example of the issues we have faced in a year of surveying the field. The archive blog at the university library notes: 'We do not have a discrete collection of Willa Muir papers, but there are letters from Willa in the Papers of George Mackay Brown, David Daiches, Hamish Henderson, Tom Scott, and Vernon Watkins' (Barnaby, 2019). There is evidence that some of this content has been digitised and can be read online, but that content is incomplete. The women can be seen to be fragmented – these are literary records which do not hold fast to themselves. It is only the very famous, the overt exception, who has managed to stay united in her own papers; as Ralph Waldo Emerson (1803-1882) notes:

> A woman in our society finds her safety and happiness in exclusions and privacies. She congratulates herself when she is not called to the market, to the courts, to the polls, to the stage, or to the orchestra. Only the most extraordinary genius can make the career of an artist secure and agreeable to her. Prescriptions almost invincible the female lecturer or professor of any science must encounter.
>
> (2013, p.1764)

Producing and Sustaining Digital Archival Spaces of Women's Writing

In our survey of digital records of women's writing in the long nineteenth century we have, to date, found 120 unique sites or spaces of deposit; these included archives, databases, websites, blog caches, and catalogues. As dismissively noted by Emerson above, we found it only to be the 'extraordinary' who had archival spaces of their own; in many cases the writing of women is siloed together. For example, the 14 subjects of the *Women's Travel Diaries* collection held at Duke University together comprise 162 unique items. The siloing of these writers, whilst in some ways suggesting a layer of similarity or homogeneity of content, can also enable tangential and opportunistic digital serendipity. For example, the user is able to move in one step, or click, from the famous missionary Mary McCornack Thompson (1858-1936), of whom there is a wealth of information contained in 91 discrete items (duke:74829-74917), to the unknown Ethel Grace Cooper and her, single item, scrapbook of missionaries (duke:248795). Thus, this siloing facilitates user interaction with lesser known and smaller archival materials which may have been overlooked had the material not been grouped together in the same archival space.

Of the sites identified to date, 65 have some component of digitised material and of these collections, 51 stated that they were digitally accessible to everyone and 17 databases were behind a paywall. How are we meant to further and develop our understanding of the many people who have shaped histories and our world history if 'her' story is reduced, hidden and monetised? Within the survey period itself we were often unable to follow up on each other's work due to search failures; in the space of six days between one member of the team's work on the survey and another, six links resulted in 404 errors (an HTTP error which indicates that the page you are looking for is not found), and five links no longer worked. Link rot has been a perennial and is an expanding problem in web resourcing (Zhou et al., 2015). For example, the brilliant *Victorian Women Writers Project*, which we accessed through three different distinct links, is now accessible through a completely different route, and the previous links we identified do not work and do not provide suggestions for how to access the site. This is not to lay blame in any way on those resources that are available. People have worked hard to make these writings seen. However, budgets are often finite, and there is not money to sustain such projects as live. A paywall can facilitate the long-term maintenance of a site, for example with the exemplary *Women Writers Project*. Their work is only possible because of the paywall: using the monies earned to continue to develop and better the site, to identify further women writers and to image, transcribe and edit these works, though such paywalls mean it is often the least marginalised who have access to the primary materials and resources to re-negotiate histories.

We also came across sites that were no longer being maintained: sites in which the hard work to digitise and bring together sources were only maintained for the length of a project or specific period of time and then removed. One such example is *Uncommon Lives*, an innovative approach to biography based on governmental documents. Of note was the work done on suffragette and human rights campaigner Jessie Street (1889-1970) and civic interior designer Ruth Lane Poole (1885-1974). The intentions of the site had been to continue to create profiles of people who were part of Australia's national memory, to show how Commonwealth records could be used to construct personal histories, and possibly at some point in the future allow people to deposit their own stories. The project ultimately only ran for four years from 2003 to 2007, and the resource was removed *in toto* by the National Archives of Australia (NAA) in 2019. To have lived such a short existence belies the incredible amount of effort and work which went into creating a digital resource such as this. As Kate Bagnall, project manager of the site, said in 2019: 'it is disappointing that the NAA no longer seems to understand the value of these websites as tools of both archival and historical understanding and exploration' (2019). The records of people's lives are not so much erased from history as left to become fallow. *Uncommon Lives* is also notable as an example of a digital source which is not explicitly an archive but uses archival material to tell stories of people, some of whom are from groups traditionally under-represented in the historical record.[3]

Thanks to the Internet Archive Wayback Machine this work has not been totally lost, but it is a clunky and aborted version of what had originally been intended. It suggests that there is greater work to be done in the recording and gathering of marginalised stories. To take from recent work on defunct online virtual worlds, some of these online records 'continue to exist as abandoned or semi-abandoned spaces, largely forgotten, but often still home to a dwindling group of users who doggedly persist' (Miller and Garcia, 2019, p.437). There are many projects like this still in existence, but like digital ruins, they are:

[A]n absent presence. On one hand, these places are often only a few mouse clicks away. Yet at the same time, they are almost completely absent from the contemporary negotiation of a web which has become coalesced through the algorithmic regulation of its traffic.

(Miller and Garcia, 2019, p.440)

In what Michelle Moravec calls 'environments of abundance' it is difficult not only to grasp these absences but to understand why it is important that such sources are not totally abandoned, especially when search engines can

---

3   Including Dhakiyarr Wirrpanda, a Yolngu elder from northeast Arnhem Land, who was the first Aboriginal Australian to appeal a conviction in the High Court.

often provide overwhelming responses to queries (2017). Although the wealth of information should be providing new knowledge structures and frameworks, it is, in its very indiscriminateness, subsuming the narratives of those who are marginalised or not recognised by the dominant knowledge structures.

It is also understandable that there are some institutions which want to hold on to the cultural capital of their items and so whilst they do facilitate digitisation, they then make access to those digital items only available in their own premises (Dong, 2012). Unfortunately, this does not facilitate wider access to multiple histories and is predicated on people being financially able to travel to archives. Archives can be sites of conflict; with those who provide access having the power to shape and remediate cultural knowledge, they 'mediate between individuals and how they access heritage materials' (Dong, 2012, p.268). In the same breath there is an imperial element – an entitlement – to demanding such open access digitisation which assumes it is correct to have access that is open and free at the point of use (Agostinho, 2019). The creators of the original content may never have wished to make their writings public, let alone available internationally on the web, had they known what that was (Moravec, 2016). Or, the cultural protocols of the creators of the content may strongly inhibit such sharing (see the software Mukurtu as an example of a project which is ethically-minded and community-focussed on sharing digital heritage in a responsible way). Digitisation and access can be expressly problematic since what is often forgotten is that the very act of digital curation is an act of editing within itself. Digital curation and its frequent partner, transcription, are not acts without critical critique and engagement:

'Because interpretation is a social act – a specific deed of critical reflection made in a concert of related moves and frames of reference (social, political, institutional) that constitute the present as an interpreted inheritance from a past that has been fashioned by other interpreting agents.

(McGann, 2014, p.78)

How will it be possible to facilitate the next generation of researchers who are likely to have even tighter budgets and restrictions than us? It is too much to put the weight on their shoulders, to repeatedly say that there are women in the archives. We must tell their stories, we must engage with their narratives, and we must look to reposition them in the grander narrative arcs of history, if we cannot find them.

Reading to Find the African Woman in the Circulation of the Digital Record of Exploration

Having noted that there are limits in what is accessible, that which we can find in the digital archive facilitates women in the historical record being read and identified in new ways. An example of the subsuming of women's narratives in the archival record can be located in David Livingstone's journals, particularly in his writings about Halima, the manumitted slave and expedition cook. Halima was one of David Livingstone's primary staff on his travels across Africa. Livingstone himself called her the 'best spoke in the wheel' of his group (1874, p.193), and evidence of her importance to his team is given in the Field Diary entry for 20th February 1872, which records that Livingstone paid seven of the people working with him, including Halima, roughly 40 yards of white cloth each (Livingstone, 1872). Such a large wage suggests the value that Livingstone placed on these people and their importance to his expeditionary group.

Halima exemplifies women who are noted in the records of others, who had a background role in someone else's narrative, or are women who we now know were there but are not mentioned in the official transcript of the event or moment. By acknowledging their presence, it becomes possible to renegotiate the historical record and to destabilise existing interpretations. Digitising critical heritage permits the cultural record to be read in new ways, which in turn enables a more complicated and ambiguous reading of history. By asking irregular questions of the sources, it 'enables us to look beyond hegemonic stories and currently circulating narrative frameworks to explore the background and context to these stories' (Woodiwiss, 2017, p.15). Stories are political, with inherent power dynamics which may not necessarily be obvious on first reading. In digital repositories, archives, and libraries are the essential elements to encourage disruptive and counter-consensus readings of history. In this particular example, this access allows researchers to move beyond the economic commodification of Africans as a constituent element of European exploration, to instead see and identify their role in the socio-cultural network of the expeditionary group. At the point missionary-explorers met people, the colonial encounter, a new historiography was created: an encounter not dictated by those presiding and organising at the imperial metropole, but by those who physically encountered each other. The relationships between event, time, location, people, agency and medium are manifested in the documents or items that are catalogued, and how those relationships are read is down to the digital user; the user can exploit the digital to shatter exploitative historical frameworks and constructs.

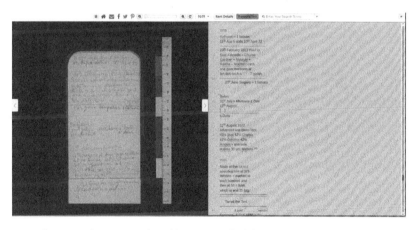

A page from David Livingstone's Field Diary in which he notes the amount in cloth he has paid the primary members of his team, who are travelling with him in the Unyanyembe region of what is now Tanzania.[4]

When Livingstone died just over a year later, Halima did not make it into the

4   Livingstone, David, 1813-1873. "Field Diary XIV, 14 November 1871-14 September 1872." Livingstone Online. Adrian S. Wisnicki and Megan Ward, dirs. 2020. Web. Image Credit David Livingstone Birthplace Trust, Blantyre. Creative Commons Attribution-NonCommercial 3.0 Unported (https://creativecommons.org/licenses/by-nc/3.0/).

final 'official' narrative about bringing back his body to the coast of Africa before it was shipped back to Britain. She was part of the event, but she is not part of the narrative of the history that is told. Halima was a foundational part of the group and we must re-present her agency. Critical research shows how engaged and complex European and southern and central African working relationships on expeditions of supposed exploration were, but it is noticeable that they do not talk about the role of women in such journeys. It is sometimes almost possible to believe these western European explorers never met a single woman on their travels, so limited are the mentions of women. When southern and central African women are mentioned, they are often presented as ethnographic specimens, mute and immobile.

Mangana Ethnic Group, Africa. 'Ivory Lip Ring, May 1859'.[5]

How should we engage with women who are tangential to the digital record – an issue of particular note in the record of exploration? These women are often written as passive recipients of the imperial agency which describes and maps their bodies as sites of 'otherness' and preconceived exotic or orientalised behaviours and representations. The political imperative of the value of the imperial endeavour is in some ways predicated on this

5   Livingstone Online. Adrian S. Wisnicki and Megan Ward, dirs. 2020. Image Credit David Livingstone Trust. Object images used by permission. May not be reproduced without the express written consent of the David Livingstone Trust. Image of the object from the Trust is © Roddy Simpson. Creative Commons Attribution-NonCommercial 3.0 Unported (https://creativecommons/org/).

presumed lack of agency of non-western people. To have been seen to travel alone reifies ideas of the proscribed 'racial' hierarchies of European and notably Britain's nineteenth-century global outlook. The above lip ring was acquired by David Livingstone in May 1859, and little was known about it. Did a woman take it out of her mouth to give or sell? Was it taken from her? Was the lip ring made as a souvenir to sell to passing trade? All that could be observed is that in this thing is a narrative of acts unlikely to be recovered. Matthew Battles says that '[a] collected object is a kind of vessel, freighted with an irredeemable record of acts and things, inaccessible worlds of sense and event, a tissue of phenomenal dark matter caught up in time's obliterative machinery' (2013). Without context, this item and its original owner are 'other'. For years it has sat in a museum display case, a relic of a different space, part of the weight of material brought back to the UK as specimens, examples, drawings and souvenirs that show the supposed alterity of Africa and its people. This 'otherness' is documented in nineteenth-century British narratives that ensured a trenchant iconography which has continued to the present day. Yet, to engage with the lip ring and its value in identifying a marginalised narrative digitally is to enable a small element of 'her' story to be revealed.

Whilst it is not possible to uncover the person behind the lip ring, it is the digital repository of a single 'great white' historical male that has facilitated the uncovering of a letter which makes the woman present. The letter is written by David Livingstone to his daughter on 28th February 1860, from Kongone:

My Dear Nannie
I send this home By Mr Rae our Engineer whom probably you may see. I send at the same time a box with a few objects of natural history for Robert and Thomas and a few rings for you, one is a lip ring, and if you like to wear it as the women up the Shire do, Mr Rae will shew you how. I bought it and the woman took it out of a hole in her lip & gave it very sorry I thought to part with a thing that made her so "brave."

(Livingstone, 1860)

By using the digital repository to show the multiple threads of personal encounter and perspectives that Livingstone and others actually recorded, it becomes possible to begin to break down the previously artificially constructed separation between nineteenth-century European and African individuals and, importantly, the arbitrary divide between men and women.

Re-curating Knowledges in the Digital Archive

Why has the ability to excavate the minutiae of the digital corpus as yet not been comprehensively utilised in pulling women out of the depths of the colonial record of nineteenth-century European exploration of Africa? Is it because those voices are not there, although contemporary research would suggest that they are, or is it that – as we have established in our survey of women's writing – no-one has wanted to spend the time searching to find the records that facilitate this interaction when it involves so much work with so many errors, lost links, failed sites and content rot? Yet those previous histories are what subsequent histories are built on. To wit, to take the idea to the n-th degree: why does 'her' story matter when we have reached where we are without the need for it? The argument must be more than that she was also there. 'With traditional institutionalized archives, everything collected and represented has been selected by "experts" according to some disciplined knowledge system. These experts have thus managed the scope of society's dialogues with its memory' (Ibrus and Ojamaa, 2020, p.51). We must look across archives and space and place, to re-constitute, re-present and re-configure the archive as a place of held narratives. As such, we need to create these bigger arguments which show the memory of society to be wrong. What is maintained is a constructed narrative.

In the next half century, the digital archival space will have greater importance and all users and creators have a responsibility to actively work to negate the problems that have followed the archive out of the physical realm and into the digital. To understand how to re-construct the narratives of societal memory, specific things need to be taken into account by both digital archival space creators and users. It is important to understand the scope of what is trying to be achieved, to define the nature of the context of the archive. It is vital to not only understand what is in the archive, but also what is not, and to make this explicit. Emphasis should be placed on facilitating access. However, this does not always mean full and complete data-heavy access but, rather, access that is suitable to the greatest number of users' requirements, not just to the requirements of the project itself. We also must understand the risks inherent in what the archive holds and what its holdings represent and who they affected. It should be a prerequisite of all digital archival spaces to know and publicly identify who has technical responsibility for the data, to understand what access is providable and maintainable and to understand the completeness of what has been digitised. The process of navigation should be made complete and transparent. The user needs to know how they got from one item to another – the physical distance jumped digitally, and the physical arrangement of what has been digitised. Finally, training people to use and maintain the archive and to take responsibility for the acknowledgement of volunteer or graduate work in the development of the archive is essential to continue this work.

The digital archival space has to be different; the same building blocks can be reshaped to allow new interpretations, new histories, and new narratives to be read. Such digital renegotiation with the archive has the capacity to fill in the lacunae, to renegotiate the resources and materials utilised in the construction of knowledge and to provide the histories of under-represented or marginalised groups, the absent presences.

BIBLIOGRAPHY

Agostinho, D., 2019. Archival encounters: rethinking access and care in digital colonial archives. *Archival Science*, [e-journal] 19(2), pp.141-165. https://doi.org/10.1007/s10502-019-09312-0.

Agostinho, D., D'Ignazio, C., Ring, A., Thylstrup, N.B. and Veel, K., 2019. Uncertain archives: approaching the unknowns, errors, and vulnerabilities of big data through cultural theories of the archive. *Surveillance & Society*, [e-journal] 17(3/4), pp.422-441. https://doi.org/10.24908/ss.v17i3/4.12330.

Bagnall, K., 2019. Uncommon lives in the National Archives: biography, history and the records of government. *The Tiger's Mouth: Thoughts on the history and heritage of Chinese Australia*, [blog] 24 October. Available at: <http://chineseaustralia.org/> [Accessed 25 May 2020].

Baijnath, R., 2019. Writing her in: an African Feminist Exploration into the Life Herstory Narrative of Dimakatso, a Woman Participant in the Expanded Public Works Programme (EPWP) at Leratong Hospital in Gauteng, South Africa. *South African Review of Sociology*, [e-journal] 50(2), pp. 27-42. https://doi.org/10.1080/21528586.2019.1666735.

Barnaby, P., 2019. 'This Single Song of Two': centenary of the marriage of Edwin and Willa Muir. *Archives @ University of Edinburgh*, [blog] 7 June. Available at: <http://libraryblogs.is.ed.ac.uk/edinburghuniversityarchives/2019/06/07/this-single-song-of-two-centenary-of-the-marriage-of-edwin-and-willa-muir/> [Accessed 25 May 2020].

Battles, M., 2013. Specimens: figurines, fishers, bugs and bats - how things in the world become sacred objects in a museum. *Aeon*, [online] Available at: <https://aeon.co/essays/a-museums-cabinet-of-curiosities-is-also-a-chamber-of-secrets> [Accessed 20 May 2020].

Bishop, A.P., Van House, N.A. and Buttenfield, B.P. eds., 2003. *Digital Library Use: Social Practice in Design and Evaluation*. Cambridge, MA: MIT Press.

Center for Digital Scholarship and Curation at Washington State University, n.d. *Mukurtu*. [online] Available at: <https://mukurtu.org/> [Accessed 1 June 2020].

Cloudseed Film, 2011. Russell A. Kirsch - Talks about The Variable Shaped Pixel. ANKA Gallery, Portland. Available at: <https://vimeo.com/22179638> [Accessed 25 May 2020].

Deen, H., Dargavel, J., Coltheart, L., Read, P. and Neumann, K., 2006. *Uncommon Lives*. [online] Available at: <https://web.archive.org/web/20071009194345/http://uncommonlives.naa.gov.au/> [Accessed 1 June 2020].

Dong, L., 2012. The economics and politics of international preservation collaborations: a Malian case study. *Archival Science*, [e-journal] 12(3), pp.267-285. https://doi.org/10.1007/s10502-011-9156-z.

Emerson, R.W., 2013. *Delphi Complete Works of Ralph Waldo Emerson (Illustrated)*. s.l.: Delphi Classics.

Ibrus, I., Ojamaa, M., 2020. The creativity of digital (audiovisual) archives: a dialogue between media archaeology and cultural semiotics. *Theory, Culture & Society*, [e-journal] 37(3), pp.49-70. https://doi.org/10.1177/0263276419871646.

Livingstone, D., 1860. *Letter to Agnes Livingstone.* [online] Livingstone Online. Adrian S. Wisnicki and Megan Ward, dirs. 2020. Available at: <https://livingstoneonline.org/in-his-own-words/catalogue?query=28th+february+1860&f%5B%5D=dateRangeYear_mi%3A%221860%22&view_pid=liv%3A001543&view_page=0> [Accessed 25 May 2020].

Livingstone, D., 1872. *Field Diary XIV, 14 November 1871-14 September 1872.* [online] Livingstone Online. Adrian S. Wisnicki and Megan Ward, dirs. 2020. Available at: <https://livingstoneonline.org/in-his-own-words/catalogue?query=liv_000014&view_pid=liv%3A000014> [Accessed 25 May 2020].

Livingstone , D., 1874. *The Last Journals of David Livingstone in Central Africa.* London: John Murray.

Martínez Luna, S., 2019. Still images?: materiality and mobility in digital visual culture. *Third Text,* [e-journal] 33(1), pp.43-57. https://doi.org/10.1080/09528822.2018.1546484.

McGann, J.J., 2014. *A New Republic of Letters: Memory and Scholarship in the Age of Digital Reproduction.* Cambridge, MA: Harvard University Press.

Miller, V., Garcia, G., 2019. Digital ruins. *Cultural Geographies,* 26(4), pp.435-454.

Moravec, M., 2017. Feminist research practices and digital archives. *Australian Feminist Studies,* [e-journal] 32(91-92), pp.186-201. https://doi.org/10.1080/08164649.2017.1357006.

Moravec, M., 2016. What would you do? Historians' ethics and digitized archives. *Medium,* [online] Available at: <https://medium.com/on-archivy/on-april-at-the-organization-of-american-historians-i-participated-in-a-roundtable-discussion-563213dc94a> [Accessed 25 May 2020].

Nail, T., 2019. *Theory of the Image.* New York, NY: Oxford University Press.

Price, K.M., 2009. Edition, project, database, archive, thematic research collection: what's in a name? *DHQ,* [online] Available at: <http://www.digitalhumanities.org/dhq/vol/3/3/000053/000053.html> [Accessed 25 May 2020].

Rekrut, A., 2014. Matters of substance: materiality and meaning in historical records and their digital images. *Archives and Manuscripts,* [e-journal] 42(3), pp.238-247. https://doi.org/10.1080/01576895.2014.958865.

Sallie Bingham Center for Women's History & Culture, n.d. *Women's Travel Diaries.* [online] Available at: <https://repository.duke.edu/dc/womenstraveldiaries> [Accessed 1 June 2020].

The Digital Scholarship Group, n.d. *Women Writers Project.* [online] Available at: <https://www.wwp.northeastern.edu/> [Accessed 1 June 2020].

The Trustees of Indiana University, 2020. *Victorian Women Writers Project.* [online] Available at: <http://webapp1.dlib.indiana.edu/vwwp/welcome.do> [Accessed 1 June 2020].

Theimer, K., 2015. Digital archives. In: Duranti, L. and Franks, P.C. eds. 2015. *Encyclopedia of Archival Science.* Lanham: Rowman & Littlefield.

Wisnicki, A.S. and Ward, M., 2020. *Livingstone Online.* [online] Available at: <https://livingstoneonline.org> [Accessed 1 June 2020].

Woodiwiss, J., 2017. Challenges for feminist research: contested stories, dominant narratives and narrative frameworks. In: Woodiwiss, J., Smith, K. and Lockwood, K. eds. 2017. *Feminist Narrative Research: Opportunities and Challenges*. London: Palgrave Macmillan, pp.13-37. https://doi.org/10.1057/978-1-137-48568-7_2.

Zhou, K., Grover, C., Klein, M. and Tobin, R., 2015. No more 404s: predicting referenced link rot in scholarly articles for pro-active archiving. Joint Conference on Digital Libraries. In: 2015. *JCDL '15: Proceedings of the 15th ACM/IEEE-CS Joint Conference on Digital Libraries*. [e-book] New York, NY: Association for Computing Machinery. pp.233-236. https://doi.org/10.1145/2756406.2756940.

NOÉMIE FARGIER

Global Sound Archive: Soundmaps Projects and the Perspective of Future

Since Google Earth was launched in 2005 and following its development over the past 15 years, every square kilometre of the earth has been documented and we can get a view of almost any location. Thanks to the Google Earth global collection of photographs, which are regularly updated, we can see changes in the landscape and virtually visit the most remote areas of the world.

Online soundmaps use this webmap technology to display field recordings in their geographic location. Most of the collections are local and collaborative, but also temporary. However, some of the soundmaps, constantly fed with contributions, gather recordings from all over the world and from the past four decades. They display 'sonic time capsules' with both patrimonial and historical goals: 'preserving sounds before they disappear' and building a global sound archive which can be studied by future generations (Montreal Soundmap, n.d.).

The soundmaps can thus provide precious material for the humanities of the future. They already enable reflection on the way we document the world, especially if we compare those sound collections with the Google Earth photographs with which they are linked. Sounds are not presented as objective reflections of reality but as contextual recordings. This is to say that soundmaps add a human and subjective dimension to webmap technology. They invite us not only to listen to what the world sounded like, but also to think about the making of archives.

In this respect, I will question their potential use throughout time. I will mainly focus on Aporee, the oldest and largest global soundmap using the Google Earth service, which appears as a case study. I will discuss the selection, the conservation, and representativeness of the sound archive that it is constructing. I will also examine the soundmapping itself, looking into its audio-visual framework and questioning its representation of space.

A model: Aporee

The growing Aporee sound collection, fed by a 'community' of almost 2,000 contributors, gathers more than 51,000 sounds from more than 45,000 places. We can find some recordings from the 1980s to today and from almost all the countries in the world. The soundmap not only allows us to listen to today's sonic environments, but preserves the sounds of yesterday for tomorrow and stores them in the digital library 'Internet Archive'. Aporee, also called 'Radio Aporee', started as an online platform in 2000 and turned into an online soundmap when Google Earth was launched; it was the first soundmap project to use the webmap technology and, in a way, grew simultaneously.

It uses the webmap as a tool to reinforce the connection between the field recording and 'its places of origin' (Noll, 2019). The sound collection, although huge and open to almost every collaborator, is homogeneous because of the curator's guidelines. The sounds they expect – location sounds, from the outside or public space (either urban, rural or natural) – avoiding 'extensive chunks of music', should be an authentic *picture* of reality (Noll, 2019). The sound, recorded with some good quality gear, should be unedited and unprocessed. The recordist appears as a witness who shares with a community of listeners a testimony and an experience. The written information they give about the context of the recording and the gear used should attest to the documentary purpose.

This sound collection's methodology, and its limitations, are to be understood in the cultural heritage of the World Soundscape Project, created by the musician Raymond Murray Schafer and a group of composers at Simon Fraser University (Vancouver) in the late 1960s. Acoustic ecology, which was both an artistic movement and a school of thought, introduced a care for sonic environments by listening to, recording, archiving and studying them and by fighting against noise pollution. The 'soundscape', the sonic equivalent of landscape, can refer, according to Schafer (1977), either to a real sonic environment or to its sonographic rebuilding based on field recordings. It could also be a musical composition evoking a specific location. It is, in any case, an 'acoustic field of study' (Schafer, 1977, p.7). The soundscapes collected on the Aporee soundmap are raw field recordings of the *real* soundscape we could have heard if we were there; the view of their geographic location contributes to testify to their veracity and to their scientific usefulness.

The Aporee global soundmap aims to offer a ready-to-use collection of sonic environments for researchers and for artists. The search filters (by place, by contributor, by type of sound, by year) present it as an organised sound archive, of which location is the most visible criterion. The web design, in addition to the Google Earth graphic standards, appears as neutral. Created by a German artist, Udo Noll, Aporee combines the collaborative culture of the open source web and the seeming neutrality of an institutional archive collection. It is considered an unequalled and inspiring model of its kind. However, this is a model that could be questioned, regarding its audio-visual framework and its prospect of building a global sound archive.

Objectives and perspectives

Today
Collaborative global soudmaps following the Aporee model combine two contradictory archive sources: a digital company which is one of the 'Tech Giants' (Google), and a plurality of individuals (the contributors). Whilst the soundmap's creators are using a free service offered by the digital company, the contributors are also sharing free data which can be used and sold by it (as Aporee's privacy settings make clear). Their contributions are made under the rules of the digital company which they help to expand. That being said, let's look into the audio-visual synergy that this association of two contradictory representations of space generates.

Instead of offering an alternative cartography, where the sonic dimension would prevail, soundmaps following the Aporee model are pinning sounds on a map which pretends to reflect an objective and immediate reality. Even if they are not contesting the view-from-above's dominant representation of space, they still offer a counterpoint. The sounds, recorded from the ground by a plurality of individuals, complete and contradict the visual webmap at the same time.

When visiting those soundmaps, in contrast to the photographic reproduction where we can zoom in to get closer and closer, or jump, by clicking, from one country to another, we need to take the time to listen to the recordings which are embedded in different locations. This listening time is one we can't speed up; a time we need to experience as the recordist experienced the location. They were not only *there*, they also made the recording from a specific position and at a certain distance, producing, as in photography, a sense of scale. The recordist can choose to focus on a specific detail of the space, a specific event, or aim at an overall 'picture'. Even if the microphone doesn't have the same selectivity as the human ear, and though there is no sonic equivalent for the term 'point of view',[1] sound recording is still an act of framing.

The parallels between photography and sonography are contradicted by the use of photography in the webmap, because what we see appears as a continuous and real-time reproduction of the Earth, instead of an archive collection. Google Earth's aerial photographs assembly (taken from a satellite, a plane or a drone, depending on the scale) doesn't seem to involve any human being but, rather, seems to be the mere product of an all-powerful technology. The world, seen from above, is presented as an unquestionable perception of reality, making us forget that it is still a representation, led by a specific system of values. However, the introduction of a sonic dimension implies a change of perspective which can be the first step for a change of paradigm.

Location recordings cannot pretend, as the image does in webmaps, to reflect a permanent space. However, their temporality can overcome the recording context. Soundscapes vary according to the moment and to

---

1   Rick Altman calls 'point-of-audition' a sound that, in a film, might be heard by a character (1992).

86

the listener, but they are also evolving over the years. Location recordings, although embedded in a 'gridded map', allow the representation of a *lived space* and therefore participate in what Jean-Marc Besse calls a 'lived geography' (Besse, 2010; Anderson, 2016). Location recordings not only create a change in perception, they open the way to experience: the experience of an individual, captured at that specific place at a certain time, which can be shared with some remote listener at any place and time. The web soundmap is a device of data and experience sharing. The virtual experience of space it enables is not only shaped for *remote in space* users, but also *remote in time*.

Beside the added value of experience, introducing subjectivity and sensitivity into an apparently objective and functional representation of space encourages us to question the mapping and making of archives. In fact, the Aporee soundmap not only combines two perceptions of space (from above/from the ground, objective/subjective, continuous/ fragmented), it also points out the soundmaps' historicity, by displaying sounds as recordings (unlike the seemingly immediate visual reality) and giving information about how they were made. As a collection project, the soundmap plays a role in conserving sound recordings and selecting them. Among the issues related to creating an archive, the representativeness of those recordings and their relevancy for future generations are some of the main points of discussion.

Tomorrow

If those sound collections are to be kept from a historical perspective, we have to be very aware of what they tell and what they omit. Any collection of archives implies an act of selection and classification. In this respect, we could wonder if the typology of sounds and the collecting mode do not fit with some ideological or aesthetical standards, setting apart some undesirable or less remarkable sounds according to the prevailing sonic culture.

As discussed earlier, the Aporee project conforms with acoustic ecology's pedagogic ambitions but also its aesthetic standards. That causes a lack of diversity in the typology of sounds which is reinforced, Jacqueline

Waldock argues (2011), by the social homogeneity of the contributors, who are mostly men, familiar with recording devices and collaborative media. Not only women, but also social groups untrained to the field recording practices are, in a way, silenced by this model of collaborative soundmapping. Waldock draws attention to the subjectivity of listening, not only as a psychological and individual act, but as affiliated to a specific culture or a social position. In this respect, women might hear and record spaces in a different way, as might 'minorities'. According to Waldock, the relevancy of the sound collected lies in its 'personal relationship' to the contributor, which should be explained 'either by written narrative or by aural description' (2011).

Following those critiques, widening the contributors' social profiles would improve the representativeness of the sound collection. As field recording and collaborative soundmapping are still niche practices nowadays, collecting sounds during field recording workshops with underrepresented social groups could introduce new objects of aural attention. The second option is to open the collection to types of sounds other than strictly environmental sounds. Should the soundmap also contain speeches, music, sounds from machines and political events to enrich the collection?

The British Library's huge sound collection, a small part of which is displayed on the UK soundmap, has clear historical and anthropological goals, covering 'the entire range of recorded sound: music, drama and literature, oral history, wildlife and environmental sounds' (British Library, 2019), which are all classified in subcategories. The British Library has undertaken a vast digitisation of ancient recordings (phonograph cylinders, disk records, magnetic tapes) in order to preserve their content before the original equipment becomes obsolete.[2] Today's researchers can already listen to some lost sounds, such as urban or rural soundscapes, ancient machines, or vocal accents. The British Library's growing sound collection will be a mine of information for the historians and anthropologists of future times. If mapping is not the first goal but instead one of the classification parameters, the UK Soundmap, which includes soundscapes, wildlife

---

2   See the British Library's 'Save our Sounds' project: https://www.bl.uk/projects/save-our-sounds.

sounds, accents and dialects, and traditional music from England, draws attention at a local scale to British sonic diversity and its ongoing erosion. To what extent could a global and collaborative soundmap offer an exhaustive sound-from-the-world collection and represent the world's cultural and social diversity? If the means of production, as we can attest from the history of art and techniques, have never been spread equally within the population, studying collaborative archive collections requires extra attention to its production. Therefore, in a historical and anthropological prospect, the *who* and the *where from* of the recordist is almost as significant as the *where* and the *what* of the recording; or, in other words, the relationship between the place of living and the place of recording is a significant clue in understanding the audio document itself and in exploring the role of familiarity and strangeness in the way we listen to the world.

The day after tomorrow
On a long-term scale, there are preservation concerns arising from the fact that soundmaps rely on web archiving. Most webmaps projects vanish from the visible web after a few years. When they are led by individuals instead of institutions or libraries, the recordings they have collected may be stored in places researchers are unable to reach. Udo Noll, who created the Aporee soundmap, thought from the beginning about saving the contents of his website. Firstly, because in the future the website's data capacity will be reached, and there may not be enough space to load new sounds or sounds of an uncompressed format (wav); and secondly, in order to ensure a copy of the collection exists. With that intention, Udo Noll collaborated with the Internet Archive, a non-profit transnational organisation, which aims at 'building a digital library of Internet sites and other cultural artifacts in digital form' and providing 'Universal Access to All Knowledge' (Internet Archive, 2014). The Internet Archive is also a pioneer of its kind, as it started in 1996, a few years after the World Wide Web was created, by archiving this new medium itself, and was the first transnational web library to be created. Its headquarters are located in San Francisco, and the data are stored in three data centres in California (San Francisco, Richmond and Redwood

City). To avoid a loss of the collections, and in case of a catastrophe, a mirror backup has been created in the Bibliotheca Alexandrina, Egypt, established in 2002 to commemorate the lost antique library, with both national and international prospects. From the Aporee platform created by the German Udo Noll, to the global sound collections stored in California and Egypt, the local recordings, coming from all over the globe, can be listened to online from anywhere, at any time, and are concretely stored on two continents. The association of a virtual space and 'real places' are part of the web paradox, which is reinforced in global soundmaps by the virtual ability to travel and to be immersed in some remote places.

This experience of ubiquity cannot really be reproduced by the web archive. As Niels Brügger alerts us, we can't expect the web archive 'to be an identical copy on a 1:1 scale of what was actually on the live web at a given time' (2011, p.32).

> When archiving newspapers, film, radio, and television, the main choices are related to the selection of the material, while the archiving process itself *grosso modo* consists of taking a copy out of circulation and storing it; no matter who stacks the newspapers or presses the record button on the video recorder, the archived copies are identical to what was once in circulation, just as all copies are identical. In contrast, with web material, choices have to be made in relation to both selecting and archiving, and we always do more than just remove the web material from circulation; the material is never totally unchanged.
>
> (Brügger, 2011, pp.32-33)

In fact, when we go to the Aporee collection page on the Internet Archive website, there is no longer a map. All we can see is a collection of sonograms, sorted by view, title, date archived and creator. We can look for specific sounds in the collection by key words, thanks to the search engine which will search in the metadata. When we write, for instance, 'rain brazil', four different sonograms appear. If we click on one of them, for instance, 'Tauary (Amazonian Rainforest) – Screaming Piha in the Amazonian Rain Forest' by Félix Blume, we can listen to it and read more information, including the location data. When clinking on the link, nothing new appears, but when copying it on to Google Maps, the exact place is pinpointed on the map, as in the original soundmap. However, the search engine has swiftly demonstrated its limits: first, I haven't found a sound of rain, but of the rainforest; second, I made my search in English, assuming that most of the metadata would be in English, but if I do the same search in French, I find one more result. In fact, the limits are not posed by the search engine but by the precision of the metadata and the language used there. The entire sound collection can't be explored by catching a glimpse of sound; as a first step, words are not only helpful but necessary to find a sound and recognise what it is.

Beyond that, the recording format itself can pose a problem for future use by humanities researchers. How can we ensure they will be able to play the recordings? And how can we ensure the digital data is sustainable on a long-term scale? Won't the collection be too large at that point? Shouldn't the criteria for inclusion be more selective to ensure the collection's lasting relevance?

Echoes from the planet

Among environmental soundmaps, some collections prove more specific than others in terms of the typology of sounds presented and in the modality of contributions. The Nature Soundmap, created by the Australian field recordist and photographer Marc Anderson, gathers sounds from wild environments made by professionals from all over the world. Recorded with high-quality material and using binaural technology (a pair of stereo microphones which reproduce the spatial perception of two ears), they aim at producing a sensation of immersion. The remote webmap visitor, while listening through headphones, is plunged into an environment that seems to surround them. They can close their eyes, concentrate, and virtually travel through listening. The power of those sonic environments adds another dimension to the visual webmap. The place where the sound is pinpointed is only an indication of where we are landing or diving. The temptation to click on a new place every 15 seconds is absent, compared to Aporee, because the sounds we are listening to are not only recordings that document a place, they are also dealing with sensations and have the capacity to make the listener feel that they *are there*.

This immersive nature soundmap collection echoes back to the work of Bernie Krause, an American musician and bio-acoustician who has been recording natural soundscapes since the 1960s. Krause has created the Wild Sanctuary in California, where 'a vast and important collection of whole-habitat field recordings and precise metadata' is stored (Wild Sanctuary, n.d.). Through conferences, books and exhibitions, he has brought awareness to the endangered *biophonies* of the planet,[3] documenting their ongoing loss and showing their richness from an environmental and aesthetical perspective. In his opinion, field recordists have a role to play in the preservation of sonic biodiversity – first, by presenting each specific biophony as a whole sonic ecosystem. He terms this the 'niche hypothesis': the idea that 'in order to be heard, whether in urban, rural, or wild habitats, vocal organisms must find appropriate temporal or acoustic niches where their utterances are not buried by other signals' (Krause, 2015, p.40). The combination of different frequencies, mixing with each other in order to be heard, makes him compare sonic ecosystems to symphonies. Beside this musical approach, he asserts the need, for scientific use of the recorded data and metadata, to give precise information about biodiversity in the recorded environments.

The second role that field recordists could play, according to Bernie Krause, is to give evidence of biodiversity loss throughout the years by comparing two recordings of the same environment several years apart. Ultimately, the sonic medium, and its ability to trigger emotions, can be used to alert audiences and governments to the need to preserve ecosystems. If listening to an environment introduces a care for it, listening to it from the perspective of its extinction may not only change the colour of our emotions but also introduce a real and urgent concern about its preservation.

3   Bernie Krause calls biophony 'the collective sound produced by all living organisms that reside in a particular biome' (2015, p.11). A natural soundscape is also characterised by its geophony, 'the non-biological
natural sounds produced in any given habitat, like wind in the trees or grasses, water in a stream, waves at
the ocean shore, or movement of the earth', and often conflicts with anthropophony, 'all the sounds that we
human generate', most of which, in his opinion, is 'chaotic or incoherent – sometimes referred to as noise'
(Krause, 2015, p.12).

Though designed as a collection of wild soundscapes, Anderson's Nature Soundmap has secondary historical goals. In fact, because of climate change, deforestation, natural extractions, and sound, air, earth, and water pollution, wild soundscapes have been changing over the past 50 years. In this respect, this sound archive lacking human presence still documents humanity's impact. The clear goals implied by the type of sonic environments targeted, and the limiting of contribution to professional nature field recordists, means that the Nature Soundscape avoids, in part, the problem of seeking to be representative. However, we can argue, as more than 95% of the contributors are white men, the lack of women in sound practices is still reinforced by the image of the solitary explorer braving the dangers of the wild world to record it.

Global/Local

If the typology of sounds and the identity of the recordist are two of the main issues implied in the making of a global sound archive, the soundmapping itself also has to be discussed. The maps studied, which I called the Aporee model, are based on a webmap service (here, Google Earth); and most of the existing global soundmaps follow this model, as if there is no alternative. However, soundmapping existed before Google Earth, and different way of intersecting the visible and the audible have been explored.

If we understand a map as a visual or graphic representation of space, representing a sonic environment can be done in many ways. Peter McMurray, in his 2018 article 'Ephemeral cartography: on mapping sound', gives alternative models of soundmapping throughout history. In the late 1960s, at the same time as Raymond Murray Schafer was developing his notion of soundscape and was mapping the increase of noise pollution in Vancouver, 'a group of urban planners and designers in Boston, led by Michael Southworth and Kevin Linch, developed a much more city-friendly notion of soundscape, articulated in a number of soundmaps as well' (McMurray, 2018, p.125). They used an original graphic vocabulary to map the different type of sounds in the city, 'including music, chimes, police officers and vehicles', and to display their locations and superpositions (McMurray, 2018, p.125). These data visualisations, McMurray argues, 'are key materialisations of soundscape for Schafer' (2018, p.125). But if Southworth is mapping 'about sound', Schafer provided in *The Vancouver Soundscape* and its associated LP (1973) 'the first systematic attempt to make a map of sound – that is, a map comprising not merely visual representations of sound but recordings of the sounds themselves' (McMurray, 2018, p.127). Since the 1980s, sound and visual artists have looked for alternative ways of mapping sound. Annea Lockwood's field recording projects about rivers, which she called 'Sound Maps', were not only released on records (*A Sound Map of the Hudson River*, 1989) but also in visual and sonic installations (*A Sound Map of the Danube*, 2005).

According to sound artist Isobel Anderson, 'if we are to harness sound as a creative and expressive cartography, we must map listening rather than solely fixed sound' (2016). As an example, she describes the installation she made at Belfast's Metropolitan Arts Centre, with the songwriter Fionnuala Fagan, about Belfast's disappeared Sailortown. Instead of using a 'gridded map', they wrote songs inspired by their interviews with members of the Sailortown Regeneration Group (SRG), and 'began to map the streets and buildings that have now disappeared' (Anderson, 2016). The exhibition combined 'songs alongside composed soundscapes, objects, images, and text' (Anderson, 2016). The visitor could listen to each song 'through headphones mounted on the walls at different locations in the space' and explore, at the same time, some 'photographs and objects from Sailortown' (Anderson, 2016). This intermedial project is far removed from a sonic data collection following the Aporee model. However, it still documents a territory and reveals 'voices that had been silenced in traditional maps of the city' (Anderson, 2016).

Nevertheless, all these attempts for an alternative sonic cartography have local scales and specific targets. This is to say, mapping local sounds at a global scale is an almost impossible challenge. What would an alternative global soundmap look like? Would it be interactive? Kinetic? Would it render a subjective perception of space? And how can the ephemeral qualities of sound be rendered? Nowadays, some of the most advanced cartographers in alternative representation of space, such as the French *Terra Forma* group (Aït-Touati, Arènes, and Grégoire, 2019), aim at mapping an 'inhabited planet', and the way we interact with space, territories and ecosystems, mostly focuses on local scales.

Should we understand those global web soundmaps for what they are – a collection of local sounds pin-pointed in their geographic location – without seeking for an alternative representation of space and using the webmap device as a frame or a tool? In every respect, global soundmaps have two main advantages: making their remote visitors travel through space and time and making them think of the way one's listening to the world could be shared and represented.

BIBLIOGRAPHY

Aït-Touati, F., Arènes, A. and Grégoire, A, 2019. *Terra Forma. Manuel de Cartographies Potentielles.* Paris: Éditions B42.

Altman, R. ed., 1992. *Sound Theory, Sound Practice.* London: Routledge.

Anderson, I., 2016. Soundmapping beyond the grid: Alternative cartographies of sound. *Journal of Sonic Studies,* 11 [online]. Available at: <https://www.researchcatalogue.net/view/234645/234646 > [Accessed 12 May 2020].

Besse, J.-M., 2010. Le paysage, espace sensible, espace public. *META: Research in Hermeneutics, Phenomenology, and Practical Philosophy,* 2(2), pp.259-286.

Besse, J.-M., 2018. *La Nécessité du Paysage.* Marseille: Parenthèses.

British Library, 2019. *Save our sounds.* [online] Available at: <https://www.bl.uk/projects/save-our-sounds> [Accessed May 24 2020].

Brotton, J., 2013. *A History of the World in Twelve Maps.* London: Penguin Books.

Brügger, N. and Schroeder, R. eds., 2017. *The Web as History: Using Web Archives to Understand the Past and the Present.* London: UCL Press.

Brügger, N., 2011. Web archiving – between past, present, and future. In: M. Consalvo and C. Ess, eds. 2011. *The Handbook of Internet Studies.* Chichester: Wiley-Blackwell. pp.24-42.

Droumeva, M., 2017. Soundmapping as critical cartography: engaging publics in listening to the environment. *Communication and the Public,* 2(4), pp.335-351.

Droumeva, M., Jordan, R. eds., 2019. *Sound, Media, Ecology.* London: Palgrave Macmillan.

Internet Archive, 2014. *Internet archive.* [online] Available at: <https://archive.org/about/≥ [Accessed May 24 2020].

Krause, B., 2015. *Voices of the Wild: Animal Songs, Human Din, and the Call to Save Natural Soundscapes.* London: Yale University Press.

Leloup, R., 2017. Les enjeux de la cartographie sonore par rapport à la frontière de la neutralité. *Intersections,* 37(2), pp.59-72.

McMurray, P., 2018. Ephemeral cartography: on mapping sound. *Sound Studies,* 4(2), pp.110-142.

Montreal Soundmap, n.d. *Montreal soundmap.* [online] Available at: <https://www.montrealsoundmap.com/≥ [Accessed May 24 2020].

Noll, U., 2019. *Info & help.* [online] Available at: <https://aporee.org/maps/info/#about> [Accessed May 24 2020].

Noll, U., 2020. *Radio aporee.* [online] Available at: <https://aporee.org/maps/≥ [Accessed May 24 2020].

Schafer, R.M., 1970. *The Book of Noise.* Wellington: Price Milburn & Co.

Schafer, R.M., 1977. *The Tuning of the World.* New York, NY: Knopf.

Sterne, J., 2003. *The Audible Past: Cultural Origins of Sound Reproduction*. Durham, NC: Duke University Press.

Thulin, S., 2018. Sound maps matter: expanding cartophony. *Social & Cultural Geography*, 19(2), pp.192-210.

Varghese, S., 2020. The Noise of Time. *New Stateman*, 21-27 Feb., pp.41-43.

Waldock, J., 2011. Soundmapping: critiques and reflections on this new engaging medium. *Journal of Sonic Studies*, 1 [online]. Available at: <https://www.researchcatalogue.net/view/214583/214584> [Accessed 12 May 2020].

Wild Ambiance Pure Nature Soundscapes, 2020. *Nature soundmap*. [online] Available at: <https://www.naturesoundmap.com/> [Accessed May 24 2020].

Wild Sanctuary, n.d. *Wild sanctuary*. [online] Available at: <http://www.wildsanctuary.com/index.html> [Accessed May 24 2020].

ELIZABETH FORD

Steil's Tavern and the Musick Club: Recreating the Historical Memory of Edinburgh

Introduction

The Musick Club, the precursor to the long-running Edinburgh Musical Society has been accurately described as 'shadowy' (Emerson and MacLeod, 2014, p.45), although it is generally assumed to have been the beginning of concert life in Edinburgh from the late seventeenth century. There are no surviving archival sources documenting its existence. No such group is mentioned in any newspapers of the time. Without an accurate membership roster, or even a passing mention of the name of any person who might have participated, looking through personal papers is directionless and unproductive. The precise location of the Cross Keys Tavern, where it is reputed to have met, is not known. Although there are plenty of maps of Edinburgh from this period, there is nothing that describes or indicates the positions of various buildings other than the major landmarks that still stand. Research then has been dependent on secondary sources, most of which repeat the same information that is quite likely inaccurate.

Working with the AHRC-funded 'Space, Place, Sound, and Memory: Immersive Experiences of the Past' project in the University of Edinburgh Reid School of Music, I recreated an evening at the Cross Keys from around 1717. This research and reconstruction show how the space in which music is made influences decisions for the musicians, and the audio virtual reality allows audience members to experience the music in a different, more participatory way than simply attending a performance or listening to a recording.

Documenting the The Musick Club

All histories of music in Edinburgh agree that a group of musicians meeting at the Cross Keys Tavern preceded and directly led to the formation of the Edinburgh Musical Society in 1727, but there is almost no evidence that this group even existed. The only contemporary mention of the so-called Musick Club is Allan Ramsay's 1721 poem 'To the Musick Club'. This poem is much discussed in histories of music in Scotland for what it suggests, not about informal music making, but about the unification of the rustic and the civilised:

> Then you who Symphony of Souls proclaim
> Your kin to Heaven, add to your Country's Fame,
> And shew that Musick may have as good Fate
> In Albion's Glens, as Umbria's green Retreat:
> And with Correlli's soft Italian Song
> Mix Cowdon Knows and Winter Nights are long.
> Nor should the Martial Pibrough be despis'd,
> Own'd and refin'd by you, these shall the more be priz'd.
>
> (Ramsay, 1721)

Although Ramsay does not describe a meeting of the Musick Club, its members, or give any other information related to it, this poem is taken as evidence that such a group existed and as a basis for their repertoire.

Hugo Arnot, writing in 1779, places the club at Steil's tavern, the Cross Keys. He says:

> The musical Society of Edinburgh, whose weekly concerts form one of the most elegant entertainments of that metropolis, was first instituted in the year 1728. Before that time, several gentlemen, performers on the harpsichord and violin, had formed a weekly club at the Cross-keys tavern (kept by one Steil, a great lover of musick and a good singer of Scots songs), where the common entertainments consisted in playing the concertos and sonatas of Corelli, then just published, and the overtures of Handel.
>
> (Arnot, 1779, p.379)

Arnot was writing 50 years after the events he describes took place and so was likely able to interview people who remembered the music at the Cross Keys.

Writing in 1792, William Tytler describes a concert that took place on St Cecilia's Day in 1695. This essay is a dubious and problematic source, as has been noted elsewhere.[1] Peter Holman, by looking at the dates of the men Tytler lists as having participated in the concert and the dates of the repertoire they were reported to have played, has determined that Tytler's dating of the St Cecilia's Day event is off by 15 years (Holman, 2004). Unfortunately, most scholars of music in eighteenth-century Edinburgh rely uncritically on Tytler's essay and combine his list of musicians with the repertoire from Ramsay's poem and the location in Arnot's history of Edinburgh to form the story of the Musick Club.[2]

Writing in the middle of the nineteenth century, Robert Chambers in *Traditions of Edinburgh* says:

One is disposed to pause a moment on Steil's name, as it is honourably connected with the history of music in Scotland. Being a zealous lover of the divine science, and a good singer of the native melodies, he had rendered his house a favourite resort of all who possessed a similar taste, and here was actually formed (1728) the first regular society of amateur musicians known in our country. It numbered seventy persons, and met once a week, the usual entertainments consisting in playing on the harpsichord and violin the concertos and sonatas of Handel, then newly published.

(Chambers, n.d., p.178)

In the *Domestic Annals of Scotland*, he reports on Tytler's St Cecilia's Day concert, and in his listing of events for 1718, he states:

---

1   Especially regarding the history of the flute in Scotland (Ford, 2020).

2   Tytler's essay should not be treated as fiction or as totally inaccurate, but greater scrutiny of his dates and authoritative claims would be prudent by the scholarly community. For example, Holman observes that Tytler grew up near where some of the gentlemen musicians he describes lived and that he may have heard them playing in Edinburgh as a teenager. Tytler could be a valuable first-hand source, but his tendency to misdate (and the fact that he was very elderly when he wrote this in 1792) should instill caution.

We learn that there was now a weekly meeting of amateurs at the Cross Keys Tavern, kept by one Steil, who is noted as an excellent singer of Scottish songs, and who appears to have possessed a collection of instruments for the use of his guests. This meeting admitted visitors of both sexes, and was a point of reunion for the beau monde of Edinburgh in days while as yet there were neither balls nor theatres.

(Chambers, 1874, p.432)

Chambers' sources were clearly Arnot and Tytler, though the mention of ladies at the Cross Keys is interesting, as women generally did not visit taverns, unless for a specific purpose (Carr, 2014). This could then imply that the meetings of the Musick Club were private events where ladies would be welcome; Fraser-Harris notes that ladies were recorded as having been present at the concerts at the Cross Keys. This suggests that it was not the all-male convivial atmosphere of the other tavern-meeting Edinburgh clubs, although, Fraser-Harris provides no evidence of these records (Fraser-Harris, 1899, p.260).

Chambers takes Tytler's list of musicians playing on St Cecilia's Day to be the same as those who played at the Cross Keys, as he specifies that the Lord Colville mentioned was Lord Colville of Ochiltree, who played organ and harpsichord, not his contemporary Lord Colville of Culross (Chambers, 1874, pp.434-5). Marie Stuart does the same when she lists the musicians as the Laird of Newhall on viola da gamba, Lord Colville on harpsichord, and Sir Gilbert Elliott of Minto on flute (Stuart, 1952, p.59). Henry Graham adds Lord Haddington to the list of musicians and specifies that the meetings began in 1718 (Graham, 1969, p.101).

The most significant recent work on the Musick Club is by Jenny MacLeod and Roger Emerson. They provide, as an appendix, a list of Musick Club members. This list comes not from any surviving source but from the names mentioned by Tytler and Harris (Emerson and MacLeod, 2014, pp.45-106; pp.65-67). Several of the men listed – Sir John Clerk of Penicuik, Sir Gilbert Elliot of Minto, Lord Colville of Ochiltree – are known to have been musicians, and it is likely many of the others they list were as well.

David Johnson, in his overview of concert life in Edinburgh prior to the official formation of the Edinburgh Musical Society, lists a few contemporary references to Steil's concerts and the musical evenings at his tavern. Unfortunately, those sources have since disappeared, though the scrapbook in the Edinburgh Public Library that he listed as missing has been located (Johnson, 2003, p.33). Johnson, too, relies heavily on Tytler for the history of social music in Edinburgh.

Murray Pittock takes Tytler's report a step even further and claims that the Musick Club met weekly at Steil's tavern. He believes that Ramsay's poem does not so much detail what was occurring as it describes the hybridisation of music that occurred in eighteenth-century Scotland, what David Johnson calls the 'Scots Drawing Room' style. Pittock argues that the Musick Club moved to St Mary's Chapel because their events had become too large, with 61 subscriptions to concerts in the 1726-1727 season (Pittock, 2018, p.160).

No available records show these data, but records for the Edinburgh Musical Society, meeting in St Mary's Chapel, commence in 1727, with 67 paying members (Sederunt Books of the Edinburgh Musical Society). This conflation of Ramsay, Arnot, and Tytler by nineteenth-century and modern scholars has constructed an idea of the Musick Club and the history of concert life in Edinburgh. Some of this may be loosely based in fact, but without any corroborating early eighteenth-century sources, few definitive and authoritative conclusions can be reached.

The Cross Keys Tavern

'Kept by one Steil, a great lover of musick and a good singer of Scots songs.' (Arnot, 1779, p.379)

More evidence for Steil's tavern, the Cross Keys, survives, but again only in secondary source materials. Father and son, Patrick and John Steil, kept it in turn, and so their identities are sometimes confused. Arnot was the first writer to locate the Musick Club at the Cross Keys, but he may have had access to sources or people living earlier in the century who would have known. Marie W. Stuart writes:

A tavern particularly associated with music was the "Cross Keys" with its gilded sign in what is now called the Old Assembly Close, "Steel's, who bears the double keys, of plenty sign," where Dr Pitcairne had proclaimed *Nunc te clavigeri delectent pocula Stili.* Its early eighteenth century landlord, Patrick Steil (after whom the Close was then named), was a great music-lover and singer of Scots songs, also a violin-maker [...] in February 1729 all the pictures, music books and musical instruments of John Steil (apparently Patrick's heir) were sold by auction. [...] Patrick played quite an important part in city life, adding the duties of a Captain in the "Trained Bands" to his other activities.
(Stuart, 1952, pp.58-59)

No evidence, however, of Patrick's membership in the 'trained bands' or violin making survives.[3] The tavern of Patrick's time may also have been associated with politics: opponents of the Act of Union are said to have met at Pate Steil's Parliament to debate their views over a drink (Stuart, 1952, p.59; Pittock, 2013, p.99), and it is also where everyone retired for a drink after debating the Roxburgh Amendment to the Act of Security on 16 July 1703 during the final sitting of the Scottish Parliament (Fry, 2013, p.47). Pate Steil's Parliament was apparently a well-known informal opposition body to the Union, but very little contemporary evidence of it survives either (Pittock, 2018, p.163).[4] In Edinburgh, tavern keepers tended to be men of substance, so it is likely Steil had means (Cooke, 2015, p.49). David Fraser-Harris describes Steil as 'not a nobody in Queen Anne's Edinburgh', as he was listed as a merchant burgess when he inherited property in Writer's

---

3 Steil's name is conspicuously absent from *Scottish Violin Makers* (Honeyman, 1910). The records of the trained bands do not survive prior to the middle of the eighteenth century, though Fraser-Harris reports that they met in Steil's tavern, and Steil's area of patrol was the west side of Warriston's Close to the west side of Fleshmarket Close (Fraser-Harris, 1899, p.261).

4 Murray Pittock describes this as an 'anti-Union debating society'. David Fraser Harris, citing the Domestic Annals of Scotland, says that the phrase Pate Steil's Parliament appeared in correspondence of the era (Fraser-Harris, 1899, p.262).

Court in 1681 (Harris, 1899, p.261).

Archibald Pitcairne's poem 'Edinburgh Taverns' instructs the reader to 'let the cups of key-bearing Steil delight' (Pitcairne, 2009, pp.110-111).[5] John and Winifred MacQueen identify this Steil as John Steil, the musician and subscriber to Ramsay's works, but it could have been either of the two.[6] Murray Pittock is inconsistent as to which Steil operated the Cross Keys at the time of the Musick Club meetings. In *Material Culture and Sedition*, he names Patrick as the proprietor of the tavern, and claims that Patrick subscribed to Allan Ramsay's poems (Pittock, 2013). In his earlier ODNB entry on Allan Ramsay, however, Pittock claims it was John Steil's tavern that Ramsay and the Musick Club frequented and that John Steil subscribed to the poems (Pittock, 2010). The surviving subscribers' list to Ramsay's poems shows that it was indeed John Steil who supported the work.[7] In Ramsay's 'Epistle to Robert Yarde of Devonshire, Esquire', he in turn says that one 'can in Cumin's, Don's, or Steil's, be serv'd as plenteously and civil, as you in London at the Devil' (Ramsay, 1721). This would make John contemporary with the activities of the Musick Club.

John Steil was a singer who performed in Edinburgh with the violinist Adam Craig and harpsichord player Henry Crumbden between 1700 and 1711 at St Mary's Chapel. This trio also performed at Skinner's Close in July 1710. David Johnson believed Steil's musical activities ceased around 1719, when he inherited the Cross Keys, but there is no evidence for when he took over the tavern (Johnson, 2003, p.33; n.d.).[8] In 1708, Patrick Steil was still in charge, as he is listed as a vintner in an advertisement in the Edinburgh Evening Courant for a sale of malt and mallow (Edinburgh Evening Courant, 1708).

An advertisement for one of Steil's performances survives pasted into a

5   Poem 19, 'Nunc te Clavigeri delectent pocula Styli, Quem genuit Baccho pulchra Garumna patri.' / 'Now let the cups of key-bearing Steil delight you, whom the beautiful Garonne bore to father Bacchus.' (Pitcairne pp.110-111; pp.342-3).

6   Pitcairne died in 1713, so there is a slightly stronger case for Patrick as the Steil referred to in the poem.

7   Subscribers' lists survive to Ramsay's poems in the National Library of Scotland, L.C. 1149.

8   The repertoire mentioned in Johnson's notes from the Tatler are songs from the opera *Hiddaspes* by Steil (presumably performed by rather than composed) and solos performed by Craig. Johnson found these issues of the Edinburgh Tatler in the Edinburgh Public Library, but they have now gone missing. References to Steil's concerts with Craig that Johnson found in the MS Transcriptions of St Mary's Chapel Session Books are also missing.

scrapbook of musical materials in the Edinburgh Public Library. It reads:

For the Benefit of Mr Steil.
At Mary's Chapel in Niddry's-Wynd, on Friday the 11th Instant, will be performed a Consort of Vocal and Instrumental Music. Tickets are to be had at the Coffee-Houses, and at the Door of the Hall, at Half-a-Crown each. The Consort begins precisely at Six a Clock.
No Plaids.
Vivat Rex.

The compiler of this scrapbook annotated the advertisement with 'circa 1700' and 'very rare'. It is undated, and the source is not known.[9]

John Steil may have had incurred financial hardship in the latter years of the 1720s. After the Musick Club moved to St Mary's Chapel and evolved into the Edinburgh Musical Society in 1727, they maintained a relationship with Steil. The Edinburgh Musical Society Sederunt Books show 'charges to Steils' in 1727 and 1728. No explanation of what the charges are for is given, and the first entry is to Steils and for wax (Sederunt Books of the Edinburgh Musical Society). The loss of the musicians may have been bad for business: in May of 1728, the creditors of John Steil were invited to meet at his house in order to determine how best to collect what was owed to them. On 26 February of the following year, Steil's possessions, including 'pictures, prints, musick- books and musical instruments' were sold at auction (The Caledonian Mercury, 1729). This is the last mention of Steil in any record. As John Steil had performed with many of the founding musicians of the Edinburgh Musical Society, his tavern was the obvious place for musicians to meet and play informally. He may have even had a harpsichord, and its proximity to Niddry's Wynd would have made it easy to go back and forth between their original and new venues.

---

9 Edinburgh Public Library, WML 46, vol. 1. This scrapbook is mentioned by David Johnson as 'untraced' (Johnson, 2003, p.33).

Old Assembly Close (Photo credit: Elizabeth Ford)

Foundations near the Fringe office (Photo credit: Elizabeth Ford)

Music: how to interpret the repertoire of a group who left no records

'[…] the common entertainment consisted in playing the concertos and sonatas of Corelli, then just published, and the overtures of Handel' (Arnot, 1779, p.379).

In 'To the Musick Club' Ramsay mentions the composer Arcangelo Corelli, pìobaireachd, and the song 'The Broom of Cowdenknowes'.[10] Given the lack of any other evidence, this, along with Arnot's later mention of Handel, must be taken as representative of the Musick Club's repertoire.

These choices are quite similar to the repertoire known to have been performed at the concerts of the Edinburgh Musical Society later in the century (MacLeod, 2001, pp.90-92). Corelli remained popular for most of the eighteenth century, and song was always included in the Edinburgh Musical Society programs.

The only surprising choice in Ramsay's poem is 'Pibrough'. As Matthew Gelbart notes, pìobaireachd would have been very foreign music in lowland Scotland in the eighteenth century (Gelbart, 2007, pp.1-13). A literal understanding of Ramsay's use of pìobaireachd as cèol mòr is, however, somewhat implausible, given the realities of playing the Highland pipes indoors and that there is very little evidence that Highland music was known in Lowland Scotland c.1720.[11] It is far more likely that Ramsay used pìobaireachd in its other meaning: piping in general. Murray Pittock, however, uses Ramsay's references to piping as a symbol of the union of the rustic and the civilised, describing it as 'fanciful', saying no pipers were present, and this refers to pipe music set for violin (Pittock, 2018, p.160). Without any evidence either way, and with the popularity, especially among the upper class, of small pipes, Border pipes, and pastoral pipes, there is no reason to suppose that pipes were not present at the Cross Keys.

Hugh Cheape details the rise of the pastoral pipes in Scotland in the eighteenth century. This was in effect a new instrument that had been developed during the eighteenth century, for a society interested in pastoral themes. Cheape goes on to argue that, as traditional music began to appeal to polite society in Scotland, so too would the gentler pastoral pipe (Cheape, 2010, pp.78-101). Ramsay's poem implies civilisation of the 'martial pibrough' by the Italianate preferences and tastes of the Musick Club, who will 'own' and 'refine' the music. This can be seen as a meeting and melding of the pastoral and urban cultures in polite society. Cheape calls attention to

10   1653-1713.

11   Pìobaireachd has two meanings in Gaelic. It can refer to cèol mòr, the highly structured formal music of the pipes, or can mean piping in general.

an anonymous drawing from 1728 showing a performance of *The Beggar's Opera* accompanied by bagpipe, suggesting that the pipes were exotically rustic in polite circles (Cheape, 2010, p.93). The pastoral pipes were so popular among gentlemen amateur musicians that John Geoghegan tapped into the market around 1746 by writing the first tutor for the pastoral pipes, with music. This was the first printed collection of music for pipes, showing a growing musical literacy among pipers. Geoghegan explicitly mentions gentlemen as his target audience and remarks that the lack of musical notation had been holding back some aspiring pipers. Geoghegan says that they have been 'hindered from what their Inclinations so urged them to, by this Instrument's wanting a Scale or Gamut to learn by', which all other Musical Instruments of any Value have' (Geoghegan, 1724, quoted in Cheape, 2010, p.86). The pipes had, by 1746, been acknowledged as the equals of the flute, violin, and harpsichord. It is therefore entirely to be expected that a gentleman piper would have played at the Cross Keys.

The Cross Keys Tavern, designed in virtual reality by Rod Selfridge

The virtual reality reconstruction of the Musick Club

The Cross Keys Tavern does not survive, nor is its precise location in Old Assembly Close known. Rod Selfridge, the project's software developer, and I visited the close and picked a location near the Royal Mile entrance, adjacent to the back entrance to the Fringe box office. The tavern room was based on the White Hart Inn, one of the oldest pubs in Edinburgh. The current building is from the 1740s, and it has always been a tavern. Little in the way of material culture from taverns from the early eighteenth century survives, so later objects and images were consulted with the assumption that drinkware and seating in public spaces was unlikely to have changed very much in 50 years.

The music was recorded acoustically, rather than anechoically,[12] in a practice room at the University of Glasgow; it was layered with pub sounds from the BBC sound archive, including a dog fight and a horse and cart on cobblestones, and with recordings of Allan Ramsay's poems referencing the Musick Club and Steil being read. The result is a unique immersive experience.

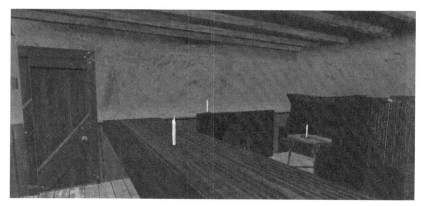

The Cross Keys Tavern, designed in virtual reality by Rod Selfridge

Repertoire

Marie Stuart, in her description of the musical events at the Cross Keys, describes a trio sonata texture.[13] This works well in the setting (an informal, small space), suits the repertoire, and showcases the newly-fashionable

---

12 Virtual reality is usually recorded anechoically, with musicians playing alone and then later edited together. We opted for a more natural environment and recording in a sound-deadened room, partly because it is impossible to fit a harpsichord into an anechoic chamber.

13 '[...] echo to the strains of its aristocratic patrons when the Laird of Newhall played on his viol da gamba, Lord Colville on the harpsichord, Sir Gilbert Elliot on the German flute' (Stuart, 1952, p.59).

transverse flute.[14]

The entirety of the chosen repertoire derives from the descriptions given by Ramsay and Arnot, along with what is known to have been popular in early eighteenth- century Edinburgh. The trio sonata in G minor, WoO 10 by Arcangelo Corelli has concordances in the Scottish manuscript sources GB-KETmmc 353.[15] 'Water Music' was first performed in 1717 and would almost certainly have been known in Scotland soon thereafter. The Scottish songs are from the *Tea-Table Miscellany* (Ramsay, 1724; McCue, 2017).

Scottish small pipes were used for the piping section. The tune 'Jingling Geordie' is very old and would have been in the repertoire of Lowland and Border pipes in the early eighteenth century (Seattle, 2011).

Musicians

David Johnson argues that the music teachers in Edinburgh did double duty, teaching at the schools and giving private lessons at country houses. Therefore, the populace would have had similar music educations to the gentry (Johnson, 2003, pp.30-31). The singer representing John Steil is a trained musician, but not a specialist in eighteenth-century or Scottish repertoire.[16] The harpsichord player, flute player, soprano, and violinist are all specialists in historical performance practice.[17] The viola da gamba player may be the best representation of a gentleman amateur musician: he is a professional cellist, but had never played bass viol until his mother, who was originally going to play, had a conflict, and he stepped in. This mix of specialisations, training, and background should represent the relative skill levels and musical educations of the players at the Cross Keys.

---

14 The flute was one of the most popular instruments in eighteenth century Scotland, especially with gentlemen amateur musicians (Ford, 2020).

15 This manuscript book in the collection of the Duke of Buccleuch and Queensberry consists of tunes from theatre, Scottish tunes, minuets, and extracts from Lully, Purcell, and Corelli transposed for solo recorder. It dates from c.1715. 'Tunes for a flute in manuscript.' GB-KETmmc 353.

16 Steil was portrayed by Donald Ferguson.

17 The musicians who participated in this reconstruction were Allan Wright, harpsichord; Katy Lavinia Cooper, female vocals; Donald Ferguson, male vocals; Andrew Bull, violin; Tim Cais, bass viol; and Ziexuan Qiao, small pipes. I played flute.

Conclusions

Concert life in Edinburgh began informally in a tavern and developed into the long-running Edinburgh Musical Society. This was an informal musical culture, not unlike a modern folk session at a pub, meaning impromptu music based around those musicians attending. This type of music making was and is rarely planned in advance or documented, due to not being, strictly speaking, a performance. The evolution of the Edinburgh Musical Society from the Musick Club can then be understood in that way: the men playing at the tavern attracted enough of an audience that they decided to give concerts and turned from a group of friends making music into a formal concert series. The venue then changed from the tavern, where they would presumably have been playing near the bar in cramped conditions, to St Mary's Chapel, which was a former church and established concert venue, eventually building St Cecilia's Hall in 1768.

Because nothing about the Musick Club was documented, all previous research has been speculative and reliant on anecdotal sources. This research into the relationship between the Cross Keys Tavern and the Musick Club has established where fact and legend diverge in this significant, but shadowy, aspect of musical culture in eighteenth-century Edinburgh. Even with this lack of hard evidence, the sound environment of informal music-making in early eighteenth-century Edinburgh can be understood using virtual reality reconstruction. This new use of technology will have wide implications for audience engagement with music of the past, especially as COVID-19 forces the performing arts to rethink the future of live performance.

BIBLIOGRAPHY

Arnot, H., 1779. *The History of Edinburgh*. Edinburgh: Printed for W. Creech.

Broadie, A., 2011. *The Scottish Enlightenment: The Historical Age of the Historical Nation*. Edinburgh: Birlinn.

Buchan, J., 2012. *Capital of the Mind: How Edinburgh Changed the World*. Edinburgh: Birlinn.

Burns, M. and Oliver, J.W. eds., 1944-1973. *Epistle to Robert Yarde* and *To the Musick Club*. In: *The Works of Allan Ramsay*. Scottish Text Society. Proquest Online Literature.

Carr, R., 2014. *Gender and Enlightenment Culture in Eighteenth-Century Scotland*. Edinburgh: Edinburgh University Press.

Chambers, R., 1874. *Domestic Annals of Scotland: From the Reformation to the Revolution*. Volume 3. Edinburgh: W. & R. Chambers.

Chambers, R., 1969. *Traditions of Edinburgh*. Edinburgh: W. & R. Chambers.

Cheape, H., 2008. The pastoral or new bagpipe: piping and the Neo-Baroque. *The Galpin Society Journal*, 61, pp.285-304.

Cheape, H., 2010. *Bagpipes: A National Collection of a National Instrument*. Edinburgh: National Museums Scotland.

Cooke, A., 2015. *A History of Drinking: The Scottish Pub Since 1700*. Edinburgh: Edinburgh University Press.

Daiches, D., 1964 *The Paradox of Scottish Culture: The Eighteenth-Century Experience*. London: Oxford University Press.

Daiches, D., 1977. *Scotland & the Union*. London: Book Club Associates by arrangement with John Murray.

Daiches, D., 1986. *The Scottish Enlightenment: An Introduction*. Edinburgh: Saltire Society.

Edinburgh Evening Courant. No. 424. 17-19 March 1708.

Edinburgh Musical Society, n.d. *Sederunt Books: [1728-1795]*. Volume 1. Edinburgh: University of Edinburgh.

Ellis, M., 2004. *The Coffee House: A Cultural History*. London: Weidenfeld & Nicolson.

Ellis, M., 2010. *Tea and the Tea-Table in Eighteenth-Century England*. London: Pickering & Chatto.

Emerson, R. and MacLeod, J., 2014. The Musick Club and the Edinburgh Musical Society. *Book of the Old Edinburgh Club*, 10, pp.45-106.

Ford, E.C., 2020. *The Flute in Scotland from the Sixteenth to the Eighteenth Century*. Oxford: Peter Lang Press.

Fraser-Harris, D.F., 1899. *St Cecilia's Hall in the Niddry Wynd: A Chapter in the History of the Music of the Past in Edinburgh*. Edinburgh: Oliphant Anderson and Ferrier.

Arnot, H., 1779. *The History of Edinburgh*. Edinburgh: Printed for W. Creech.

Broadie, A., 2011. *The Scottish Enlightenment: The Historical Age of the Historical Nation*. Edinburgh: Birlinn.

Buchan, J., 2012. *Capital of the Mind: How Edinburgh Changed the World*. Edinburgh: Birlinn.

Burns, M. and Oliver, J.W. eds., 1944-1973. *Epistle to Robert Yarde* and *To the Musick Club*. In: *The Works of Allan Ramsay*. Scottish Text Society. Proquest Online Literature.

Carr, R., 2014. *Gender and Enlightenment Culture in Eighteenth-Century Scotland*. Edinburgh: Edinburgh University Press.

Chambers, R., 1874. *Domestic Annals of Scotland: From the Reformation to the Revolution*. Volume 3. Edinburgh: W. & R. Chambers.

Chambers, R., 1969. *Traditions of Edinburgh*. Edinburgh: W. & R. Chambers.

Cheape, H., 2008. The pastoral or new bagpipe: piping and the Neo-Baroque. *The Galpin Society Journal*, 61, pp.285-304.

Cheape, H., 2010. *Bagpipes: A National Collection of a National Instrument*. Edinburgh: National Museums Scotland.

Cooke, A., 2015. *A History of Drinking: The Scottish Pub Since 1700*. Edinburgh: Edinburgh University Press.

Daiches, D., 1964 *The Paradox of Scottish Culture: The Eighteenth-Century Experience*. London: Oxford University Press.

Daiches, D., 1977. *Scotland & the Union*. London: Book Club Associates by arrangement with John Murray.

Daiches, D., 1986. *The Scottish Enlightenment: An Introduction*. Edinburgh: Saltire Society.

Edinburgh Evening Courant. No. 424. 17-19 March 1708.

Edinburgh Musical Society, n.d. *Sederunt Books: [1728-1795]*. Volume 1. Edinburgh: University of Edinburgh.

Ellis, M., 2004. *The Coffee House: A Cultural History*. London: Weidenfeld & Nicolson.

Ellis, M., 2010. *Tea and the Tea-Table in Eighteenth-Century England*. London: Pickering & Chatto.

Emerson, R. and MacLeod, J., 2014. The Musick Club and the Edinburgh Musical Society. *Book of the Old Edinburgh Club*, 10, pp.45-106.

Ford, E.C., 2020. *The Flute in Scotland from the Sixteenth to the Eighteenth Century*. Oxford: Peter Lang Press.

Fraser-Harris, D.F., 1899. *St Cecilia's Hall in the Niddry Wynd: A Chapter in the History of the Music of the Past in Edinburgh*. Edinburgh: Oliphant Anderson and Ferrier.

Fry, M., 2013. *The Union: England, Scotland and the Treaty of 1707*. Edinburgh: Birlinn.

Gelbart, M., 2007. *The Invention of 'Folk Music' and 'Art Music': Emerging Categories from Ossian to Wagner*. Cambridge: Cambridge University Press.

Gelbart, M., 2012. Allan Ramsay, the idea of 'Scottish Music' and the beginnings of 'National Music' in Europe. *Eighteenth Century Music*, 9(1), pp.81-108.

Graham, H.G., 1969. *The Social Life of Scotland in the Eighteenth Century*. 5th ed. London: Adam & Charles Black.

Harris, B. and McKean, C., 2014. *The Scottish Town in the Age of the Enlightenment, 1740-1820*. Edinburgh: Edinburgh University Press.

Hillman, M., 2017. *Thomas Sanderson's Account of Incidents: The Edinburgh Musical Society 1727-1801 and its Impact on the City*. Edinburgh: The Friends of St Cecilia's Hall.

Holman, P., 2004. An early Edinburgh concert. *Early Music Performer*, 13, pp.9-17.

Honeyman, W.C., n.d. *Scottish Violin Makers: Past and Present*. 3rd ed. Dundee: The Honeyman Music Publishing Co.

Johnson, D., 2003 *Music and Society in Lowland Scotland in the Eighteenth Century*. 2nd ed. Edinburgh: Mercat Press.

Johnson. D., n.d. Unpublished notes. s.l.: Courtesy of John Purser.

MacLeod, J., 2001. *The Edinburgh Musical Society: its membership and repertoire 1728-1797*. Ph.D. University of Edinburgh.

McCue, K. ed., 2017. *Musick for Allan Ramsay's Collection of 71 Scots Songs*. Columbia: University of South Carolina Libraries.

McElroy, D.D., 1969. *Scotland's Age of Improvement: A Survey of Eighteenth-Century Literary Clubs and Societies*. Washington WA: Washington State University Press.

Pitcairne, A., 2009. *The Latin Poems*. Edited and translated from Latin by J. MacQueen and W. MacQueen. Tempe AZ: Arizona Center for Medieval and Renaissance Studies.

Pittock, M., 2010. Ramsay, Allan (1684-1758), poet. In: B. Harrison, ed. 2004. *Oxford Dictionary of National Biography*. [e-book] Oxford: Oxford University Press. https://doi.org/10.1093/ref:odnb/23072.

Pittock, M., 2013. *Material Culture and Sedition: 1688-1760*. Basingstoke: Palgrave Macmillan.

Pittock, M., 2018. *Enlightenment in a Smart City: Edinburgh's Civic Development 1660-1750*. Edinburgh: Edinburgh University Press.

Ramsay, A., 1721. *Poems*. Edinburgh: Printed by Mr. Thomas Ruddiman.

Ramsay, A., 1724. *The Tea Table Miscellany, or, a Collection of Choice Songs, Scots and English*. Edinburgh: The Author.

Scott-Moncrieff, G., 1947. *Edinburgh*. London: B. T. Batsford Ltd.

Scrapbook of Musical Cuttings. [manuscript] WML 46, vol. 1. Edinburgh: Edinburgh Public Library.

Seattle, M. ed., 2011. *The Master Piper: Nine Notes That Shook the World.* 3rd ed. s.l.: Dragonfly Music.

Skinner, R.T., 1947. *The Royal Mile.* Edinburgh: Oliver and Boyd.

Stuart, M.W., 1952. *Old Edinburgh Taverns.* London: Robert Hale Limited.

Taylor, J., 1903. *A Journey to Edenborough in Scotland.* Edinburgh: William Brown.

The Caledonian Mercury. No. 1198, 1257, 1382 and 1383. 18 December 1727, 2 May 1728, 18 and 20 February 1729.

Tunes for a flute in manuscript. GB-KETmmc 353.

Tytler, W., 1792. On the fashionable amusements and entertainments in Edinburgh in the last century, with a plan of a grand concert of music on St Cecilia's Day, 1695. *Transactions of the Society of Antiquaries of Scotland.* Edinburgh: William Creech. pp.499-511.

SAM COHN

The Future of History and its Recent Past: In Praise of Boredom

Historical trends over the past 50 years

I think of myself as an empirical historian who entertains theory and models. This essay, however, will be of reflections and almost empty of empirical research. Instead, the major source of my essay is myself. I do not think that this datum (i.e. myself) is entirely inappropriate for the subject at hand – historical trends over the past 50 years. That timescale encapsulates my development as a historian. Both trajectories – mine and the historiography – illustrate the unexpected twists and turns that history-writing can take, even over a relatively short-term.

Circa 1970, the French *Les Annales* school was at its pinnacle, and during my graduate training with David Herlihy, first at the University of Wisconsin, then at Harvard University, the French reigned supreme. *Les Annales* melded historical research with social-science theories, models, and methods. Moreover, it could be physical geographic at its heart – most famously portrayed in Fernand Braudel's *La Méditerranée et le monde méditerranéen à l'époque de Philippe II* (1949). With this, we need to appreciate that environmental and climatic history, employing scientific methods, are not new to the twenty-first century. They were pivotal to historical research at the time of IASH's foundation.

In that year, 1970, the Annalist historian Emmanuel Le Roy Ladurie famously predicted that future historians would need to become computer programmers and that their research would have to change fundamentally. They would leave their library carrels as isolated scholars and begin working in *équipes* composed of technicians, postgraduates, and multidisciplinary experts, all, of course, hierarchically organised. They would come to resemble their white-coated colleagues across town in new shiny laboratories.

Yet already in the early 1970s, new trends were developing. In 1972, in an office with five graduate student desks, I remember a guru graduate, a decade older than the rest of us, coming to my desk and telling me to forget my chi-squares and regressions. That stuff was passé. I now needed to read Foucault. To be sure, I did not find any serial analysis in Foucault. Instead, one symbol such as Jeremy Bentham's Panopticon could form the core for spinning a sharp break in epistemes, differentiating one age from another. By the end of the 1970s, the dominance of *Les Annales* had slipped and the journal itself had changed, entertaining more 'l'histoire des mentalités' than the prices of wheat. I even produced an article for *Annales* on medieval art history, although I snuck in a few numbers. Perhaps, the best landmark of this change in mentality was Lawrence Stone's 'The Revival of Narrative: reflections on a new old history' in *Past and Present* (1979), which coined the term 'the narrative turn', and ever since, we have become dizzy from one turn after another. By the 1980s, the large regional studies of the Annalists – the Beauvaisis, the Mâconnais, Languedoc, etc., almost always in two volumes, of which the second comprised tables, charts, and poorly drawn maps – had disappeared. Now the interdisciplinary beacons were literary theory and cultural anthropology. Historians could return to the quiet of their mahogany desks.

Most emblematic of this return to tranquillity was 'microhistory', ingeniously initiated by Carlo Ginzburg's *Il formaggio e i vermi: il cosmo di un mugnaio del '500* (1976). But soon, in less gifted hands, it became a more-or-less formulaic process to produce a short book quickly: a theoretical or anthropological introduction, followed by a handful of documents spied in the archives to tell a story.

The turn from the Annalists has had welcoming surprises. One has been the revival of diplomatic history (at least for the Renaissance and early modern period). The revival was not a return to the questions set by Garrett

Mattingly and others in the 1950s that tied the presence of residential embassies with the growth of bureaucracy and state development. Rather, the enormously rich, voluminous diplomatic correspondence is now being tilled to investigate networks of information, spying, emotional history through linguistic analysis, and early developments in ethnography. One task of a new diplomat in a foreign place was to report back on the nature of the people (their diet, clothing, habits, religious customs, social organisation, even hairstyles), as in a Venetian dispatch sent to the Council of Ten in 1521 on the 'savage peoples of Cornwall'. No diplomatic historian of the 1950s would have bothered transcribing those pages.

In the twenty-first century, certain trends of the 1980s began to wane. Most symbolic of that late-twentieth-century historiography was the decline of microhistory. This is not to say that this approach has become moribund. A friend of mine at the University of Toulouse has just published an entertaining book on a snowball fight on the island of Murano on 27 January 1511, but I do not now hear historians asking: "have you read the latest ground-breaking microstoria by so-and-so?" Instead, historiography has moved in the opposite direction towards global histories, creation and use of big data, histories that break the canonical chronological boundaries, and developments in digital humanities. In a sense this is a return to Le Roy Ladurie's prediction of 1970. Even if no historian I know is a computer programmer (or needs to be), large-scale histories conducted by *équipes*, often utilising models and methods from the natural sciences, especially genetics, are the ones catching media attention and winning big grants. With this current transition, the signposts have not been as clear as they were in the 1970s and 80s. I know of no seminal work to have tilted the scales from microstoria to new global histories. Perhaps most instrumental in this transition has been the moves of national and international funding agencies and especially those of the European Research Council, initiated in 2007 with their section on 'the study of the human past'. For these, applications for the million-plus-Euro grants follow the same format as those in the natural and biological sciences, stressing 'ground-breaking' hypotheses and new methodologies. Perhaps, as a result, those trained in the scientific disciplines of late have been the ones to scoop up the lion's share.

Historical trends in research at IASH

Let me now turn to one sliver of empirical data that I had hypothesised would support the two transitions described above. Ben Fletcher-Watson has kindly allowed me to inspect the IASH secret archives of the previous thousand-plus fellows – their names, countries of origins, institutions, and titles of their IASH projects. I have picked out the historians. Of course, from these files it is often difficult to surmise the type of research, much less approaches or methods. For instance, the 2013 project title of the classicist David Konstan (who happens to be a friend) was 'Beauty and the Greek'. From the title, you would not have known that it was groundwork for a history of emotions, utilising current psychological theories. At any rate, medievalists are specialists in working with incomplete data. From the limited IASH archive, I can confess that it does not correspond with the trajectories I have plotted above. For the 1970s and 1980s I find no historians at IASH working on topics with an *Annalist* stamp: no regional histories, even economic histories, or ones based on serial analysis or the hallmark of Annalist histories from that epoch – demography. No family reconstitutions. Even more astounding, during the first 37 years of IASH fellows, I do not find any on questions of migration, so central for Scottish history. The first study on migration comes only in 2007, and it derives from a scholar in an education department, not history. Afterwards, I find fifteen scholars with topics involving migration, but again these are dominated by non-historians in departments of Religious Studies, Art History, English Literature, Political Science, Social Policy and others. Perhaps the early IASH fellows were ahead of the curve, having already progressed beyond the Annalist paradigm? However, for the next transition – topics crossing the humanities/science divide – none of the history fellows appear at this forefront. The first fellow with an environmental history topic was in 2004, and I do not find another until 2018. Climatic history also lagged behind. The first climatic one I spotted at IASH was in 2014-15. It involved sophisticated techniques for recreating wind patterns in the Shetlands during the seventeenth century, made possible by software that this IASH fellow had developed. But he (in fact, IASH's one thousandth fellow) was a geographer, not a historian. The first historian to appear with 'climate' in the project title appears only in 2018.

Envisioning the future

I wish now to peer into the future, where no one can contradict me, at least, for the moment. There are, in fact, two futures. First, the one I envisioned in July 2019 when I submitted my proposal for the now-cancelled 50th anniversary symposium panel and, secondly, the one for our present, post-COVID-19 future. For the first, I would stress the continuing strength of historians crossing the humanities/science divide, as we are now seeing at IASH with growing interests in aDNA, genome sequencing, and readings from phylogenetic trees. In the current decade, I expect more historians to be asked to join *équipes* of geneticists, physical anthropologists and evolutionary biologists. Given the surprises within the past 50 years, I would also predict reactions to current trends concerning funding and working practices. In December 2019, I had the good fortune of meeting the architect and architectural historian Adrian Forty, who wrote the award-winning *Concrete and Culture: A Material History*. It is difficult for me to think of many scholars more interdisciplinary than Adrian, a practising UK architect who collaborates with chemists and structural engineers and whose cultural history extends from cinema to philosophical notions of time. Adrian confessed that he has never participated in a team grant and argued strenuously that the most productive mode for historians is to collaborate but to work individually. I know many others who think the same and have been quietly critical of humanities disciplines forced into models of research standardised for the natural sciences.

With the outbreak of Covid-19, as we are now seeing for the sciences, money is pouring into immediate research for cures and vaccines, and epidemiological modelling is high on the agenda. I also suspect for the humanities it will be a good time for those interested in economic, psychological, political, and cultural questions about plagues in the past. I have already thought of four or five PhD dissertation topics. Time allows mentioning only one: I know of no work on the economic consequences of the Great Influenza of 1918-19 for any country, despite its massive lockdowns across the globe that lasted months. One worry that appeared in newspapers when the pandemic was declining in November 1918 was the terrible prospect facing life insurance companies, with predictions that the massive pay-outs would soon sink the entire industry worldwide. By the end of 1919, a curious surprise had emerged: the industry was booming as never before. Those from the lower middle classes and workers began purchasing policies for the first time. They had learnt some lessons from history, even if journalists and economists (at least circa November 1918) had not.

I wish to end with another lesson, this one from historiography as I have experienced it over the past 50 years. Of course, what is happening in the present always influences history writing, not only in the topics chosen but on methods and approaches. However, I think history writing also possesses its own internal dynamics. Once a trend of historical research becomes deeply entrenched and predictable, historians get bored and begin to think in different boxes. Thank God for boredom!

BIBLIOGRAPHY

Braudel, F., 1949. *La Méditerranée et le monde méditerranéen à l'époque de Philippe II*. 3 vols. Paris: Écrits sur l'histoire. Translated into English 1972 and 1973 by Sian Reynolds.

Forty, A., 2012. *Concrete and Culture: A Material History*. London: Reaktion Books.

Ginzburg, C., 1976. *Il formaggio e i vermi: il cosmo di un mugnaio del '500*. Turin: G. Einaudi. Translated into English 1980 by J. and A. Tadeschi.

Le Roy Ladurie, E., 1973 and 1978. *Le territoire de l'historien*. 2 vols. Paris: Gallimard. Translated into English 1979 by B. and S. Reynolds.

Stone, L., 1979. The revival of narrative: reflections on a new old history. *Past & Present*, (85), pp.3-24.

NATALIE GOODISON AND DEBORAH MACKAY

An Unlikely Research Partnership between a Medievalist and a Geneticist: Working Across Disciplines

Introduction

This paper explores the benefits of interdisciplinary research from the perspectives of an epigeneticist and a medievalist. A mutual friend introduced us in an email concerning a rare birth described in a medieval romance (think fiction, faery story), and soon the emails were whirring back and forth. Perhaps to our surprise, we discovered that the medieval romance was likely rehearsing well-known cases of a *mola matricis,* what is referred to today as a hydatidiform mole. Eventually, we published our findings in the *Medical Humanities BMJ* (Goodison, Mackay and Temple, 2018), and the publication has continued to garner substantial interest. According to *BMJ*'s metrics as of June 2020, the article abstract has been viewed 2,749 times, the full article 389 times, and the pdf downloaded 132 times. In 2019, it received an attention score in the top tenth percentile in BMJ metrics. Such a collaboration has impacted our separate careers and research in significant ways. This article will be divided into two sections, with each author writing individually on the way the partnership has affected their research and their (re)conception of their field.

This paper honours the 50th anniversary of the Institute for Advanced Studies in the Humanities at Edinburgh. At the heart of our research partnership is interdisciplinary collaboration, and this paper is a testament to both the benefits of interdisciplinary research as well as what IASH promotes in its research networks. This paper also reflects the interests of

IASH as it centres on the benefits of the medical humanities. To date, IASH is the only research centre at the University of Edinburgh – throughout all its schools, departments, or institutions – that has promoted the medical humanities as a research strength. Finally, our collaboration, happening to centre on a woman's abnormal experience of childbirth, also reflects another of IASH's research focuses: gender. This paper then, with its focus on gender, the medical humanities, interdisciplinary research, and cross-school collaboration celebrates the heart of what IASH so assiduously and generously promotes.

Background

The text on which we conducted our research is *The King of Tars*, found in the fourteenth-century Auchinleck Manuscript located in Edinburgh's own National Library of Scotland (Chandler, 2015). The story is written in Middle English, and while this romance is fictional, at least eight historical accounts testify to some version of this story (Hornstein, 1941). The story tells of a Christian Princess who willingly marries a Saracen (pagan) Sultan in order to save her own people from destruction. The Sultan makes their marriage conditional upon the Princess's conversion to his religion, wearing his religion's clothing, and praying to his gods. The Princess does this, although the texts make the caveat that that she does not do so in her heart. The couple are wed and nine months later the Princess gives birth – not to a healthy child, but to a lump of flesh. The text describes the lump as a gobbet of flesh, without ears, eyes, limbs, mouth, or nose, completely unlike human form in either Spirit or Flesh – the two important animating principles in medieval theories of generation. The Sultan immediately blames his wife, telling her the child is indicative of her lack of faith. The Princess in turn blames her husband's religion. They agree to a test of the gods: each will pray to their god to animate the child, and the loser must convert. The Sultan prays to his gods, with vigour, but they do not respond to his prayers. The Princess retrieves a priest from jail, has the priest baptise the lump of flesh, and as the waters of baptism are conferred upon the lump, it transforms into a healthy baby boy. The Sultan must now convert, and as he prepares to undertake the rite of baptism, the priest bestows upon him a new name. This naming changes the Sultan's skin from black to white, whereupon, seeing the power of the Christian God, the Sultan truly believes. The romance manuscript, unfinished due to its damaged condition, concludes with the Sultan partnering up with his father-in-law to wage war against pagans.

Deborah

As I remember, our collaboration began with a two-line email introduction from a colleague, to whom Natalie had mentioned her work on *The King of Tars*. My research is tangentially connected to moles, and our mutual colleague urged me to collaborate with Natalie because the Princess's monstrous birth might be a mole, and because I am 'a medievalist at heart'. Perhaps I am a medievalist at heart; but since I'm contributing as an epigeneticist by trade, I will start by explaining how moles arise as an epigenetic phenomenon.

Every cell of your body contains two copies of your genome. The genome is a string of three billion letters in the form of a one-dimensional 'text' that is copied faithfully from cell to cell, from the one-cell embryo to the fifty trillion cells of an adult.[1] The genome is a one-dimensional instruction book to make you as a four-dimensional organism. Within the genome, approximately twenty thousand genes encode the constituent parts of your cells, from the light-receptors of your eye to the keratin of your toenails.[2]

Every cell in your body contains the same DNA, but every cell does different things with it: your eyes make light-receptors and your toes make toenails, but not vice-versa. In each cell, epigenetic changes (on or around the DNA) cause the one-dimensional genome to change its three-dimensional shape. Some genes adopt an open, accessible form, and these are highly used; other genes have a closed, inaccessible form, and these parts

---

1   The tables on http://www.ensembl.org/Homo_sapiens/Info/Annotation are updated live with statistics on the human genome; https://www.youtube.com/watch?v=OjPcT1uUZiE&list=PL999A2EBDB5049A16&index=1 (the first 90 seconds) offers a visual representation.

2   These statements are approximately true! Not every cell contains 2 complete copies of DNA: for example, eggs or sperm carry one copy ready to transmit to the next generation, while mature red blood cells jettison their nuclei for the sake of nimbleness. And not every genome is completely identical because copying any text is an error-prone business. But it is a pragmatic approximation to say every cell in your body contains the same genome.

are not used.[3] Over your lifetime, your cells express a common genomic text in an uncommon diversity of ways: as an adult with some fifty trillion cells that in their individual lifespans express permutations of some twenty thousand genes in abundances that can vary some ten-thousandfold, you can objectively describe yourself as a person of infinite variety.

Particularly dramatic epigenetic changes occur between generations. In every individual, some cells undergo highly-specialised epigenetic programming to become gametes – eggs and sperm – and when the gametes fuse, the resultant zygote erases the epigenetic marks of gametes and establishes the marks of totipotency, the unique capacity of the zygote to develop into every cell type of the developing organism (Mackay and Temple, 2017).

It is this last epigenetic transformation that is aberrant in a mole. Its DNA complement is normal, but its epigenetic marking is not;[4] what develops is not a healthy embryo, but a non-viable mass resembling extra-embryonic (placental) structures. Hydatidiform moles develop in approximately one in 1,000 pregnancies. Risk factors include maternal nutrition, ethnicity and age – it is more common in very young and older mothers. I study very rare families where women have adverse reproductive outcomes, including children with congenital disorders and nonviable outcomes like molar pregnancy. One of these women was the Princess in *The King of Tars*. I wish to outline some of the things I learned – both scientifically and intellectually – from the case of the princess.

Firstly, the representation of epigenetics that I have given here is one that has developed directly out of this collaboration. In order to communicate concepts of epigenetics and reproduction to my non-specialist collaborator, I had to re-examine, criticise, crystallise, integrate and re-narrate them. I believe this has been a great aid to my clarity of communication in the forums – lay, medical and scientific – where I share epigenetic ideas.

Secondly, the new insight I gained during this collaboration drove me

3   https://www.youtube.com/watch?v=mHak9EZjySs&list=PL999A2EBDB5049A16&index=2 offers a visual representation of open and closed DNA.
4   I am focusing here on a specific group of moles, where cells contain both maternal and paternal genomes, but the maternal DNA is epigenetically programmed like paternal DNA. In the majority of cases, reproductive errors around the time of fertilisation result in the molar cells containing two paternal genomes.

to revisit cases that had been set aside as insoluble: children with ultra-rare congenital disorders caused by disturbed epigenetic programming. I had been studying the DNA of the affected families for several years, searching (fruitlessly) for genetic changes in the children's DNA that could account for their disorders. But the Princess's experience prompted me to go back to these DNA sequences, focusing not on the children's DNA, but their mothers', and here I saw a shared pattern of genetic changes. These genetic changes in mothers reduced their eggs' capacity for epigenetic reprogramming, with outcomes ranging from unwell children to miscarriages, periods of infertility and – like the Princess – molar pregnancies.

I was amazed by these findings: after all, my genetic training taught me to look for the genetic change and the clinical problem in the same person! Because our prevailing concepts of genetics have little place for maternal-effect mutations, I had stared at these cases for literally years before Natalie handed me the lens of historical perspective that brought them into focus. Our collaboration has led to the identification of new genetic mutations causing epigenetic disorders, an increasing number of new publications (e.g. Begemann et al., 2018), and most importantly, diagnoses for affected families.

Thirdly, the research made me aware of a more general unmet need in medicine. Humans have a significant burden of subfertility, but fertility is currently a relatively low priority for medical care and research. I think this is partly because subfertility is not an 'autonomous' disorder: if a couple have multiple miscarriages, they don't need a doctor themselves, because they are healthy – it is their offspring that are affected. Nonetheless, fertility issues cause distress and illness. I am contributing to reviews and position statements on this issue (e.g. Gheldof et al., 2019), in the hope that wider understanding of reproductive genetics may lead to advances in diagnosis, prognosis, counselling and care for couples with stories like that of the Princess and the Sultan.

Finally, I offer an 'epigenetic' view of interdisciplinary collaboration. I mentioned earlier that epigenetic changes enable our cells to shape their shared linear 'text' of DNA into unique, emergent, adaptable three-dimensional architectures, in which genes that are linearly far apart are brought into proximity and expressed together. This epigenetic mechanism for juxtaposing genes gives us our extraordinary capacity – from the level of cells and tissues to humans and populations – to live and thrive by expressing emergent responses to our changing and sometimes hostile environment.

As a medical researcher I work almost exclusively among colleagues that think in the same ways as I do. For me, interdisciplinary collaboration juxtaposed me with ideas that I would never otherwise have encountered and gave me an 'epigenetic' creative space where extant observations could be synthesised in novel ways.

Natalie

I was shocked to discover that the fictional romance of *The King of Tars* might accurately depict congenital abnormalities. The field of medieval romance, in which *The King of Tars* sits, is full of the marvellous – of knights defeating an insurmountable number of opponents, of giants who are impossibly large, of women turning stepsons into werewolves, of enchantresses turning themselves into stone. The genre is littered with the unlikely: Gryphons, swan-children, Green Knights, revenants and wraiths, magic rings – these are the stock-motifs of romance. Thus, whilst reading *The King of Tars*, I was firmly convinced that the birth of a lump of flesh was merely one more fabulous instance amid a genre that was fabulous. In fact, romance is so far removed from reality that it has even been termed 'escapist literature'. The romance of *The King of Tars* is filled with unlikely events: a lump of flesh transforms into a child, the Sultan's skin changes from black to white. Why would the birth of a lump of flesh be any different from these other implausible occurrences?

Fast-forward several months later to my meeting Deborah, who read the analysis of the birth of a lump of flesh and told me that not only did such things happen, but also how they were genetically formed. Deborah has explained the genetic process of how a woman might give birth to a lump of flesh. This phenomenon is well documented in literature from the nineteenth century under the term 'hydatidiform mole' (Ross, 1898; Roberts, 1924) – but was this well documented in the Middle Ages? Scholars in the medical humanities have recently turned away from identifying past descriptions of diseases, so much so that it has been deemed a waste of time. So how were we to interpret the possibility of a hydatidiform mole recorded in a medieval text?

The answer came almost at once: I was to look in medieval gynaecological literature to see if other such phenomena were described. I looked in *De Secretis Mulierium, The Sickness of Women,* and the writings of Albertus Magnus and Nicole Oresme, and all faithfully testified to the rare phenomenon of a woman giving birth to a lump of flesh, called a *mola matricis* or uterine mole.[5] It turns out that rare births were considered a divine sign and were carefully analysed in medieval literature. Texts even hypothesise as to how these rare births were formed. The *mola matricis* has a long history, mentioned by Hippocrates, Galen, and Aristotle.[6] Uterine moles recur throughout medieval discourses, including writings on theology, philosophy and women's health – all of which treasured abnormalities. It seems possible, even likely, that the recorder of *The King of Tars,* who would have been someone literate, likely someone clerical and located in London (the hub of intellectual medieval discourse), may have read the great-authors and intellectual debates of his day – including Aristotle and Albertus Magnus, both of whom wrote on the *mola matricis.* This changed my perception of the romance. Suddenly, *The King of Tars* was no longer dealing with the fabulous and the un-real, but instead it was drawing on very real fears that a woman may encounter during childbirth. Romance has often been heralded as a genre that enacts wish-fulfilment: the knight is ultimately victorious, the lady is saved, the knight and lady marry, they live happily ever after (Frye, 1957, p.186). However the genre also does the opposite: by focusing on abnormalities that are real it presents the fulfilment of nightmares. In other words, the birth of a lump of flesh, giving birth to that which cannot be classified as human, draws on very real fears surrounding pregnancy, and these fears are showcased in this romance.

---

5   For De Secretis Mulierium see Lemay (1992) pp.67-68; for The Sickness of Women see Green and Mooney (2006), pp.455-568, especially pp.533-536 (Chapter 11, ll: 1348-1437); for Albertus Magnus (13th CE), see Kitchell and Resnick (2018), Book 10. Ch. 4, pp. 839-841; and for Oresme see Hansen (1985) pp.228-231 and pp.236-237.

6   i.e. Aristotle's De Animalibus Historiae: Libri X: Graeci et Latine (Schneider, 1811), see Tome 4, p.474.

This discovery made me question whether other instances of abnormal pregnancy in romance reflected wider cultural discourse on women's conception and childbearing. Romance abounds with abnormal births – twins, septuplets, those fathered by faery or demon. My research at IASH focused on the relationship between mother and abnormal offspring, specifically whether the mother's sin or salvation influenced the child's form. For example, the romance *Chevalere Assigne* castigates women who give birth to multiple offspring, as each child is thought to be fathered by a different man (Anon., 14th CE, p.149-70). In the case of the romance's septuplets, it indicates that the mother has had seven different sexual partners. As I began to research whether or not this was a commonly held belief in medieval thought, I discovered another point which is reflective of wider medieval theories of conception: a woman was thought to conceive if she orgasmed. If these theories are applied to the romance *Chevalere Assigne,* then the woman in question has not merely committed adultery, but enormously enjoyed doing so, enough to generate seven different children. The romance seems to support this as the Queen Mother vilifies her daughter-in-law the moment she successfully gives birth to her seven children. Thus, our research collaboration has made me reconsider how much of what romance presents is untrue or unlikely and to what extent romances draw upon the widespread hopes and fears that affect their audience, readership, and community.

Our partnership also made me analyse the extent to which romance may reflect prevalent theories of conception. During my time at IASH, I began to unpick this topic, only to discover the paucity of writings on medieval abnormal generation, on the role of female pleasure in medieval conception, and on pre-Modern notions of inheritance.

Our collaboration also made me reconsider the *longue durée* (or history that extends beyond human record) of medical problems circulating around the globe from time out of mind. Between the Classical Era and the early twentieth century, a great intellectual debate occurred in the works and reception of key thinkers and writers. Debates on generation can be traced from Antiquity (i.e. Aristotle, Galen) to their medieval reception (Albertus Magnus), to their Early Modern reanalysis, to Modernists' discussions, demonstrating how the same idea was treated over centuries. The remodelling of the university syllabus after the Second World War meant a dismantling of this 'conversation between the greats'; indeed, the curriculum in literature has moved so far forward as to utterly discard this 'great conversation', to ensure that is entirely dismantled, within efforts to decolonise the curriculum.

Specifically, in dismantling this *longue durée* of medicine, thinkers deliberately change the names of diseases, such as *mola matricis* shifting to *hydatidiform mole*. This cuts short the narrative of women who have experienced and faced such congenital abnormalities over time, discards the methods each era adapted to this condition, and bypasses the views of how past peoples clinically responded to uterine moles. I will always applaud Deborah for not laughing when she heard that the romance's medieval response was to heal the lump-child through a miracle; instead, Deborah applauded their endeavours to use a religious force to counteract what modern medical terminology would classify as not-even-human. She even pointed out that medieval medicine had the ability, at least in the historical sources, to heal the lump of flesh into a child – something, she was careful to point out, that not even modern medicine, with all its innovations, can do.

As Deborah indicated, looking at a medieval response to a congenital birth defect caused her, and others, to re-examine the way she viewed modern medicine. Having, in the words of C.S. Lewis, 'the clean sea breeze of the centuries blowing through our minds' allows us to use past considerations of similar problems to re-conceive the dataset a whole new way (1946, p.7). As Gasper, Smithson and McLeish (2017) point out in their interdisciplinary work, working with humanities scholars causes scientists to view problems from entirely different, previously unconceived angles. Deborah affirms such reports. Thus, expanding beyond the narrow confines of our own discipline and being willing to look at a problem from another's perspective fosters the ability to reconceptualise and solve what were termed as insurmountable problems.

However, I think that several things must be present in order for this kind of collaboration to be successful. The first is genuine intellectual curiosity, almost for the sake of itself. In a Scientific Study of Manuscripts workshop hosted in Durham, Dr Lucia Burgio, Senior Scientist in the Victoria and Albert Museum's Conservation Department, emphasised that genuine curiosity led to some of the greatest research breaks of her career. I had the good fortune to meet a geneticist who was fascinated by what I was working on, not because it had any immediate benefit to her, but because she genuinely found the problem fascinating.

The second requirement helpful to interdisciplinary collaboration is the ability to discuss the discourse of your field outside the terms your field uses. Wonderfully, Deborah was able to sit down with me and explain the science behind rare cases of congenital abnormalities in extremely understandable terms. Since meeting Deborah, I have read article upon article in the sciences in an attempt to increase my knowledge of epigenetics, but often I have been unable to understand what the articles are saying because the language of the field's discourse is so precise. Though it is perhaps necessary for scientific communication, it nevertheless detracts from comprehension for outsiders. As I could not understand that language of academic papers, it was essential that I sat down with Deborah, read her emails, and listened as she deconstructed something very difficult into terms I could use. Thus, this emphasises that there is learning to be done and research connections to be made that cannot be carried out via the written, published academic word, but must be done in conversations, at dinners, over tea and coffee, on walks, etc., or would otherwise be largely unintelligible. This is the beauty of the 'conversation among the greats': as they all wrote in Latin, the terminology was largely the same. Thus, a *mola matricis* described by Hippocrates (c.370 B.C.) can be responded to by Albertus Magnus (d.1280), over 1500 years apart. The loss of a common academic language means losing the ability to understanding what others mean. In some ways, I think this common academic tongue is at the heart of IASH's lunches every Tuesday, where Fellows congregate over platters of sandwiches and salads. At these, IASH Fellows habitually discuss their research with people entirely outside of their discipline and must communicate their research in a clear language.

I promised to end this my section with possible suggestions for interdisciplinary collaboration. To translate the ideas discussed in this paper beyond IASH, my suggestion, although I suspect it will be met with laughter, is to host dinner parties with people of different schools, departments, and methodologies, with people who are intellectually curious, and see what occurs after a bottle of wine. The breeze of the centuries that ripples through our mind, as Lewis goes on to demonstrate, unshackles us from the lie so prevalent in culture that 'we in this modern moment are right and all that is past is wrong'; or, in his words, what he calls 'chronological snobbery', 'the uncritical acceptance of the intellectual climate common to our own age and the assumption that whatever has gone out of date is on that account discredited' (Lewis, 1955, p.161).[7] Each generation believes the present age to be the best, but when we are aware of our own 'chronological snobbery', it shows us that our own viewpoints too are unstable. A humble engagement with the past may not only show where our own thinking is flawed but may also provide us with the answers to solve current problems.

Conclusion

Our research collaboration has allowed us to accomplish far more together than in the isolation of our own fields. To date it has, for Deborah: 1) led to the identification of very rare genetic diseases; 2) provided diagnostics and treatment to those affected; 3) instigated research into human's significant burden of subfertility; 4) provided 'epigenetic' creative spaces that allow for thinking outside discipline structures; 5) proven that historical perspectives can lead to scientific, medical breakthroughs.

For Natalie the partnership has caused her to: 1) re-evaluate romance to consider the fantastic in light of cultural relevance for medieval audiences; 2) realise that romance genuinely engages in prevalent fears surrounding congenital abnormalities in *The King of Tars*; 3) investigate whether other abnormal births are reflective of wider medieval theories of generation, birth practices, or well-documented medical phenomena; 4) reconsider the *longue durée* of congenital abnormalities birthed by women; 6) examine the science of abnormal conception in medieval thought; and 7) question the dismantling of 'the great conversation', especially in renaming medical terms, as it seemingly cuts off the voices of those who experienced similar

7   On chronological snobbery, see C. S. Lewis, *Surprised by Joy* (1955).

problems and curtails approaches, responses, remedies, and solutions to these abnormal births applied over time.

From our experience, interdisciplinary collaboration 1) has been shown to successfully enable considerations of problems from an entirely new perspective and framework, which solves seemingly insurmountable obstacles; 2) provides us with a common language of understanding, thereby fostering connections between research ideas; 3) pushes us to reconsider the readability of the precise language of our specific discourse; 4) might be best fostered in situations where this field-specific discourse is socially discouraged (i.e. meals); and 5) works best when the question of our own benefit is temporarily suspended and we have a genuine interest in fields outside our own.

BIBLIOGRAPHY

Anon., 14th CE. *Chevalere Assigne*. In: D. Speed, ed. 1993. *Medieval English Romances*. 3rd ed. Durham: Durham Medieval Texts.

Begemann, M. et al., 2018. Maternal variants in NLRP and other maternal effect proteins are associated with multilocus imprinting disturbance in offspring. *Journal of Medical Genetics*, 55(7), pp.497-504. http://dx.doi.org/10.1136/jmedgenet-2017-105190.

Chandler, J.H. ed., 2015. *The King of Tars*. [e-book]. Kalamazoo, MI: Medieval Institute Publications. Available at: Robbins Library Digital Projects <https://d.lib.rochester.edu/teams/text/chandler-the-king-of-tars> [17 July 2020].

Frye, N., 1957. *Anatomy of Criticism*. Princeton, NJ: Princeton University Press.

Gasper, G., Smithson, H., McLeish, T., 2017. The next scientific breakthrough could come from the history books. *The Conversation*, [online] Available at: <https://theconversation.com/the-next-scientific-breakthrough-could-come-from-the-history-books-73553> [17 July 2020].

Gheldof, A., Mackay, D.J.G., Cheong, Y. and Verpoest, W., 2019. Genetic diagnosis of subfertility: the impact of meiosis and maternal effects. *Journal of Medical Genetics*, 56(5), pp.271-282.

Goodison, N., Deborah M. and Temple, I.K., 2018. Genetics, molar pregnancies, and medieval ideas of monstrous births: the lump of flesh in *The King of Tars*. *Medical Humanities BMJ*, 45(1), pp.2-9.

Green, M.H. and Mooney L.R. eds., 2006. Sickness of women. In: M.T. Tavormina, ed. 2006. *Sex, Aging, and Death in a Medieval Medical Compendium: Trinity College Cambridge MS R.14.52, Its Texts, Language, and Scribe*. Tempe, AZ: Arizona Center for Medieval and Renaissance Studies. pp.455-568.

Hansen, B. ed., 1985. *Nicole Oresme and the Marvels of Nature: A Study of his 'De causis mirabilium', with Critical Edition, Translation and Commentary*. Toronto: Pontificate Institute of Mediaeval Studies.

Hopwood, N., Flemming, R. and Kassell, L. eds., 2018. *Reproduction: Antiquity to the Present Day*. Cambridge: Cambridge University Press.

Hornstein, L., 1941. New analogues to the *King of Tars*. *Modern Language Review*, 36, pp.433-442.

Kitchell, K.F. and Resnick, I.M. ed., 2018. *Albertus Magnus On Animals: A Medieval Summa Zoologica*. Translated by K.F. Kitchell and I.M. Resnick. Columbus, OH: Ohio State University Press. Book 10. Ch. 4, pp. 839-841.

Lemay, H.R. ed., 1992. *Women's Secrets: A Translation of Pseudo-Albertus Magnus' De Secretis Mulierum with Commentaries*. Albany, NY: State University of New York Press.

Lewis, C.S., 1946. Introduction. In: Athanasius, ed. Sister Penelope Lawson. 1946. *On the Incarnation*. Translated by a religious of C.S.M.V. New York: Macmillan.

Lewis, C.S., 1955. *Surprised by Joy*. Reprint 1998. Glasgow: Fount.

Mackay, D.J.G. and Temple, I.K., 2017. Human imprinting disorders: principles, practice, problems and progress. *European Journal of Medical Genetics*, 60(11), pp.618-626.

Roberts, A.B., 1924. A case of Hydatidiform Mole. *British Medical Journal*, 2(3339), p.1198.

Ross, D., 1898. A fatal case of Hydatidiform Mole. *British Medical Journal*, 2(1981), p.1814.

Schneider, G. ed., 1811. *Aristotelis de Animalibus Historiae: Libri X: Graeci et Latine*. Lipsiae: Bibliopolio Hahniano.

SORAYA DE CHADAREVIAN

DNA and History

'Transforming the Humanities Initiative'

The epistemic and disciplinary separation of the biological sciences and
the humanities is strongly guarded. Most scholars in the humanities view
any infringement of this separation with suspicion. The example often held
up for its nefarious implications are the biological theories of human races
in the late-nineteenth and early to mid-twentieth centuries. The critical
reception of sociobiological explanations of human behaviour in the 1970s
is a further example. What then can we say of recent attempts to use genetic
evidence to reconstruct historical events?

This question lay at the basis of a multidisciplinary seminar funded
by a grant from the Mellon Foundation 'Transforming the Humanities
Initiative', convened by the medieval historian Patrick Geary and myself
at the University of California, Los Angeles about ten years ago. The
seminar brought together faculty from the humanities (historians,
linguists, archaeologists) and the natural sciences (population geneticists,
biostatisticians) to learn from each other and discuss the opportunities
and challenges of genetic history.[1] Many of the most spectacular results
of genetic history, which are regularly reported in the press, concern the
pre-historic period. Yet in the seminar we were specifically interested in
the use of DNA technologies to study the historic period of the last 4,000

---

1   For a fuller description of the project, see http://www.sscnet.ucla.edu/historyandgenetics/.
See also de Chadarevian (2010).

years or so, when textual evidence next to linguistic and archaeological evidence is available to inform, back up and confront genetic evidence. The genetic technologies that were available at the time of our discussions included improved protocols for work with ancient DNA (aDNA) and next-generation sequencing technologies that allowed for full genome sequencing.

In the seminar we worked towards a critical assessment of the promises of genetic history. Participants agreed that genetic techniques can only provide evidence for a very specific set of historical questions. Rather than providing final answers, genetic studies establish probabilistic relationships between possible historical interpretations. Therefore, genetic evidence can never stand alone and must always be considered in the context of other evidence. More generally, an important premise for a fruitful conversation between the disciplines is that genetic evidence is not understood in essentialist, deterministic or reductionist terms.

The Longobard Project

With this critical assessment in mind, the aim was to explore the possibility of a collaborative project in which historians and geneticists worked together from the very beginning to avoid some of the pitfalls of genetic historical studies. Unlike in most genetic history projects, historians along with archaeologists and linguists would be involved in all stages of the work – from the initial formulation of the historical questions to decisions about sampling and the interpretation of the results. We convened a special workshop with experts from the humanities and the biological sciences to settle on a project that could serve as a pilot for such an approach. The decision fell on a study of the migration history and social organisation of the Longobards, a population that according to historical records migrated from central Europe to Northern Italy in the sixth century. The plan was to extract and characterise ancient DNA from individuals from a number of cemeteries in Central Europe (Hungary, Czech Republic, Austria) and Italy, identified culturally as Longobard, as well as from nearby cemeteries that culturally seem to belong to 'non-Longobard' populations. A clear premise was that 'Longobard' is a cultural identity and that the project, while it could study such topics as mobility and kinship, could not identify any of these populations as 'Longobards'.

In the past ten years, Geary has dedicated himself fully to this project, collaborating closely with population geneticists and archaeologists to analyse the data emerging from the genetic study. The interdisciplinary team published its first results in *Nature Communications* in 2018 and most recently received a multi-million grant to continue its efforts (Amorim et al., 2018). For the occasion of my brief contribution here, I have interviewed Geary to talk about his experience of working with scientists and the ongoing challenges and broader implications of the effort to use genetic evidence in history.

The first point that Geary reiterates is that for most historical questions, genetic tools are completely irrelevant. It is only for a very specific set of quite basic questions that genetic evidence can provide some clues. In the case of the Longobard-era project possible questions were: do people with a certain genetic background marry people with a different genetic background? Do they treat their dead in the same way? Do they dress in the same way? In many ways, such questions depend on the availability of genetic tools. Yet, at the same time, any genetic evidence relies on input from other approaches, like cultural archaeology or textual evidence. In this restricted sense, genetic evidence does allow historians 'to examine deeper structures within populations' (Geary, 2020). Even while highlighting the challenges of genetic history and the danger of simplified and essentialising interpretation, Geary believes that genetic history based on aDNA studies and next-generation sequencing techniques, in combination with historical, archaeological and isotope dating techniques, 'does work' (Geary, 2020). At the same time, Geary is very aware of the dangers of using genetic evidence for essentialist claims. Only continuous vigilance and the close collaborations of geneticists and (critical) historians can avoid such pitfalls. Or, as he likes to say, 'genetics has to be tamed to be used as a historical tool' (Geary, 2020; in press).

There is interest but also scepticism around this work among historians. Not much has changed in this respect. The biggest interest in his work, Geary notes, is in Germany. It is also in the German context that a robust historical and philosophical discussion has developed around genetic historical approaches.[2] Yet as Geary also observes, German historians are more interested in *talking about* rather than *doing* genetic history themselves. Both the interest in the subject and the reluctance to actually undertake genetic history projects may have obvious historical reasons. At the same time, the presence of the Max Planck Institute for Evolutionary Anthropology in Leipzig, where Svante Pääbo has long been working with aDNA, has raised interest in the field. However, Pääbo is interested in evolutionary history rather than in more recent historical times. Other geneticists have also been moving into this field, above all Johannes Krause, one of the two founding directors of a new Max Planck Institute for the Science of Human History in Jena. The funding of the Max Planck Gesellschaft has thus been instrumental for advancing the study of aDNA in Germany.

Geary sees himself as interlocutor for the scientists. He is centrally involved in formulating the historical questions that they then tackle with their tools. He has become conversant in talking about the genetic technologies, but he does not actually do the analysis and the modelling. Yet against the claim by some geneticists that historical results just jump out of the genetic data, he insists that genetic data do not speak for themselves (Wade, 2014; Geary, in press).

As for the publication pattern, the genetic studies appear in scientific journals such as *Nature Communications* or the *European Journal of Human Genetics*, with Geary appearing as co-author (Amorim et al., 2018; Vai et al., 2019). He makes sure the historical questions are in step with current scholarship and claims are not over-blown. He then takes these articles and tries to explain the technologies and results in a step-by-step fashion to fellow historians and archaeologists.[3] Currently, he is at work on a monograph that takes the Longobard project as a case study to introduce historians to the various genetic approaches and discuss their statistical nature and validity. In that respect, his work could be viewed as that of an

2   See, for instance, Bösl, 2017; Feuchter, 2017; Bösl and Feuchter, 2019; Feuchter, 2019 as well as the dedication of two fora with several contributions dedicated to the issue in the history of science journal *Zeitschrift für Geschichte der Naturwissenschaften, Technik und Medizin* (N.T.M.) (Schenk, G.J. et al, 2018; Lipphardt, V. et al, 2019).

3   See, for example, Geary and Veeramah (2016) and Geary (in press).

interpreter between the world of science and history.

If sequence analysis can provide insight into the historical structure of human populations, could we then regard genetic information as historical to start with and thus as a 'boundary object' between history and genetics (Star and Griesemer, 1989)? This provocative suggestion makes sense to Geary. The specific genetic sequences that genetic technologies reveal are, at least in part, traces of decisions made by people based on complex cultural norms and ambitions. In turn, genetic analysis can help to reconstruct these patterns. Rather than biologising history, this would amount to humanising biology. Geary is at ease with this suggestion.

Conclusion

We can venture to say that to succeed and become a useful tool for historians, genetic history needs dedicated historians like Geary, who are open to collaborating with scientists, and scientists who see the value of interacting with historians. It will only provide evidence for a very particular set of historical questions and this evidence must be carefully weighed against other evidence. Genetic analysis is not restricted to human remains. For instance, genomic analysis together with new approaches in protein analysis are opening up new ways of studying books as material artefacts linked to local geographies, livestock economies, and trade, while also providing insights into the handling of books.[4] Such studies have the potential to reframe the relations of the human and biological sciences by pointing to the hybrid nature of objects like DNA and books.

Acknowledgements

I wish to thank Patrick Geary for generously sharing and discussing his recent work with me in preparation for this essay.

---

4   On the new field of biocodicology, see Fiddyment et al. (2019). For earlier biological approaches to the study of books and the cross-disciplinary collaborations it produced, see, for instance, Musil-Gutsch and Nickelsen (2020).

BIBLIOGRAPHY

Amorim, C.E.G. et al., 2018. Understanding 6th-century barbarian social organization and migration through paleogenomics. *Nature Communications,* [e-journal] 9(1), pp.1-11. http://dx.doi.org/10.1038/s41467-018-06024-4.

Bösl, E., 2017. *Doing Ancient DNA: Zur Wissenschaftsgeschichte der aDNA Forschung.* Bielefeld: Transcript.

Bösl, E., and Feuchter, J., 2019. Genetic history – eine Herausforderung für die Geschichtswissenschaften. *Neue Politische Literatur* 64(2), pp.237-268.

de Chadarevian, S., 2010. Genetic evidence and interpretation in history. *BioSocieties* 5(3), pp.301-305.

Feuchter, J., 2017. Mittelalterliche migrationen als gegenstand der 'Genetic History'. In: F. Wiedemann, K.P. Hofmann and H.-J. Gehrke, eds. 2017. *Vom Wandern der Völker: Migrationserzählungen in den Altertumswissenschaften.* Berlin: Edition Topoi. pp.347-70.

Feuchter, J., 2019. The middle ages in the genetics lab. In: C. Jones, C. Kostick and K. Oschema, eds. 2019. *Making the Medieval Relevant.* Berlin: de Gruyter. pp.99-112.

Fiddyment, S. et al., 2019. So you want to do biocodecology? A field guide to the biological analysis of parchment. *Heritage Science,* 7, pp.35-45.

Geary, P. and Veeramah, K., 2016. Mapping European population movement through genomic research. *Medieval Worlds,* 4, pp.65-78.

Geary, P., (in press) Herausforderungen und Gefahren der Integration von Genomdaten in die Erforschung der frühmittelalterlichen Geschichte. In: (in press). *Berlin-Brandenburgische Akademie der Wissenschaften–Das mittelalterliche Jahrtausend.* Volume 7. Berlin: de Gruyter.

Geary, P., 2020. *Interview with Patrick Geary by author.* Interviewed by Soraya de Chadarevian. [in-person] 8 April 2020.

Lipphardt, V., Bösl, E., Bauch, M. and Krischel, M., 2019. Forum genetic history II. *N.T.M.,* 27, pp.165-199.

Musil-Gutsch, J. and Nickelsen, K., 2020. Ein Botaniker in der Papiergeschichte: Offene and geschlossene Kooperationen in den Wissenschaften um 1900. *N.T.M.,* 28, pp.1-33.

Schenk, G.J., Haak, W., Schiffels, S., Meier, M., Patzold, S., Keupp, J., Feuchter, J. and von Rummel, P., 2018. Forum: genetic history. *N.T.M.,* 26, pp.301-350.

Star, S. and Griesemer, J., 1989. Institutional Ecology. 'Translations' and boundary objects: amateurs and professionals in Berkeley's Museum of Vertebrate Zoology 1907–1939. *Social Studies of Science,* 19(3), pp.387-420.

Vai, S. et al., 2019. A genetic perspective on Longobard-era migrations. *European Journal of Human Genetics,* 27, pp.647-656.

Wade, N., 2014. Tracing ancestry: researchers produce a genetic atlas of human genetic mixing. *The New York Times*, 13 February, Section A, p.10.

TOMASZ ŁYSAK

Holocaust Studies in the
Era of Climate Change

> As long as this specific future is undesirable it must be prevented.
> The long history of prediction from ancient divination and prophesy
> to modern forms of prognosis is largely a history of methods and
> institutions designed to recognize future threats and to circumvent
> them.
>
> (Horn, 2018, p.175)

At first glance, the pairing of the Holocaust and climate change may strike one
as odd. On the one hand, Holocaust studies, as an academic field, deal with
the historical event itself and its cultural and societal aftermath, including
but not limited to a philosophical reassessment of Western civilisation,
literary and artistic representations of mass murder, the psychoanalytical
treatment of mass trauma, and the sociology of violence. On the other
hand, the reality of climate change has yet to dawn upon us, as its trajectory
is at present an unfolding dark prophecy. While the full force of climate
change is still to reveal itself in the future (Vermeulen, 2017; Rohloff, 2011),
there is no denying that Holocaust commemoration is a future-oriented
cultural endeavour, since remembering the victims and identifying the
causes of state-sponsored violence were meant, from the outset, to prevent
a repetition of this historical trauma. It is not my intention to assess the
efficacy of these efforts, in part because it would involve assigning blame
for political failures (to stop ongoing genocides) to academics, writers, and

other actors engaged in commemoration. Instead, I would like to point out the convergence between the two fields in question. Understandably, there is a need to use existing knowledge to prevent a historical event from repeating itself and to alert the public to future catastrophes, conflicts, and bloodshed. Such an approach is dubbed 'learning lessons from the past'. Conversely, casting the path that led to the Holocaust in a new light is not assessed herein for its historical accuracy but rather as a contemporary response to an impending climate catastrophe.

Despite a tacit agreement among scholars and writers that the Auschwitz-Birkenau concentration camp (typically referred to simply as 'Auschwitz') represents a novel form of violence, there is no consensus as to the viability of drawing lessons for humanity from this experience. Lissa Skitolsky (2012) identifies three philosophical approaches to the Holocaust: 'redemptive', 'nihilistic', and 'narcissistic'. The 'redemptive' approach assumes that the damage inflicted upon inmates and victims is reversible, while the 'nihilistic' stance rules out learning from the Holocaust as its negative meaning invalidates any productive application of this knowledge. The latter position leads to a pedagogical conundrum: 'Is it possible to draw any useful lessons from a situation of useless and gratuitous violence that cannot be represented through moral categories and theoretical concepts?' (Skitolsky, 2012, p.83). In Skitolsky's view, Giorgio Agamben's 'narcissistic' philosophy may serve as a lodestar as it 'does not attempt to conceptually comprehend nor deliberately obscure the nature of Auschwitz but, rather, to bear witness to the form-of-life which suffered under its assault' (2012, p.85).

These nuanced discussions posit an inherent difficulty in conceptualising the Holocaust, and yet there are scholars who argue that Holocaust commemoration has a longstanding political angle, serving a variety of needs (Novick, 2000). One path to lifting the taboo on interpreting the Holocaust in history and cultural studies, in order to help it generate 'compassion for strangers', has been delineated by Patrick H. Hutton (2016). A mere two decades ago, Berel Lang envisioned the future of the Holocaust as two parallel threats, namely genocide and omnicide. The latter is usually understood as the result of a nuclear conflict, but Lang concentrates solely on the possible annihilation of human life, as if the deployment of nuclear weapons were of no consequence to other life forms on the planet (1999, pp.40-61). Therefore, there are ample precedents for talking about current pressing societal and political issues by drawing parallels with the historical event of the Holocaust. More generally, the question of drawing lessons from past events in the Anthropocene – including deceptively named 'natural disasters' – lies at the core of scholarly work in ecocriticism as an interpretive endeavour (Rigby, 2015).

Zhiwa Woodbury proposes reassessing climate change as climate trauma, highlighting a necessary shift in the perception of trauma as an event in the past to a continuous threat, rechristened 'an entirely *new order of trauma*' (2019). And yet, the current position of trauma studies as an academic field would be difficult to grasp without Holocaust studies, as its methods were to a large extent honed while explaining the suffering of Holocaust survivors. Last but not least, the concerted efforts of survivors, educators and politicians to render the Holocaust as a warning to humanity endowed the memory of this event with a symbolic power. Given the grave danger climate change poses, it seems fitting to consider the convergence of the pessimistic re-evaluation of Western civilisation in the wake of World War II and pre-emptive thinking about a looming catastrophe in the future. In the following argument, I posit that recent theoretical work on the intersection of the Holocaust and climate change can be productively linked to a body of earlier commemorative literary texts and fiction films. Furthermore, the vocabulary of survival, mass violence, and scarcity of resources – ubiquitous as it is in Holocaust memoirs and fiction – comes in handy in drawing attention to future environmental catastrophes. Nowhere is this more pronounced than in science fiction, which is why I demonstrate that Primo Levi's sci-fi literary side-project expresses similar concerns to his autobiographical writings. Finally, I draw attention to the intersection of science, futuristic thinking, and the unintended consequences of technological advances.

Linking the Holocaust to the Study of the Environment
What are the origins and the current state of debate on the Holocaust and

climate change? Eric Katz opens up a discussion about the relationship between the study of the Holocaust and environmental policy with two research questions: 'Does my work as an environmental philosopher have any relevance to an understanding of the evil of human genocide? Can the study of genocide teach us anything about the human-induced destruction of the natural world, what is sometimes called the process of "ecocide"?' (1997, p.79). Katz conceptualises the link between these two, at first glance, divergent phenomena, applying the concept of domination. Historically, he perceives a similar drive to rule over nature and human beings in Nazi ideology. Additionally, he criticises anthropocentrism for its oppressive practices, since at its core it legitimises domination and oppression against those categorised as subhuman (Katz, 1997, p.84). Truth be told, the initial conceptualisation of genocide by Raphael Lemkin included destruction of the environment and culture, a trait downplayed or obscured by his commentators (Crook and Short, 2014). Speaking from the perspective of environmental studies, Jacek Małczyński and others maintain that linking the Holocaust with the study of the environment contributes 'to the cultivation of environmental virtues and the promotion of ecologically sound behaviour' (Małczyński et al., 2020, p.185). In addition, this team of scholars believes that the geological aftereffects of the Holocaust are going to unfold long after the biographical horizon of commemoration.

The new geological era of the Anthropocene was so named to account for a host of changes humans have been causing at the planetary level. The term has stirred an ongoing debate including, but not restricted to, an unfair assignment of guilt for the damage to the natural environment. In order to correct the view that humans as a species are to blame, two other criteria have been identified: the capitalist mode of production (Capitalocene) and the plantation system (Plantationocene) (Craps et al., 2018, p.500). Rosanne Kennedy qualifies the application of the moral vocabulary of the Holocaust to talk about species extinction as a typical trope described in memory studies, by virtue of which the past 'shape[s] moral discourses and advocacy in the present' (Craps, et al., 2018, p.506). Pointing to Andreas Huyssen's observation that the Holocaust may give an impulse to remember 'other traumatic events' at the cost of downplaying their specificity, Kennedy argues that memory studies inherited paradigms from Holocaust studies, something which facilitates the use of Holocaust analogies in talking about non-human species (Craps et al., 2018). The solution to this dilemma is to invite reflection on 'nonhuman species as objects, if not subjects, of memory' (Craps et al., 2018, p.506).

John K. Roth – an eminent American philosopher working on ethics and the Holocaust – takes up the idea of climate change in his discussion of Alan Weisman's 2007 book *The World Without Us*. Roth grapples with the idea that, in a geological timeframe, human events may seem insignificant, yet he asserts that for Weisman it is all the more important 'to appreciate intensely that human life is distinctive and precious, that what we think and do makes a huge difference' (2017, p.160). Given Weisman's assumption that history and memory are predicated on human consciousness, Roth feels compelled to admit that the disappearance of humans from the globe would render all events – including the Holocaust – of no significance. However, this realisation does not nullify the call to remember the dead as their demise was, at the same time, world-shattering and of no consequence to the existence of the world. By this token, Roth invites his readers to face death with Charlotte Delbo – a famous French Auschwitz survivor – whose recollection of the disfigured face of an unidentified victim signifies the dark core of the Holocaust. At the same time, Roth harbours no illusions as to the practical and political effectiveness of remembrance, comparing it to the constant, tragic toil of Sisyphus (2017, p.163). It must be noted that the geological perspective does not cancel out the efforts of activists and educators in the present and, likewise, the moral pessimism stemming from the events of the Holocaust does not translate into pedagogical nihilism. On the other hand, our relationship with 'distant posterity' is heavy with the unknown, and while we assume we are making an educated guess about the future, it might as well be a shot in the dark (Rescher, 2018).

In order to open up the possibility of a fruitful exchange of ideas between Holocaust studies and genocide studies, Raz Segal acknowledges that by concentrating solely on the Holocaust the former field of study 'creates a hierarchy of mass violence' (2018, p.109). And yet, Segal is quick to notice that climate change – a by-product of 'development' in the Global

South – 'has resulted since World War II in displacement, dispossession and group destruction that has affected *tens of millions of people*' [emphasis in the original] (p.110). Timothy Snyder's re-reading of Hitler's war on the Jews in ecological terms, as a backlash against universalism that was meant to end conflict on earth, especially over land and food, prompts Segal to investigate the ideological underpinnings of criticising Hitler for his pastoral view of natural agriculture. And yet, the Western belief in rationality, as expressed in the agricultural revolution, is one of the key reasons for suffering in the Global South (Segal, 2018, p.125). 'Food insecurity, malnutrition and starvation, which constitute central elements in Snyder's work on mass violence in twentieth-century Europe, still function as policies of destruction outside of Europe today' (Segal, 2018, p.126). Segal debunks Snyder's optimism (expressed in *Black Earth*) that yield-intensive agriculture could have prevented the war, since Hitler would have had no need for extra land to feed his growing population, on the basis that present-day evidence shows that monocultures do not prevent suffering. Furthermore, he believes that 'the hard and tedious work of preserving humanity' falls on the shoulders of those 'who understand not the Holocaust, but precisely the structural genocidal violence of the late modern period' (Segal, 2018, p.130).

On a side note, Jean Solchany undermines Snyder's rereading of National Socialism through the prism of ecological thought as 'a dangerous futurology' (2017, p.XXXI). Solchany argues that such an undertaking is a fallacious application of concepts unknown at the time, as well as a simplified diagnosis of military conflicts in the second decade of the twenty-first century (2017). Such an argument is also put forward by Jeffrey Herf in his review of Snyder's book (Berenbaum and Herf, 2017, pp.230-232). In Segal's view, ideology ceases to be the only source of violence, which instead stems from deep-seated inequalities in capitalism and industrialised agriculture. In actual fact, Solchany criticises Snyder for foregoing historical methodology in favour of ecological activism, whereas Segal takes issue with the ill-founded technological optimism that pervades Snyder's thinking regarding agriculture.

Historically, a bucolic vision of a return to premodern agriculture has been a double-edged sword. One of the unrealised provisions of the Morgenthau Plan – proposed by United States Secretary of the Treasury Henry Morgenthau Jr. in 1944 and delineating the course of action toward the defeated Third Reich – stipulated that post-war Germany should be deindustrialised and effectively turned into a primitive agrarian society. Thus, by sentencing German society to live the Nazi dreams of *Blut und Boden* (blood and soil), the nation of perpetrators was meant to repent for their guilt (Ubertowska, 2017, pp.140-141). Aleksandra Ubertowska uses Anselm Kiefer's series of paintings entitled *Morgenthau Plan* (2012) to analyse the ethical viability of this agrarian punishment. While Ubertowska has reservations when it comes to accepting the magnitude of the punishment as being justified, Kiefer embraces this dystopian vision. For the German painter 'regression to nature' constitutes 'a purifying measure, which is culturally elevating' (Ubertowska, 2017, p.145). Kiefer's artistic reinterpretation of this aborted environmental experiment may be seen as a meditation on reducing human impact on the environment, a strategy of degrowth. In this manner, post-Holocaust art contemplates how violence against humans is indicative of terracide.

In the above-mentioned discussions one can identify several intellectual strategies. First, there is a reinterpretation of Nazi history to include ecology by scrutinising the Nazis' system of government as well as the production of necessities of life (Neumann, 2012), and a linking of agriculture to Nazi ideology and the present-day reality of yield-intensive farming. Second, a timeframe is set for the future relevance of the Holocaust beyond the biographical context of commemoration. Despite this novel approach, the very discussion of the future of the Holocaust can still be construed within the 'Never Again' political paradigm. The integration of the history of the Holocaust into a new geological era of the Anthropocene takes into account the latter's appetite for destruction and the drive to subject others to its logic of progress.

Primo Levi's Multifaceted Response to the Crisis of Humanity at Auschwitz

In his assessment of the present-day state of memory studies, Stef Craps

(2017) proposes that the field in question should become future-oriented. Studying climate fiction (or cli-fi), he argues that there is a hard-to-miss connection between the pre-emptive pedagogy of Holocaust studies/ memorialisation and the looming ecological catastrophe: 'Just as the memory of the Holocaust can allegedly help prevent future genocide, so the proleptic memory of climate catastrophe can perhaps function as a spur to action that would prevent the anticipated catastrophe from actually coming to pass' (Craps, 2017, p.488). In this context, 'anticipatory memory' is conceived as a call to action in which mourning over future, unfathomable losses serves as a precondition for activism (Craps, 2017, p.489). Even though Primo Levi's account of his survival at Auschwitz and its moral consequences typically take centre stage in criticism, recently the onus has shifted to treat his other works more seriously, including his science fiction. My intention here is to pinpoint a common thread across the genres, namely, the relation between humans and their nonhuman environment: water and carbon.

Levi's account of Auschwitz-Birkenau in *Survival in Auschwitz* provides an insight into the impact of limited resources on social bonds and morality. However, there is an inherent paradox when it comes to water in the camp: potable water is not available to the majority of prisoners (and was replaced by soup and ersatz coffee for the purposes of hydration), yet, at the same time, inmates fight an uphill battle against superfluous water that turns the camp into one big muddy bog. Upon arrival, after a four-day train journey from Italy, Levi takes a sip from a tap, ignoring the prohibition above it: 'I have to spit it out, the water is tepid and sweetish, with the smell of a swamp' (1996, p.22). Ironically, the prisoners use this contaminated water to maintain their hygiene. Given the inadequate protection against the elements, those working outside have to battle inclement weather (rain, wind, and cold) with no possibility to dry their wet camp uniforms when their shift is over. As a chemist by training, Levi cannot ignore the proposition that 'the Lager was pre-eminently a gigantic biological and social experiment' (1996, p.87). Given the size of the group in question, it was possible 'to establish what is essential and what adventitious to the conduct of the human animal in the struggle for life' (1996, p.87).

The scenarios of global warming predict the rise of sea levels causing large-scale flooding, change to shorelines, and the disappearance of island nations in some parts of the globe. Conversely, this hyperobject – to use Timothy Morton's term (2013) – also leads to droughts, desertification, and a dearth of drinking water elsewhere. Therefore, a situation in which a group of inmates was intentionally subjected to scarce water and the rage of the elements may serve as a model for a global catastrophe in which it is difficult to say who is to blame. However, what is being compared here is a historical event with a non-event (Horn, 2018, p.55). The chance discovery of a water pipe at Auschwitz features prominently in Levi's last book, *The Drowned and the Saved*. Having assessed that this source of water would be insufficient for the whole work team, Levi decides that he can only share the find with one friend (2017, pp.66-67). This episode presages the necessity of allocating scarce resources to a lucky few and the moral conundrum of deciding who should miss out.

Primo Levi's collection of dystopian short stories *The Sixth Day and Other Tales* ends with 'Excellent is the Water', in which a laboratory technician discovers some irregularities in the viscosity of distilled water. Initially, he discounts them as a measurement error in the lab, but later observations of the qualities of water in a local stream confirm that something has changed. A preliminary observation perceives no change to the basic qualities of water: 'He touched it, tasted it: it was fresh, limpid, it had no taste, gave off the usual swampy odor, and yet it was strange' (Levi, 1991, p.252). A further examination identifies a heightened level of viscosity. This local phenomenon spreads around the globe leading to the destruction of crops in some areas and their flourishing elsewhere. Gradually, the grim effects of this change start to manifest in humans: 'we die at thirty or forty at the most, from edema, pure fatigue, fatigue at all hours, without mercy and without pause, a fatigue that weighs within us since the day of our birth, and impedes our every rapid and prolonged movement' (Levi, 1991, p.255). This natural catastrophe even deprives humans of the physiological response to stressors: 'We do not weep: the lacrimal liquid dwells superfluous in our eyes, and it does not form in teardrops but oozes out like a serum that robs our weeping of dignity and relief' (Levi, 1991, p.255). Therefore, an at-first-glance insignificant change in the physical properties of the universal solvent destroys not only the natural world and reduces human life expectancy but also precludes a humane response to the ongoing disaster. In this context, it is easy to make a comparison to the world-shattering experience of the Nazi camps which destroyed lives, communities, the belief in progress, and forced numerous survivors into a state of stupor, debilitating their power of self-expression. Furthermore, this short story is a departure from other dystopian science fiction stories penned by Levi which primarily target technological progress gone-wrong and were meant as social activism (Mori, 2015). Levi also questions the optimism of science as regards its power to control the outcome of technological experiments (Farneti, 2006, p.728).

The final short story – entitled 'Carbon' – in the autobiographical collection *The Periodic Table* traces the trajectory of a single atom of carbon released from a block of limestone by a man with a pickaxe in 1840. After having been trapped in a slab of rock for millennia, it attains a gaseous form and is sent airborne through a chimney. Inhaled by a falcon and released into the air, it continues its journey by sustaining biological life via the process of photosynthesis. Levi then proceeds to extol the virtues of carbon dioxide, pointing out that its almost insignificant presence in the air is indispensable to organic life. Having commented upon a variety of life-forms the carbon bonds with, Levi argues, 'the death of atoms, unlike ours, is never irrevocable' (1994, p.231). He also muses on a future technology that would allow the sourcing of carbon from the air rather than using carbon trapped in the fossilised products of photosynthesis: coal and petroleum. 'Photosynthesis is not only the sole path by which carbon becomes living matter, but also the sole path by which the sun's energy becomes chemically usable' (Levi, 1994, p.231). To offer a temporary coda to this ceaseless journey of a single atom, Levi places it inside a glass of milk which he drinks only to have it absorbed into his brain. Thus, Levi's intellect and creativity are part and parcel of the movement of matter in the universe. 'Carbon' highlights a basic unity between humans and nature on the atomic level, a harbinger of the posthumanist theories of the early twenty-first century (Malewitz, 2016). Catalina Botez argues: 'In *The*

Periodic Table, man is perceived as part of the natural world and subject to constant and constructive interaction with other natural elements through technological work or *techné* (2012, p.716). Furthermore, Botez identifies Levi's preoccupation 'with the nature of postcatastrophic humanity' as one of the key concerns in his works (2012, p.722).

Gassing, Environmental Pollution, and Capitalism

Despite the fact that the East German feature film *Der Rat der Götter* (*The Council of the Gods*) (1950) is clearly a communist propaganda piece, aimed at discrediting American imperialism and industrialism by tying it to the wartime crimes of the German company IG Farben, it correctly zeroes in on the industrial preparation that preceded the Holocaust. Before the outbreak of World War II, principled chemist Dr Scholz is dared to witness an experiment carried out at the IG Farben plant. Four animals have been locked in an airtight compartment to be asphyxiated with 'mustard gas': a lamb, a puppy, a duck and a hen. The agony of the animals is shown in a take/counter-take sequence of shots, with the lamb drawing its final breath in the foreground. The experiment is dated in the film to September 1939, but the editing ties this episode to Dr Scholz's later discovery that Zyklon B cans are being shipped to Auschwitz. Thus, the film stages an experiment predating the application of poison gas to human subjects. Its daring representation of the extermination would be impossible without replacing human victims with laboratory animals. The Allied victory in 1945 hardly dampens the spirits of IG Farben's management as the company resumes the production of explosives in preparation for another war. This development saddens Dr Scholz, who envisions a different career path for his son: 'You should take up biochemistry. Study artificial protein. [...] Instead of poison and explosives we could bake bread from thin air' (*Der Rat der Götter*, 1950). As a former employee, Dr Scholz still clings to the idea of progress offered by the pursuit of knowledge. A giant explosion at the factory then takes the lives of hundreds of workers, but the film blames management for this tragedy since they allegedly never stopped their military production. A cloud of black smoke is seen billowing over the factory town just seconds after the explosion. There is a link between Dr Scholz's about-face and

Primo Levi's forced work for the Buna factory at Monowitz: the enmeshing of applied science and chemistry in the Holocaust deprives *techné* of its purported innocence (Botez, 2012, p.717). Heretofore, laying blame at the feet of technology has served to question modernity's pedigree as a product of the Enlightenment. However, I would like to argue that the East German film and Levi's prose share a view that tainted science can redeem itself by redefining its goals and renouncing the benevolent naïveté of scientists.

Marijn Nieuwenhuis argues that the discussion of gassing as a legal and biopolitical procedure owes its gravity to the Nazis' extermination by gassing in the camps. His agenda is to shift the perception of air 'as a natural phenomenon' and to put forward 'the idea that breathing and air need to be rethought as being politically and historically contextual' (Nieuwenhuis, 2018, p.80). He adds that 'respiration constitutes and *is* the separation between corporal life and death'. Making air political helps Nieuwenhuis resolve a seeming paradox of moral horror at using gas as a chemical weapon and at the same time ignoring the lethal consequences of millions of people inhaling polluted air.

In the same vein, *Der Rat der Götter* yokes the 'necropolitics' (Mbembe, 2003) of producing poison gas (exploiting the seeming gullibility of a professional chemist) with the danger the chemical plant poses to its workers. While the film makes no overt statement about air pollution, disregard for human life is shown in the business-as-usual duplicity of the management. Therefore, it makes perfect sense to reiterate the film's central problem: the relationship between capitalism and state-sponsored violence. However, with climate change, this profit-driven policy – blind to human, non-human, and environmental costs – is by no means limited to Western capitalism, as it has become the operational logic of industrial production. Speaking of 'racial capitalism', Arun Saldanha points out that white Europeans have been the drivers and captains of capitalism and, by extension, the Anthropocene (2020). Furthermore, 'racial capitalism reproduces itself ideologically by masking its systematic violences while providing the benefits to those in power' (Saldanha, 2020, p.18). Scholars of popular representations of climate disaster argue that typical scenarios of rescue single out white Westerners by setting them apart from 'racialized others' (Gergan, Smith and Vasudevan, 2020).

The cli-fi drama *Snowpiercer* (2013) – an adaptation of a French graphic novel by Benjamin Legrand and Jean-Marc Rochette – tells the story of a botched climate engineering experiment which had been meant to reverse global warming. In its wake, the entire globe is covered with ice and the few remaining humans encircle the planet in a purpose-built train. The living conditions in the tail section of the train are harsh and the people there inhabit a concentration-camp-like space: overcrowded, dirty and furnished with bunk beds. This imagined future combines imagery typical for Holocaust films: an endless train journey into the unknown that deprives the passengers of dignity and the oppressive institution of the concentration camp (the separation of children from their parents, the periodic killing of surplus passengers, substandard food). The guards punish one of the passengers by sticking his arm out of the train so that it freezes off (in the camps, extreme weather was intentionally employed to shorten the lives of prisoners, to torture or kill them. In addition to this, medical experiments investigating hypothermia were carried out on camp prisoners who were deliberately exposed to low temperatures). Children are selected for an unknown fate by having their height measured (such selection was common upon arrival at Auschwitz to determine who should be sent for immediate extermination). Later in the film, it is revealed that children are necessary to keep the train going.

In the early days, the tail section passengers had to resort to cannibalism in order to survive. Unsurprisingly, this shattered their moral values and they became complicit in the self-sustaining logic of the train's arc. Therefore, it is hardly surprising that the film's agenda has been analysed using the notion of biopolitics, which was coined as a tool to study the concentration camps. 'In the context of the Anthropocene, *Snowpiercer* [...] represent[s] contemporary worries about overpopulation, resource scarcity, and ecological limits, which may form the basis of future biopolitical reasoning' (Andersen and Nielsen, 2018, p.616). The film's director Bong Joon-ho lays the blame for the devastation of the planet not on humanity but rather on capitalism, debunking geo-engineering as a hubristic fantasy (Streeby, 2018, p.3). *Snowpiercer* as a 'mainstream climate narrative' lacks the power to change reality but provides us with food for thought about 'the meaning of life' (Estok, 2019, p.8). Ideologically, there is a yawning chasm between the two films discussed herein and yet their creators are in agreement about the detrimental impact of capitalism on, respectively, the state apparatus of violence and planetary equilibrium. What disappears from the picture is the fact that the genocidal use of poisonous gas is a much less common phenomenon than air pollution.

Conclusions

Holocaust commemoration was meant, from the outset, to establish and retain the validity of this historical genocide for the future. However, the intended temporal horizon was limited at first to the biographical memory of those affected, while antisemitism was initially identified as the main cause of the Holocaust. Primo Levi pushes this commemorative agenda much further into a dystopian future, illuminating the cost of an all-out struggle for limited resources as well as an unchecked desire for progress. Even though Levi certainly does not lose ethnic prejudice from sight, his works call for activism, care for non-human beings, and a degree of caution in assessing the benefits of science. Forgotten left-wing interpretations of the Holocaust as a by-product of industrial capitalism appear in a different light now, given the realisation that capitalism is to blame for the destruction of the environment and will continue to be an underlying cause of climate change violence. Furthermore, new forms of racism (political and those expressed in cultural representations) may serve as a smokescreen to obscure structural causes of human misery. The ongoing debate within Holocaust studies about the inhumanity of genocide and a recent ecocritical turn in this field highlight the need to tie the question of human survival to the preservation of the non-human world. Conversely, the posthumanist perspective projects the aftermath of the Holocaust into the geological future. Thus, the aftereffects of the genocide became part and parcel of human-induced changes to the natural environment.

There is a feeling of urgency galvanising scholars and educators concerning new threats to human survival, one which taps into the moral justification of Holocaust studies. And yet, making the connection between the Holocaust and climate change is the domain of philosophy, human rights studies, and literary and film criticism, with only a minor presence in historiography. These ecological considerations have required a methodological shift, enabling scholars to include heretofore neglected aspects of the Holocaust and its impact on the victims, survivors, and the environment. Conversely, a new ecological sensitivity has become a springboard for a novel epistemology of the Nazis' genocidal project. Nevertheless, such a methodological retooling illuminates earlier commemorative endeavours, concerned with using the Holocaust as a warning for the future.

BIBLIOGRAPHY

Andersen, G. and Nielsen, E.B., 2018. Biopolitics in the Anthropocene: on the invention of future biopolitics in Snowpiercer, Elysium, and Interstellar. *The Journal of Popular Culture*, 51(3), pp.615-634.

Berenbaum, M. and Herf, J., 2017. Conflicting perspectives on Timothy Snyder's *Black Earth*. *Journal of Cold War Studies*, 19(4), pp.226-233.

Botez, C., 2012. Contiguous spaces of remembrance in identity writing: chemistry, fiction and the autobiographic question in Primo Levi's *The Periodic Table. European Review of History: Revue Européenne D'histoire*, 19(5), pp.711-727.

Craps, S., 2017. Climate change and the art of anticipatory memory. *Parallax*, 23(4), pp.479-492.

Craps, S., Crownshaw, R., Wenzel, J., Kennedy, R., Colebrook, C. and Nardizzi, V., 2018. Memory studies and the Anthropocene: a roundtable. *Memory Studies*, 11(4), pp.498-515.

Crook, M. and Short, D., 2014. Marx, Lemkin and the genocide–ecocide nexus. *The International Journal of Human Rights*, 18(3), pp.298-319.

Der Rat der Götter, 1950. [film] Directed by Kurt Maetzig. East Germany: DEFA.

Estok, S.C., 2019. Suffering and climate change narratives. *CLCWeb: Comparative Literature and Culture*, 21(5), pp.1-8.

Farneti, R., 2006. Of humans and other portentous beings: on Primo Levi's *Storie naturali. Critical Inquiry*, 32(4), pp.724-740.

Gergan, M., Smith, S. and Vasudevan, P., 2020. Earth beyond repair: race and apocalypse in collective imagination. *Environment and Planning D: Society and Space*, 38(1), pp.91-110.

Horn, E., 2018. *The Future as Catastrophe: Imaging Disaster in the Modern Age*. Translated from German by V.A. Pakis. New York, NY: Columbia University Press.

Hutton, P.H., 2016. *The Memory Phenomenon in Contemporary Historical Writing: How the Interest in Memory Has Influenced Our Understanding of History*. New York, NY: Palgrave Macmillan.

Katz, E., 1997. Nature's healing power, the Holocaust, and the environmental crisis. *Judaism*, 46(1), pp.79-89.

Kiefer, A., 2012. *Morgenthau Plan*. [paintings] (New York, Metropolitan Museum of Art).

Lang, B., 1999. *The Future of the Holocaust: Between History and Memory*. Ithaca, NY: Cornell University Press.

Levi, P., 1991. Excellent is the water. In: P. Levi, ed. 1991. *The Sixth Day and Other Tales*. Translated from Italian by Raymond Rosenthal. London: Abacus. pp.250-255.

Levi, P., 1994. *The Periodic Table*. Translated from Italian by Raymond Rosenthal. London:

Abacus.

Levi, P., 1996. *Survival in Auschwitz*. Translated from Italian by S. Woolf. New York, NY: Simon & Schuster.

Levi, P., 2017. *The Drowned and the Saved*. Translated from Italian by Raymond Rosenthal. New York, NY: Simon & Schuster.

Malewitz, R., 2016. Primo Levi's *The Periodic Table*: chemistry as posthumanist science. *Configurations*, 24(4), pp.417-440.

Małczyński, J., Domańska, E., Smykowski, M. and Kłos, A., 2020. The environmental history of the Holocaust. *Journal of Genocide Research*, [e-journal] 22(2), pp.183-196. http://dx.doi.org/10.1080/14623528.2020.1715533.

Mbembe, A., 2003. *Necropolitics. Translated by Libby Meintjes. Public Culture, 15(1), pp.11-40.*

Mori, R., 2015. Worlds of 'Un-knowledge': dystopian patterns in Primo Levi's Short Stories. Translated by Vincent Marsicano and Umberto Rossi. Science Fiction Studies, 42(2), pp.274-291.

Morton, T., 2013. *Hyperobjects: Philosophy and Ecology after the End of the World*. Minneapolis, MN: University of Minneapolis Press.

Neumann, B., 2012. National socialism, Holocaust, and ecology. In: D. Stone, ed. 2012. *The Holocaust and Historical Methodology*. New York, NY: Berghahn Books, pp.101-124.

Nieuwenhuis, M., 2018. Atmospheric governance: gassing as law for the protection and killing of life. *Environment and Planning D: Society and Space*, 36(1), pp.78-95.

Novick, P., 2000. *The Holocaust in American Life*. Boston, MA: Houghton Mifflin.

Rescher, N., 2018. Distant posterity: a philosophical glance along time's corridor. *The Review of Metaphysics*, 72(1) pp.3-27.

Rigby, C.E., 2015. *Dancing with Disaster: Environmental Histories, Narratives, and Ethics for Perilous Times*. Charlottesville, VA: University of Virginia Press.

Rohloff, A., 2011. Extending the concept of moral panic: Elias, climate change and civilization. *Sociology*, 45(4), pp.634-649.

Roth, J.K., 2017. Facing death: what happens to the Holocaust if death is the last word? In: S.K. Pinnock, ed. 2017. *Facing Death: Confronting Mortality in the Holocaust and Ourselves*. Seattle, WA: University of Washington Press. pp.156-173.

Saldanha, A., 2020. A date with destiny: racial capitalism and the beginnings of the Anthropocene. *Environment and Planning D: Society and Space*, 38(1), pp.12-34.

Segal, R., 2018. The modern state, the question of genocide, and Holocaust scholarship. *Journal of Genocide Research*, 20(1), pp.108-133.

Skitolsky, L., 2012. Tracing theory on the body of the 'Walking Dead': *Der Musselman* and the course of Holocaust studies. *Shofar: An Interdisciplinary Journal of Holocaust Studies*, 30(2), pp.74-90.

Snowpiercer, 2013. [film] Directed by Bong Joon-ho. South Korea, Czech Republic: Moho Film, Opus Pictures, Union Investment Partners, Stillking Films.

Solchany, J., 2017. Much ado about nothing? A critical look at Timothy Snyder's interpretation of Nazi and Stalinist crimes. Translated from French by Allan Macvicar. *Revue d'histoire moderne et contemporaine*, 64-4(4), pp.134-171.

Streeby, S., 2018. *Imagining the Future of Climate Change: World-Making through Science Fiction and Activism*. Oakland, CA: University of California Press.

Ubertowska, A., 2017. Krajobraz po Zagładzie. Pastoralne dystopie i wizje 'terracydu'. *Teksty Drugie*, 2, pp.132-146.

Vermeulen, P., 2017. Creaturely memory: Shakespeare, the Anthropocene and the new nomos of the earth. *Parallax*, 23(4), pp.384-397.

Woodbury, Z., 2019. Climate trauma: toward a new taxonomy of trauma. *Ecopsychology*, 11(1), pp.1-8.

MARGARET McALLISTER

Setting Rumi: Casting the Intangible

Since I arrived at the Institute for Advanced Studies in the Humanities in January 2020, my colleagues have expressed to me how arcane the discipline of music feels to them. The general consensus seems to be that music is a 'language' understandable only to the initiated. However, music is an elemental attribute of our species. None of us have to 'try' to be musical – we are musical – it is our birthright.

When attempting to define music there is a point where words are inadequate. The place in our consciousness that music inhabits and animates has no direct correlation that can be expressed by words. This may be what Stravinsky was referring to in his oft cited quotation 'Expression has never been an inherent property of music. That is by no means the purpose of its existence. If, as is nearly always the case, music appears to express something, this is only an illusion and not a reality' (Stravinsky, 1975, p.53). While volumes of prose are written about music, ultimately music is self-referential. By this, I mean that it can only be understood and experienced in terms of itself.

Knowing and accepting the limitations of words, my aim here is to share some thoughts about music and the forces that impact the decisions of a composer when composing. Specifically, I will discuss a song cycle that sets poems by the Persian poet Rumi, using words and terms that the layperson can understand. The inclusion of general background material is necessary as a framework for discussion and context. I hope to inspire my colleagues to become curious about music in general and to explore, expand and deepen their listening.

This journey is one of many compositional journeys. For the composer, the genesis of each piece brings unique challenges – practical, aesthetic and metaphysical. Each of these aspects has so many facets, that when referring to even a short piece of music one could write exhaustively about each. To clarify, by 'practical' I mean the nuts and bolts of writing a piece. For instance, an example of practical considerations are the collaborative elements: how many performers do I have, is it a vocal or instrumental piece, what is the highest note the singer can sing, and so on. By 'aesthetics' I mean the compositional techniques employed and the stylistic choices made; and by 'metaphysical' I mean those elements that cannot be described by objective experience.

Ancient origins, vocal and instrumental music
In the popular imagination instrumental music is generally thought to be the most erudite and sophisticated music, especially music that is written for the virtuoso soloist, the symphony orchestra, and to a lesser extent, the string quartet.

This was not always the case. For more than 2,000 years in Western art music, from the time of the ancient Greeks until the late Renaissance and early Baroque periods, the marrying of music and words held the highest status, and the composition of purely instrumental music was generally considered subordinate and of a lesser artistic order.

The voice is the primal musical instrument. Each human being on the planet is endowed with a unique voice, so unique that now commercial companies seek to record our voices to identify us for our own so-called security.

When teaching, I like the following simple exercise in awareness: I play a note on the piano and ask my students to sing it; I remind them that we are all singing the same pitch, vibrating at the same number of cycles per second, but the sound of each of our voices is unique. I ask them to imagine that every human in the world is singing this note and all of them have a unique vibratory signature. I am hoping that for a moment, they contemplate the immense and magical reality of it. It is just extraordinary to think about.

The ancients were serious about music. Music as a subject was a foundational and indispensable part of the education of the citizen and a preparation for the study of philosophy. They made significant achievements in the scientific aspects of music. By 500 BCE, Pythagoras had calculated the mathematical ratios of musical intervals using the monochord; the Greeks developed a sophisticated theoretical system of music, a music notation system, tuning systems and technologies in building instruments.

The musicians of the Middle Ages adopted the names of the Greek modes (scales) and other concepts in their theoretical system. The names of the scales – dorian, phrygian, lydian and mixolydian – are still with us today, and they are used not only in classical music but also in jazz and in many genres of the popular styles. The concept of the Music of the Spheres, an idea predicated on the belief that mathematical musical principles govern planetary motion and that there exists a celestial music, still fascinates thinkers and creators.

Music and the State and Inner music

To various degrees, Plato, Aristotle and St. Augustine believed that music was such a powerful force it needed to be controlled for order and piety to prevail, both in the individual soul and in collective society. This anxiety about music was by no means peculiar to Western cultures. Although developed in isolation from each other geographically and culturally, the ideas of Confucius on music, its ideal context and function for both the individual and the politics of the state, have many similarities with those of the ancient Greeks.

In Greek philosophy, the Doctrine of Ethos embraced the idea that music had the power to directly affect human behaviour, character and emotion. Perhaps this explains Aristotle's concerns about purely instrumental music: if there are no words to direct the imagination, the mind would have the freedom to freely associate and could engage in all sorts of passionate, sensual and subversive thoughts.

Likewise, the early Christians and most importantly, St. Augustine, were suspicious of music's sensual aspects and considered banning music from the early Christian church. Luckily for us, Augustine decided that music's power to uplift was greater than its power to degrade. The evocation of the mystical through musical means has intrigued composers from Hildegard von Bingen (1098-1179) and Guillaume de Machaut (1330-1377) to György Ligeti (1923-2006) and John Cage (1912-1992) and has resulted in many masterworks. In fact, I cannot think of a single composer who has not engaged in, for lack of a better term, mystical curiosity.

Much modern scholarship on music focuses on cultural and sociological aspects of musical practice, but is there a unique inner music that transcends these definitions? The ancient idea that this inner music exists, or that music can influence human character profoundly, seems implausible and old-fashioned to the modern consciousness.

However, the appropriation and control of music by totalitarian regimes, such as those of Hitler and Stalin, speaks to the power of music. Historical evidence of extreme musical oppression and musical manipulation is irrefutable. This censorship applied not only to music with words but to instrumental music as well. Why did they feel so threatened by music consisting purely of sound? Can music that is instrumental inspire an extra-musical idea, such as individuality, for instance? Can music without words stimulate feelings that could incite rebellion? Obviously these dictators thought so.

A less discussed example is the oppressive atmosphere of fear that Schubert and Beethoven were forced to navigate in Metternich's Vienna, where public concerts were controlled, and the secret police were aided by a vast network of spies. David Bretherton (2011) makes a compelling case that Schubert engages in a politically subversive subtext in his settings of Mayrhofer's poem *Es Tanzen Mond und Sterne* (*The Moon and Stars Dance*).

Stylistic options, the importance of revision, inspiration and the musical imagination
The creative options available for today's composers are unprecedented in the history of music. The twentieth century abounded in the expansion of musical vocabulary with new techniques and their resultant styles of

composition: Impressionism, Expressionism, Serialism, Spectral Music, New Complexity, Pandiatonicism, Neotonality, Atonality, Minimalism, Stochastic music, the various forms of electronic and computer music, experiments in tuning systems and microtonality, the acoustic ecology movement, ragtime, jazz, and a flowering of many genres in the popular styles. This is by no means a comprehensive list.

Additionally, the influx of music from other cultures began to influence composers in the West. Music from India, China, Japan and the Middle East not only contributed exciting timbral opportunities with new instruments but also new theoretical systems in tuning, pitch organisation and rhythm. A famous example is Claude Debussy's fascination with the Javanese gamelan orchestra that performed at the Paris Exposition Universelle of 1889. Subsequently, composers such as Olivier Messiaen, John Cage and many others were inspired by the aesthetic philosophies of music and sound as espoused in Eastern religions.

For some, unfortunately, these technical directions and stylistic movements became akin to political ideologies. Zealots of various movements believed they were composing the 'right music' and others were composing the 'wrong music.' Those powerful in academic circles strove to cultivate clones of themselves. This accomplishes nothing positive.

A whirlwind of possible compositional choices swirls around me. I am curious about everything; I always want to have an open mind. I've explored and made pieces using many different techniques. I compose using whatever techniques are needed to attain the sound that I imagine. The constants that are always necessary for my work are rhythmic flow, musical lyricism (by which I mean explicit or implied melody), and a formal structure that is directional in how it sculpts the time span. These constants are possible in any style.

Rhythm is the fundamental force in music, but its deepest affections, and its pervasive power is not definable. The attempt to capture its essence and explain it, confounds thinkers, and rhythm is one of the most researched ideas in current musicological thought. Rhythm is not only indispensable to music; it animates poetry, permeates natural places, architectural spaces, conversations, the placement of figures in a painting – rhythm has limitless possibilities. Rhythm is generally agreed to imply pulse and repetition. A multitude of stimuli can inspire a rhythmic idea: a movement, a colour, the rhythm of spoken words, the rain beating against a window, a heartbeat, a yawn. The list is endless. While rhythm cannot be easily defined, all human beings feel its presence and know it within; it is a fundamental part of our intrinsic musicality.

One of the definitions of rhythm from *Merriam-Webster's Dictionary* (2020) is 'a movement, fluctuation or variation marked by the regular recurrence of a natural flow of related elements'. As the painter/musician Paul Klee put it: 'Motion is the root of all growth' (1961, p.18). 'The pulse is felt through the sound as a structural framework over which the quantities and qualities of the musical ideas move' (Klee, 1961, p.271). The form of a piece is related to its rhythmic properties. Since music occupies a space of time sculpted with sound events, the placement of events within the form is also rhythmic.

Rhythmic flow is the perception of music unravelling itself naturally and inevitably, carrying the listener on a distinct journey. Within the form, the music unfolds in a prescribed length of time; in a sense, the composer takes the listener on a structured time journey. There may be stops and starts, detours and digressions in the musical discourse. When the composition is finished, the listener has the sense of a cognisant experience of the musical elements. I prefer constantly unfolding forms and a through-composed musical narrative. I rarely use any literal repetitions.

As it is with rhythm, defining melody is also devilishly undoable. The *Grove Music Online* entry for melody is 18 pages long. I use a *Merriam-Webster* definition, 'a rhythmic succession of notes organized as an aesthetic whole' (2020). When I refer to musical lyricism, I mean any type of melodic thread, that guides the music, and carries the listener from the beginning to the end of the piece. This may or may not be a 'tune'. Celebrated French teacher and composer Nadia Boulanger, whose students included composers Aaron Copland, Elliot Carter, Philip Glass – men composing in vastly disparate styles – called this 'le grande ligne'. She believed it to be an indispensable feature of any successful composition, regardless of style (Fauser, 2002, p.536).

Melody with all its manifestations presents the most formidable challenges for any composer. A composer cannot force melodic ideas. It is remarkable and unfathomable to me that when I compose a piece of music (either vocal or instrumental), as it unfolds there is a point when it begins to have a life of its own. In a strange and uncanny role reversal, the composer ceases to be the master and now becomes the servant, aiding the composition to unfold naturally in its own terms. This refers not so much to a specific musical idea or element, such as a particular note or a rhythm, but to the compelling forces that drive any work of art toward the inevitable completeness of its form.

One of my primary objectives when composing is that, when I finish a piece, nothing can be added or taken away from it without creating a distortion. There is no excess – nothing unnecessary. For me this involves editing, polishing and revision. It is simply remarkable how minute changes in a musical work can transform a passage. Tiny adjustments such as lengthening or shortening a duration, adding a grace note, changing one pitch or adding a rest are examples of this. The world of sound in a work of music is minutely sensitive, and the slightest manipulations can be transformative to the musical narrative.

I remember how delighted I was as a student composer fortunate enough to have access to the autograph (an autograph is the score written in the composer's hand) of Schoenberg's monumental *Gurrelieder* and to observe that he had made changes in his final score. He is not alone. Bach was still making refinements in the details of his monumental work *The Well Tempered Clavier* 20 years after it was completed. Schubert revised his tiny song '*Die Forelle*' four times before he was satisfied, and Beethoven's sketches reveal how he struggled and revised his ideas. There are many other examples, and I also made final revisions in my Rumi songs for the IASH 50th Anniversary Conference.

I am often asked, 'how do you write music – do you just hear it?' I am reminded of an image I saw of Beethoven resting against a tree by a brook, paper and pen in hand with his eyes upturned wistfully to the sky, awaiting the divine transmission to his pen. This romanticisation of the composer and the work of composing is common. Only once have I been given a

171

melody by way of a direct gift. I was commissioned to write an instrumental piece for a psychiatric conference about the rehabilitation of human trafficking victims. I was asked to write music that charted the course of the victim from the initial hope of a new life, to enslavement, despair, madness, escape, sorrow/regret and rehabilitation. I was to finish the piece with a message of hope. Kevin Bales' book *Disposable People* was my primary research source, but the stories of present-day slavery were so sobering that I found it impossible to compose an ending of hope. Everything I wrote seemed inadequate or trite. My deadline was imminent, and I was paralysed. I finally went to bed around one o'clock in the morning, and as I put my head on the pillow, I suddenly heard the melody in my mind. It was indeed a gift. I got up, wrote it down, and immediately went back to bed and fell into a sound sleep. It has never happened again. Generally, the process proceeds thus: I am imagining music, writing down what I imagine and revising and polishing it.

Collaborative input and the score as a map

Unlike the painter who has a completed work in the object of their painting, the composer imagines music and notates a graphic representation of it called a score. This score is a type of map; it indicates the pitches, durations and other details of a musical journey. The performers read and interpret the map and transform it into sound. Only then does it become music. Therefore, most music is a collaborative art form.

The collaborative aspect of music is a double-edged sword for the composer. On the one hand, the performers are bringing their own artistry and expertise to the score; they are the ones who bring it alive and transform it into music. A sensitive performer will enrich and augment the ideas of the composition with their musical insights. On the other hand, a wanton disregard for the music as the composer has written it down is quite possible. Furthermore, while the composer is grateful for accuracy, accuracy is not enough. I recall a performance by Mozart played by a respected professional string quartet. Every note was correct, the rhythm was accurate, the intonation (tuning) was perfect, but the performance was pedestrian and directionless, and as a result it lacked intelligibility.

At its best, collaboration enriches the creative process. When Béla Bartók was composing his *Sonata for Solo Violin*, for the legendary violinist Yehudi Menuhin, the composer and the performer communicated about technical issues, and Bartók adjusted his ideas to make the work more playable. The experimental composer John Cage responded in this fashion when asked how he felt when his work was performed by performers who were not committed to a conscientious performance:

> Well, last night, *Five* was played incorrectly. I didn't enjoy it. I'll tell you frankly; I was unhappy, and even disturbed. It was actually improvising – it had nothing to do with my work. I know what Karlheinz Stockhausen would have done – he would have shouted "STOP!" Now why wouldn't I do that?
>
> (Cage, 1990, p.5)

And when asked about the performer's responsibilities, Cage replied:

> I don't know what to say. What I've done is to write music, and what I hope is that it will be played as it is written; where there are freedoms the freedoms are taken there, rather than everywhere. When one writes music, one writes sounds and absence of sounds on the part of that player, and when they don't pay attention to differences, then it doesn't seem to be something that you want.
>
> (Cage, 1990, p.5)

The most important thing for me in any performance is the continuity of the timeline of the work. If the rhythm, pulse and tempos are disregarded by the performer, especially if inappropriate and exaggerated rubato (stretching) is added, the flow of the music is distorted, and the forward motion and vitality of the piece is dissolved. A wrong note or chord is something a piece can survive but when the *time* is distorted, the form and structure of the music becomes warped and misshapen. Furthermore, it is important to understand that rhythmic vitality does not necessarily mean faster, as sometimes fast music can be a static blur of sound and rhythmically dead.

Mozart's compositions in slow tempos, for instance, have a vibrant rhythmic vitality and flow.

Four Songs on Texts of Rumi

I was commissioned to compose a piece for cello and voice by cellist Rafael Popper-Keizer. While searching for texts, I happened upon four poems quoted in an essay by Harold Klemp. The poems were excerpted from *A Year of Rumi* by Coleman Barks. Jalāl ad-Dīn Muhammad Rūmī (1207-1273), Persian poet, Islamic scholar and Sufi mystic, is one of the most popular poets in the United States. Themes of spiritual ecstasy, divine love, universalism and religious syncretism permeate his poetry.

In *A Year of Rumi*, each day of the year is represented by a short poem/contemplation that Barks paraphrases from English translations of Rumi's *Mathnavi*. In the foreword, Barks' quotation from Jelaluddin Chelabi, head of the order of dervishes descended from Rumi, distills the book's message into a nutshell: 'Love is the religion and the universe is the book' (Barks, 2006, p.8).

After reflecting on the poems, I decided upon a direction. I wrote in my programme note: 'My understanding is that Rumi is speaking with humour, insight and compassion on the gratitude of the seeker for the spiritual master, the stilling of the mind, the desire for truth, perplexity, misdirected desires, creativity and the continuity of life'. My titles for the movements, in order, are: I *What I want*, II *Clear and Still*, III *These Two Insomnias*, IV *This Candleflame Instant*.

The empty page looms, and there are so many possibilities (practical, metaphysical and aesthetic/stylistic choices to be made), the elusive inner voice always being the ultimate arbiter. On the practical side, I know I will have two virtuoso performers offering a large window of options, balanced with the fact that this is a duo – a smaller window of options. The effects of the lush orchestral planes of Claude Debussy or Philip Glass will not be available. The intimacy of the ensemble suggests a piece that inhabits the interior psychological world of the seeker, where the singer and cellist are one, and rhetoric and dialectic are set aside. As a dramatic strategy, I want each of the four movements to be different stylistically, to vary in tempo, and to be able to stand alone but also to work organically as a group.

It often happens that I find the images and ideas of visual artists to be fuel for my imagination. Consider these words of Paul Klee: 'A concept is not thinkable without its opposite', and 'no concept is effective without its opposite' (Klee, 1961, p.15). Examples of such oppositions, from a host of possibilities are: loud-soft, high-low, short-long, slow-fast, consonant-dissonant, fluid-angular, transparent-dense, arrogant-timid, frenetic-languid, arco-pizzicato. The dynamic tension between opposites releases dynamic energies. Dynamic energies release flow and the direction of flow creates form. In my experience, this works.

Truth, perplexity and misdirected desires

I. _Who Makes these Changes (What I want)_
Who makes these changes?
I shoot an arrow right.
It lands left.
I ride after a deer
and find myself chased by a hog.
I plot to get what I want
and end up in prison.
I dig pits to trap others
and fall in.
I should be suspicious of what I want.

(Barks, 2006, p.298)

The pulse is fast. The expressive markings are: _agitato, emphatic, tender, desperate, with resignation, sweetly, smoothly, furtive,_ and finally _mystified._ The cello has pop-inspired bass-riff gestures and the note choices are abstract. The expanse of the vocal range is wide and dramatic; the movement ends with the singer softly asking the question 'Who?' on a very long sustained pitch, while the cello ends with a soloistic, soft agitato passage.

The stilling of the mind

II. Water and Moon (Clear and still)
There is a path from me to you
that I am constantly looking for,
so I try to keep clear and still
as water does with the moon.

(Barks, 2006, p.56)

The movement is marked, 'with humour, gently.' The tempo is moderate, the cellist strums the strings like a guitar, ad libitum (at liberty: the cellist is allowed to improvise the execution of the strums but not allowed to change the notes). The vocal range is in a narrow, non-dramatic register; the singer sings a folk-like melody that is nothing like a folk song. She ends by singing the words 'I try', and we are left with the idea that, while she is trying her best, the stilling of the mind is an ideal yet to be met.

Creativity, the desire for truth and gratitude for the spiritual master

III. When I am with you (These two insomnias)
When I am with you, we stay up all night.
When you are not here, I can't go to sleep.
Praise God for these two insomnias.
And the difference between them.

(Barks, 2006, p.69)

This setting was the most difficult for me. The tempo is medium fast, and the movement is marked, 'gently wandering and wondering.' The cello plays a constantly unfolding line in jazz-like rhythms, somewhat like the ebb and flow of a brook, and the pitches have a jazz feel. The singer sings in the lower velvety register of her voice, her rhythms are straightforward in contrast to those of the cello. She ends softly on the words 'Praise God'.

The continuity of life

IV. _The moments you have lived (This candleflame instant)_
As essence turns to ocean,
the particles glisten.
Watch how in this candleflame instant
Blaze all the moments you have lived.

(Barks, 2006, p.326)

This movement is marked _reflective:_ the pulse is slow, and the time is free. The range of both the voice and the cello is wide and dramatic; there are intricate, florid figurations for both, that are evocative of ecstatic singing. The mood is meditative and builds in intensity. The cello has multiple voices and timbres with varied orchestrations of tremolos and harmonics. The musical gestures are both meditative and passionate; there is an ecstatic ardour as the moments blaze. The last word sung is 'glisten'; the cello ends _morendo_ (dying out).

On abandonment being the first duty of the listener

Will navigating the works of the cultural theorist, the philosopher, or the music theorist enhance an individual's understandings, perceptions and enjoyment of a piece of music? Undoubtedly so, but experience tells me a certain amount of abandonment is necessary. For instance, when going to a concert of classical Indian music, I have a negligible amount of knowledge about its formal intricacies and cultural contexts. I have no choice but to let go of any preconceptions and abandon my attention to the rhythms and sounds, allowing them to envelop me. I know that it is impossible for me to edit out all my knowledge and life experience with music, but still I attempt to re-imagine this scenario of innocence whenever I hear any new piece of music. If I find the piece compelling, I will want to listen again and perhaps consider its ideas more carefully. Therefore, my advice to the listener is: 'listen with an open heart and mind and fully experience the music'.

Concluding thoughts

A vast number of variables affect the process of music composition. I feel remiss not to have discussed the role of dance, context and memory in music and especially remiss not to have addressed the prevalent idea that the experience of music is purely subjective. However, these require extensive discourse and the subjective argument cannot be refuted by logic. Therefore, I am satisfied to leave you with two provocative statements to ponder. One is from Aaron Copland, 'The precise meaning of music is a question that should never have been asked, and in any event will never elicit a precise answer' (Copland, 1952, p. 13), and the other from John Cage, 'Music is edifying for from time to time it sets the soul in operation' (Cage, 1949, p.1).

I wish you the best on your musical journeys.

BIBLIOGRAPHY

Adhitya, S., 2017. The city as a rhythmic composition. In: Adhitya, S., ed. 2017. *Musical Cities: Listening to Urban Design and Planning*. [e-book] London: UCL Press, pp.3-8. http://dx.doi.org/10.2307/j.ctv550cz9.7.

Barks, C., 2006. *A Year with Rumi: Daily Readings*. New York, NY: Harper Collins.

Botstein, L., 2005. Art and the state: the case of music. *The Musical Quarterly*, [e-journal] 88(4), pp.487-495. http://dx.doi.org/10.1093/musqtl/gdk007.

Bretherton, D., 2011. The shadow of midnight in Schubert's 'Gondelfahrer' settings. *Music & Letters*, [e-journal] 92(1), pp.1-42. http://dx.doi.org/10.1093/ml/gcq087.

Cage, J., 1949. Forerunners of modern music. Reprint 2010. In: Cage, J., ed. 2010. *Silence: Lectures and Writings*. Middletown, CT: Wesleyan University Press.

Cage, J., 1990. John Cage and the 'Glaswegian Circus': an interview around Musica Nova 1990. Interviewed by Steve Turner. *Tempo*, [e-journal] 177, pp.2-8. Available at: <http://www.jstor.org/stable/945926> [Accessed 9 June 2020].

Copland, A., 1952. *Music and Imagination*. Reprint 1961. London: Harvard University Press.

Fauser, A., 2006. Aaron Copland, Nadia Boulanger, and the Making of an "American" Composer. *The Musical Quarterly*, [e-journal] 89(4), pp.524-554 Available at: <http://www.jstor.org/stable/25172851> [Accessed 8 July 2020].

Ilnitchi, G., 2002. 'Musica Mundana': Aristotelian natural philosophy and Ptolemaic astronomy. *Early Music History*, [e-journal] 21, pp.37-74. http://dx.doi.org/10.1017/S0261127902002024.

Klee, P., 1961. *The Paul Klee Notebooks Volume 1: The Thinking Eye*. Edited by Jürg Spiller. Translated by Ralph Manheim,1961. London: Lund Humphries.

Lin, Y. ed., 1943. *The Wisdom of Confucius*. Translated by Y. Lin, 1943. New York, NY: The Modern Library.

Merriam-Webster, 2020. *Merriam-Webster Dictionary*. [online] s.l.: s.n. Available at: <http://www.merriam-webster.com/dictionary/rhythm> [Accessed 9 June 2020].

Stravinsky, I., 1975. *An Autobiography (1903-1934)*. London: Calder and Boyars.

Author Biographies

Professor Rosi Braidotti

Rosi Braidotti is Distinguished University Professor at Utrecht University, where she has taught since 1988. She was been awarded honorary degrees from Helsinki (2007) and Linkoping (2013); she is a Fellow of the Australian Academy of the Humanities (FAHA) since 2009, and a Member of the Academia Europaea (MAE) since 2014. She serves on the Advisory Board of IASH. Her main publications include *Nomadic Subjects* (2011) and *Nomadic Theory* (2011), both with Columbia University Press, and *The Posthuman* (2013) and *Posthuman Knowledge* (2019) with Polity Press. In 2016, she co-edited *Conflicting Humanities* with Paul Gilroy, and *The Posthuman Glossary* in 2018 with Maria Hlavajova, both with Bloomsbury Academic. www.rosibraidotti.com

Professor Sam Cohn

Samuel Cohn, Jr. is Professor of Medieval History at the University of Glasgow, Fellow of the Royal Society of Edinburgh, and Honorary Fellow of the Institute for Advanced Studies in the Humanities,. He has taught at the universities of Harvard, Wesleyan, Brandeis, Brown and Berkeley and was the first Federico Chabod Visiting Professor at L'Università degli Studi, Milano (Statale) in 2017. From the late 1990s, he has published and taught on two broad themes: popular insurrection in Medieval and Early Modern Europe, and the history of plague and other diseases from antiquity to the present. His most recent books include *The Black Death Transformed: Disease and Culture in Early Renaissance Europe* (Edward Arnold and Oxford University Press, 2002), *Lust for Liberty: The Politics of Social Revolt in Medieval Europe, 1200-1425* (Harvard University Press, 2006), *Cultures of Plague: Medical Thinking at the End of the Renaissance* (Oxford University Press, 2010), *Popular Protest in Late Medieval English Towns* (Cambridge University Press, 2013), and *Epidemics: Hate & Compassion from the Plague of Athens to AIDS* (Oxford University Press, 2018). He has just submitted to press *Popular Protest and Ideals of Democracy in Late Renaissance Italy*.

Dr Catherine Crompton
Catherine J. Crompton is a neuropsychologist and autism researcher, with interests in neurodiverse communication, neurodiverse interaction, and how autism-specific social skills facilitate interactions with autistic peers. She is a leader in participatory research and conducts research with and for the autistic community. She was previously on the committee of the Scottish Autism Research Group and has co-ordinated several research, practice and community events in Scotland. She was a Postdoctoral Fellow at the Institute for Advanced Studies in the Humanities in 2019-20, and her current work is in designing peer support systems for autistic people and supporting the development of autistic community spaces.

Professor Soraya de Chadarevian
Soraya de Chadarevian is Professor of History of Science, Technology and Medicine at the Department of History and the Institute for Society and Genetics at the University of California, Los Angeles. She has published widely on the history of the molecular life sciences. Her most recent book, *Heredity under the Microscope: Chromosomes and the Study of the Human Genome*, is published by University of Chicago Press (July 2020). She was a Fellow at the Institute for Advanced Studies in the Humanities in July 2016 and 2017.

Dr Noémie Fargier
Noémie Fargier is a French researcher, writer and stage director. She holds

a PhD in Theatre and Sound Studies (Sorbonne Nouvelle University, 2018) and has taught in the drama department in several universities in France (Paris Nanterre University, University of Paris 8, University of Strasbourg) since 2015. From January to August 2020 she was a Postdoctoral Fellow at the Institute for Advanced Studies in the Humanities, working on recent developments in the practice of field recording. Since 2011 she has written and directed several plays, which all question intimacy and subjectivity. She has recently developed projects associating field recordings with an exploration of sensitivity and narration.

Dr Elizabeth Ford
Elizabeth Ford was the 2018-2019 Daiches-Manning Memorial Fellow in Eighteenth-Century Scottish Studies. Her project explored the musical environments in coffeehouses and taverns in eighteenth-century Edinburgh, focusing on the Cross Keys and the Musick Club. Her PhD (Glasgow, 2016) won the National Flute Association Graduate Research Award. She was part of the team that established the RSE-funded Eighteenth-century Arts Education Research Network at the University of Glasgow. Her complete edition of William McGibbon's sonatas is published by A-R Editions, and her monograph, *The Flute in Scotland from the Sixteenth to the Eighteenth Century*, is part of the Studies in the History and Culture of Scotland Series from Peter Lang Press. In the 2020-2021 academic year, Elizabeth will hold the Martha Goldsworthy Arnold Fellowship at the Riemenschneider Bach Institute, the Abi Rosenthal Visiting Fellowship in Music at the Bodleian Libraries, and the American Society for Eighteenth Century Studies-Burney Centre Fellowship at McGill University. Her research is informed by her background as a player of historic flutes. She is co-founder of Blackwater Press.

Dr Natalie Goodison
Natalie Goodison is a medievalist who specialises in embodiment. After receiving her undergraduate degree from the University of North Carolina, she went on to obtain her masters in Medieval Studies at the University of Edinburgh and competed her PhD at Durham University. Her

research interests include the history of ideas, medieval romance, and the medical humanities, and her first project explored embodiment through supernatural transformations in English romances – what happens when the corporeal body transforms due to magic or supernatural influence. Her current project examines rare births in the Middle Ages, their causes, and their soteriological effects on mother and offspring. She asks the question: in an age where the sins of the parents might literally be visited upon the bodies of their children, what did genetically abnormal children signify? Natalie held the Junior Anniversary Fellowship at the Institute for Advanced Studies in the Humanities during its 50th Anniversary year.

Dr Colin Johnson

Colin G. Johnson is an associate professor in the School of Computer Science at the University of Nottingham. He received his PhD in 2003 from the University of Kent, which was based on computer simulations of biological evolution and the application of evolutionary-inspired ideas for problem solving in engineering, mathematics and sound synthesis. His research interests are in the development of new artificial intelligence algorithms and their application to a wide variety of topics including understanding biological and physical science problems, engineering problems in software engineering and audio engineering, and the digital humanities. A particular interest is in creative intelligence, including developing ways for AI systems to act creatively and understanding how artists and musicians have used ideas from AI in their practice. He was a Digital Scholarship Research Fellow at IASH in 2019. He is also active in science communication – he has given talks at science events such as *Café Scientifique* and *Pint of Science* as well as appeared on radio shows in the UK and Australia, discussing science and technology.

Dr Tomasz Łysak

Tomasz Łysak is based at the University of Warsaw, where his work focuses on representations of the Holocaust in relation to trauma studies and psychoanalysis. He has held fellowships at the University of Washington, Seattle, the University of Edinburgh, and the University of Chicago. He has been awarded a research grant from the National Science Centre: 'From Newsreel to Post-Traumatic Film: Documentary and Artistic Films on the Holocaust' (2013-2015). He has edited *Antologia studiów nad traumą* (Trauma studies anthology 2015) and is the author of *Od kroniki do filmu posttraumatycznego – filmy dokumentalne o Zagładzie* (2016), which was awarded as the best debut book in cinema and media studies by the Polish Association for Studies of Film and the Media. Recently he has been working on Polish popular culture and the Holocaust.

Professor Deborah Mackay
Deborah Mackay is Professor of Medical Epigenetics at the University of Southampton, UK. After undergraduate Biochemistry at the University of Oxford, she took her PhD at the Imperial Cancer Research Fund and worked postdoctorally as a molecular cell biologist at UCL before developing her current interests in the genetics and epigenetics of human imprinting disorders. Imprinting disorders disturb the epigenetic control of critical subset of genes that regulate human growth, development and metabolism. Over the last 20 years, Deborah has identified new genetic and epigenetic causes of disease, identified new disorders and new ways of diagnosing them, and worked alongside researchers, clinicians and families to develop guidelines for diagnosis and clinical care. Recently her group has identified genetic changes in the mothers of individuals with imprinting disorders; these maternal-effect variants, which are associated with a range of adverse reproductive outcomes in offspring, highlight critical connections between epigenetic marks, maternal reproductive fitness and offspring development and health. She currently has over 100 peer-reviewed publications, including papers in *Nature Genetics* and *The Lancet*, and co-authorship of reviews and guidelines. She also loves enthusing about genetics and epigenetics with support organisations, schoolchildren, lay groups and frankly anyone who will listen.

Dr Margaret McAllister
Margaret McAllister is a composer. She was the Fulbright Scotland 2019-20 Visiting Professor, sponsored by the Department of Celtic and

Scottish Studies, and a Fellow of the Institute for Advanced Studies in the Humanities at the University of Edinburgh. Her Fulbright project was to compose new works in tandem with distinguished Scottish poet Aonghas MacNeacail. Her studies in classical composition and music theory were at Boston University where her principal teachers were Theodore Antoniou and Lukas Foss. She has also worked with Milton Babbitt, Oliver Knussen, Toru Takemitsu and Gunther Schuller. She has received many distinctions for her work and commissions and performances from professional solo artists and performing ensembles including the New Millennium Ensemble, Alea III, Boston Composers String Quartet, Pandora's Vox, Tapestry, Zodiac Trio, Odd Appetite, as well as on National Public Radio and the Canadian Broadcasting Corporation. . Her work has been supported by the Fromm Foundation and Navigator Foundation. She was the co-founder of *Crosscurrents*, a new music platform dedicated to performing the works of young and emerging composers, and was the artistic director and founder of the Hyperprism concert series at Boston College. She is Associate Professor of Composition at Berklee College of Music in Boston.

Dr Kathryn Simpson

Kathryn Simpson is Lecturer in Information Studies in the School of Humanities at the University of Glasgow. She was a Postdoctoral Fellow at the Institute for Advanced Studies in the Humanities at Edinburgh University in 2018-19. She is an Associate Project Scholar and UK Outreach Director for Livingstone Online. Her current research project, entitled 'Boundaries of gender: "petticoat governments" and secondary voices in nineteenth century European expeditions of Africa', mines digital content to foreground the many women, both European and African, who assisted and enabled David Livingstone (1813-1873) in his journeys in Africa.

Supporters of Research

FULBRIGHT

THE UNIVERSITY
of EDINBURGH

ISSN 2041-8817 (Print)
ISSN 2634-7342 (Online)
ISBN 978-0-9532713-1-3

The University of Edinburgh is a charitable body,
registered in Scotland, with registration number SC005336.